BÉA GONZALEZ

The
MAPMAKER'S OPERA

HarperCollins*Publishers*

HarperCollins*Publishers*
77–85 Fulham Palace Road,
Hammersmith, London W6 8JB

www.harpercollins.co.uk

First published in Canada by
HarperCollins*Publishers* 2005

A paperback original 2006

This novel is entirely a work of fiction. The names,
characters and incidents portrayed in it are the work
of the author's imagination. Any resemblance to actual
persons, living or dead, events or localities is
entirely coincidental.

A catalogue record for this book
is available from the British Library

ISBN-13 978 0 00 720779 4

Set in Dante

For Andrew, who taught me to look up at the sky, and our dear *pingüinos*, Will and Andre, who bring such joy to our lives.

Seguiriya

No soy d'esta tierra
Ni en eya nasi:
La fortuniya, roando, roando
M'ha traio hasta aquí.

Ar campito solo
Me voy a yorá;
Como tengo yena e penas
El arma
Busco soléa.

Las cosas del mundo
Yo na la jentiendo.
La mitad de la gente llorando
Y la otra riendo.

Horas de alegría
Son las que se van
Que las penas se queden
Y duran
Una eternidad.

I'm not from this land,
Nor was I born here;
Fate, rolling, rolling
Brought me this way.

To the fields
I wander to weep;
Filled with such sorrow and grief
It is only solitude
I seek.

The things of this world,
I just don't understand
Half of the people cry,
While the other half laugh.

The happy times
How fleeting they are,
While the sad times
Last and last
An eternity at least.

Arbolito del campo	The little tree in the field
Riega el rocío	Is watered by dew
Como yo riego	Like I water the cobblestones
De tu calle	Of your street
Con llanto mío.	With the weight of my tears.
Cuando yo me muera	When I die
Mira que te encargo:	I ask you do this for me:
Que con la jebra de tu	Take a strand of your
Pelo negro	Brilliant black hair
Me amarres las manos.	And bind my hands with it.

Dramatis Personae

Emilio, *a seminarian* .... Tenor

Mónica, *governess in the house of Don Ricardo Medina* .. Mezzo-soprano

Remedios, *mother of Emilio* .... Contralto

Doña Fernanda, *wife of Don Ricardo Medina* .... Contralto

Don Pedro, *priest and confidant of Doña Fernanda* .... Baritone

Raimundo, *master of the Medina house* .... Bass-baritone

Don Ricardo Medina, *head of the Medina clan* .... Baritone

Alfonso, *bookseller and Emilio's uncle* .... Bass

Diego, *son of Mónica and Don Ricardo* .... Tenor

El Señor Raleigh, *English traveller, friend of Emilio and Diego* ..... Bass

Edward Nelson, *Diego's mentor* .... Bass-baritone

Very Useful, *Mr. Nelson's servant* .... Baritone

Sofia Duarte, *daughter of Roberto Duarte* .... Soprano

Don Roberto Duarte, *Yucatecan* hacendado, *bookseller* .. Bass-baritone

Gabriela, *wife of Roberto Duarte* .... Mezzo-soprano

Doña Laura, *mother of Roberto Duarte* .... Contralto

Aunt Marta, *Gabriela's sister* .... Mezzo-soprano

Don Victor Blanco, *henequen magnate* .... Bass

Carlos Blanco, *son of Victor Blanco* .... Baritone

Rosita, *childhood friend of Sofia* .... Soprano

Patricia, *friend of Sofia* .... Soprano

ACT ONE

Overture

It begins in a once-upon-a-time land, on a remote plain, far from the place we call home. It begins with a dreamy voice, closed eyes, and a glass of warm milk to tame the chill of a too-cold night.

In the background, the first notes sound out, preparing to lure us in.

A *seguiriya* tonight, perhaps?

"No, something livelier," she says, "something irrepressible, something joyous." She stops to think. "Ah, yes, I have it, *niños!* A *bulería* sung by the incomparable Lola Flores, all passion, all grit, a voice with which to tame the wind!"

She begins—

In a town in the heart of La Mancha, home to Don Quijote and his windmills, to long afternoons and silent, silent nights, the Clemente family lived for centuries, their fortunes tied to those of a plant: the Crocus sativus—*from whose dried stigma comes saffron, the world's most precious spice. What you may not know is that it takes 160,000 flowers to produce just one kilogram of this culinary bit of gold. When Mónica Clemente left La Mancha for the narrow streets of Seville, she carried the taste of saffron forever on her tongue. More than any bucolic recollections of childhood, Mónica's memories were imbued with the taste of saffron soups, saffron stews and most of all, the sublime paellas of her Aunt Bautista, who always knew instinctively the precise amount to be placed into the olla, where the chicken, chorizo and thirteen other ingredients blended and brewed. . . .*

Ah, here it was, the opening bars of our grandmother's favourite story, the one she would tell most often because it was full of the beautiful—forbidden love, unbearable grief, a country lost and another one found and moments of true transcendence. It was the story she would tell most often because it was true, because it was full of joy and sadness too, and the poetry, she would argue, was in the pity most of all, in all the tears shed for life's pain and life's losses.

In her accented English, with Spanish peppering the narrative— "because Spanish," our Abuela would insist, "is not only the language of love, *oigan bien,* but the language of life itself"—our grandmother would transport us to a world where we would easily lose all sense of time. With her words, the streets of nineteenth-century Seville would come alive and we swore we could see the *señoritas,* with their long black hair and their tortoiseshell combs, flirting with the men from opened windows; that we could hear the call of the water-sellers, hear the steady strokes of the brooms as the cleaners made their way through the narrow streets; that we could smell the oranges and the jasmine and even the pungent olive groves, though there were no olive groves for miles but just the hint of their scent in the air; that we could feel the *taconeo* of the flamenco dancers' feet deep inside our hearts; that we could taste the saffron in Bautista's famous *paellas* and stews.

And when she was all done with Seville she would carry us over the ocean, across a tumultuous sea—"because this is a story without borders," our Abuela would say, "a story that although rooted in place and time manages to transcend both"—and suddenly we would find ourselves in Mexico, melting in the unbearable heat of the Yucatán, tasting the *tortillas* that arrived still warm inside a hollow gourd, gazing at the sky to catch a glimpse of the area's splendid birds.

In our Abuela's capable hands we would wander into uncharted territory, passing from century to century, from vivid descriptions of a *bal costumé* to landscapes we had never seen but could depict down to the last shrub and tree—an often rocky terrain of recipes, *seguiriyas, soleares, tonás,* the poetry of Antonio Machado, the philosophical musings of Ortega y Gasset.

"A world, *niños*, a world!" she would proclaim. And we would agree, nodding our heads, seated side by side on a basement floor feasting on *galletas* imported from the distant Carmelite convents of Southern Spain.

All that is left now is the memory of her voice escaping from her empty room where her books and papers are scattered about as they have always been and where ghosts still linger on the sheets.

"*Vamos,*" she urges us from the grave. "Forget the mess left behind and get on with the tale." Because the only things you really leave behind, we hear her say, are the things that obsess you, that give meaning to your life, the things that fill you with the energy to rise up in the morning and keep you on your toes throughout the long days and even longer nights. Because we are meant to tell stories, to relate the tales that make living bearable and, when all is good and gone, there is only this, a hushed voice, a lingering note, a tale that will outlive our little selves until the last generation is done.

With that in mind we sit down to retell the story with the help of our Abuela's most cherished prop—a century-old map. Beneath the lines of longitude and latitude there is a deep blue ocean that turns reddish where land meets sea. On either side we scan the two continents—the old and the new, the past and the present, the beginning and the end. We bring forth also a black-and-white picture of the mapmaker, a certain Diego Clemente, the tenor who resides at the heart of this tale. The photograph is yellowed with age so that Diego's face appears jaundiced, as if he were suffering from one of the myriad diseases common in the tropics where he played out the last scenes of his life. But he is handsome, that we can see, his eyes are large, his bearing is refined, there is no hint of the abusive girth that has accompanied many a splendid voice but has made a mockery of a well-loved part.

We return once again to the map. It is an exquisite specimen drawn on parchment, minutely detailed with mountains, rivers, oceans and a wealth of symbols waiting to be transformed into music by our trembling, excitable minds. Along the map's borders lie the spectacular birds that beckoned to Diego from across an ocean and that accompanied him until the very moment of his death. The names of those birds had tumbled easily from our lips as children, as familiar to us as the *seguiriyas,* the arias and the *soléas* that played on our grandparents' ancient turntable with its large knobs and its heavy wooden lid. Back then, we would take turns naming the birds one by one: an Aztec Parakeet in the west, a Turquoise-Browed Motmot in the north, a Ferruginous Pygmy Owl in the east, a Violaceous Trogon to the south.

Even as children, we could see something else in the map—that it was weighed down by secrets, that there was a dark stain lying beneath the pinks and the yellows, that the oceans were murky and that shadows were cast upon the earth.

It would take us almost twenty years to piece the story together, with all of the ups and downs, the good and the bad. It would take us that much time to unearth the mysteries, to plug the holes that our Abuela had left behind, the bits and pieces that would alter the tempo of the music, allowing a tone of lamentation to weave its way through the score.

In the background we now hear our Abuela urging us along from the grave. *"Vamos,"* she says in her familiar, impatient way. We smile, remembering, and together begin to trace a path on the map—from the yellow waters of the Guadalquivir River in Seville to the alabaster jewel that is the city of Mérida—travelling happily along the musical latitudes of our childhoods as if our Abuela were here beside us once again.

As we walk on sacred ground

As always, it is best to begin with the map.

Once, centuries ago, a map was a thing of beauty, a testament not to the way things were but to the heights scaled by men's dreams. Mapmakers were not just artisans, they were artists intent on creating universes where the magical and the mythical were very much alive. On the corners of their maps they placed the wondrous creatures that guarded the entrances to heaven and hell. The world was a more mysterious place and everything was more beautifully drawn, more beautifully imagined, more beautifully named. In Europe a man would gaze uneasily to the West, fearful of drowning in the unknown sea—the *mare ignotum*. To the East lay Eden with its promise of everlasting innocence.

In the sixteenth century, a Spanish king, Philip II, obsessed with a love of God and in need of enough gold to prove it, instructed the royal cartographers to map his kingdom. Make the invisible visible, he told them, and let every European know who reigns over the New World. Within a few short years he was dead, but through engravings and woodcuts, the cartographers continued fashioning territories, travelling the spaces they sought to make real with measuring chains, wooden goniometers, compasses and their vivid fantasies—because before a land can hope to be mapped, it must first take root in our dreams.

Diego Clemente's map is to be read carefully, from east to west, from right to left, beginning at 5°59′w, 37°23′N—the red spot that marked his birth in Seville—and ending at 89°39′w, 20°58′N—Mérida, his final resting place.

It is a beautiful map, more beautiful yet when you consider the sorrows he must have conquered in order to leave behind this final testament of symbols, lines and grids. A man should wait until he is close to death before attempting to draw conclusions about the meaning of his life—so you once said, Abuela, and we cannot help but wonder if Diego had been furnished with the opportunity to inspect his handiwork, to reflect one final time on his journey from his beginnings in Seville until that very last day at a Mexican hacienda an ocean away.

Like Columbus, who believed the New World contained mysterious islands brimming with wondrous gardens and golden apples, Diego's mind had a touch of the fanciful in it, a penchant for concocting magical kingdoms, for imagining perfection, for clawing at the edges of mortality, attempting to map with his quill the mystery of existence, trying to keep death and, what is more, extinction itself at bay. We pause briefly to remember those who have disappeared forever from the skies—the Carolina Parakeet, the Passenger Pigeon, the Labrador Duck—and we lament, oh how we lament, the absence of dreamers like Diego who dared to stand up to the throngs, to the beliefs and disbeliefs of his own day and age.

But the lights begin to dim now, the words of the program become harder and harder to make out. A hush falls over the audience, a sense of expectation rises until it is met at its peak by the lowering of the baton as the first notes sound out. The curtains slowly rise and we find ourselves seated before the heavenly streets of nineteenth-century Seville. Picture a city bathed in the smell of orange blossoms in spring, jasmine in the fall. Imagine the women, their long dark hair covered by lace *mantillas*—black or white depending on the occasion—their *fiesta* dresses boasting trains, ribbons, frills and polka dots. In the distance the sounds of a guitar escape from a half-opened window—a song of love and death, for as any Spaniard will tell you, any love worth having must meet with a tragic end. Imagine too the tap-tap-tap of the flamenco dancer, arms intertwined, the music evaporating like steam, for the notes will not submit themselves to transcription and the dance vanishes forever once the passion of the dancer has been fully spent. And imagine then the heat, languorous, sultry, unbearable, the kind to be escaped in the early hours of the afternoon as shutters are closed and all retire inside for the *siesta*—those two hours of well-needed rest.

Inside the city's cathedral a tall, thin man with a prominent nose is hurrying towards the main door, dressed entirely in black, his ardent eyes focused on a distant horizon, his mind lost in unknown thoughts. See him? It is Emilio García—the man who will eventually marry Mónica Clemente—at this point a seminarian, though he will end his life as a humble bookseller in Seville.

It was Emilio's knowledge of English that would bring him much of his renown in his later days and it was this knowledge that also provided the means for the fateful meeting between Mónica Clemente and himself inside the city's great cathedral. It was here that Mónica came to say her daily prayers and it was here too that Emilio spent his mornings shepherding about the English tourists who had begun arriving in Andalucía in small numbers around this time.

Darkly dressed, sallow-skinned, large dark eyes peering out intently from beneath an unruly head of hair, the young man appeared almost cadaverous until he began to speak and then he seemed to suddenly ignite, as if a spark had entered his body and granted him the gift of life. "*Venga, venga,*" he would urge his charges, gathered dutifully by the Puerta de la Asunción. "Inside," he would enthuse, "await paintings by Murillo, Valdés Leal, Jordaens and Zurbarán. But that, gentlemen, is not all—shrines decorated with amethysts and emeralds, gold in abundance, the precious stones of Cardinal Mendoza and silver work the likes of which you have never seen before." And then he would wave them forward as if waiting inside that building were the keys to the heavens themselves, the enthusiasm in his voice increasing with every step until it reached a crescendo from where he would only slowly and reluctantly descend.

"Notice, if you will, the roof by Borja, *señores,*" he would point out to the tourists first. "A beauty, no? A marvel to behold."

"Ah yes, indeed," the tourists would respond, necks stretched awkwardly upwards trying to get a good look, their efforts interrupted abruptly by Emilio, who had already moved on to other more important things.

"And before you, the sculpture of Santa Veronica by Cornejo. Yes, splendid it is. I have no words to adequately describe such works. Magnificent, tremendous. *Señores,* you must admit that they simply fill the heart with awe."

"*So true,*" the English would agree, shaking their heads, eyebrows arched in wonder as their young tour guide charged earnestly ahead.

Emilio, to all appearances oblivious to those who trudged faithfully behind him, would continue to point out the delights of the cathedral. "On your right, the Virgin with the Christ, St. John and the Magdalena, all by Pedro Roldán. And, my personal favourite—notice, please, the stupendous statues and Corinthian pillars designed by Juan de Arce. Magnificent, *señores*, outstanding beyond compare."

The English would nod. Ah yes, ah no, of course and indeed, they would say, walking dutifully behind the young man who would saunter ahead as if fearing the great building itself was on the verge of disappearing into thin air and it was all they could do to catch this one final glimpse of it.

Later, alone in the cramped rooms of their *pensiones*, it was not the ostentatious delights of the cathedral the tourists would remember, but the enthusiastic young man who had been their guide: his passion, the quickness of his stride, his facility with English, which he spoke with such flourish and drama that it seemed in some ways a totally new language.

In the evenings too, alone in his dark room at the seminary, Emilio would pore over his books, trying with all his might to block out the gaiety of Seville. The sounds and the smells drifted into his room from the streets outside as people played, sang and declared their love for each other; because there, outside, were the sounds of life, he would tell himself and, thinking this, he would sink into despair at the sight of his narrow bed, the stained walls, the brass cross hanging over his desk and even his own pale hands turning the pages of a book by the dim candlelight.

On that particular evening, Emilio was reading the poetic works of Shelley, stumbling over the words but determined to get them right for if there was one thing that Emilio loved above all it was the sound of the English language.

English—yes, it seems strange indeed that a man who had been raised speaking the sonorous language of Lope de Vega and Cervantes felt such passion for the language he often accused of driving a person mad with its incomprehensible grammatical rules and its impossible pronunciation. But Emilio had been ensnared, seduced by English words, English cadences. Even more than the language, he loved the writers: Sir Walter Scott, above all, whose novels Emilio spent hours admiring, dictionary at the ready, or the heady outpourings of the English Romantics.

Inside the cathedral of Seville—not so much a building as a city in itself, with its staff of more than one hundred priests and sacristans, the comings and goings of peasants, tourists and nuns, the thirty Masses heard and the thirty yet to be heard in honour of Count this and *estimado señor* that, dead but nobly buried with seven priests and the most important families of Seville in attendance—Emilio would saunter along the hallowed aisles, savouring those English words as they rolled roughly from his tongue, all the while lamenting every moment that took him closer to a union with God.

It was his mother's wish that he become a priest. "You were conceived with that in mind," she had told him once. He had been born long after her other sons and shortly before the death of Emilio's father—yet another sign, she had argued, that he was meant for God, that he had come into this world to guarantee his father's passage from purgatory to heaven above and to ease the pain of her own life, a life she forever threatened was coming to an end, though the years passed and no end ever appeared imminent to those around her.

A tiny woman with a commanding voice, in her later years Emilio's mother had taken to spending much of her free time inside the churches of Seville. This habit had made her something of an authority, not, as you would think, on the architecture of these beautiful buildings, but on the many sins of the prominent dead of the city, in whose names Masses were said, bells rung and souls siphoned from purgatory by the prayers of those below.

Hoy se sacan ánimas, the churches proclaimed. *On this day souls will be set free.* To those tourists who were puzzled by things Spanish, nothing seemed more ridiculous than the thought of the numerous Masses paid by a man not yet dead in order that he be assured a place up above.

"Simply barbarous," the more critical would point out. "Proof indeed that Spain sits on the periphery of a distant century and that to Europe she surely does not belong."

To Remedios, Emilio's mother, these Masses were proof not of the barbarism of her compatriots but of another and more sinister truth, and that was this: only the rich ever secured a place for themselves in heaven. Those like her, who could not, had no choice but to find other means to ascend. It was in this spirit then that she offered up Emilio, for there was no greater reward, she knew, than the one saved for women who produced sons dedicated to the word of God.

Emilio had no desire to dedicate his life to God. Not even ten years old when his mother first informed him of her wish, he had determined from that moment on that his lot in life would be to escape, writhing and screaming if need be, from the stultifying clutches of the Church.

"Don't despair just yet," his friend Camilo would say to him years later when Emilio complained of his future as a priest in a city made for music, for gaiety—*vamos hombre,* let's just come out and say it—a city made for love.

"For remember, *amigo*," Camilo would continue, "in Spain only the clergy eat well."

For the purposes of our story, Remedios's obstinacy would prove fortuitous in the end. If she had not insisted on her son's adopting the clerical robes, Emilio would have never chanced upon Mónica Clemente as she bowed her head in prayer every day inside the great cathedral walls. Mónica and Emilio, born hundreds of miles apart in a time when people lived and died within miles of the dot that marked their entry into the world, should never have even met. And had it not been for a series of unforeseen circumstances, it would indeed have turned out that way; but fate had other things in store for them.

Mónica Clemente, a bit thin of lip, a tad long in the nose, was nevertheless blessed with a sweet face—the face of an angel, Emilio would say—though as we shall soon see, she was made of more complex matter than any angel with a golden halo and alabaster wings.

When Emilio spotted Mónica inside the cathedral for the first time, the girl had been living in Seville for less than a year. It had not taken long for the city to bewitch her with its narrow, ever-winding streets and its houses of pink, blue and yellow stucco; it was a fairy-tale setting, with its Arabic patios, its majestic fountains half-glimpsed from open gates, the weight and colour of the roses that hung from the balconies and the orange and lemon trees that perfumed its streets. Already, Seville was considered one of the true marvels of the world, immortalized in countless plays, poems and operas composed by the great European minds of the day.

To a young girl from a sleepy village in the region of La Mancha, Seville was like a magical apparition—a dream she found herself in almost by accident and in which she roamed with half-issued breaths. To breathe too deeply, she feared, would dissolve the dream in an instant, leaving her trapped once again inside the quiet village of her birth.

And how had she come to be there? Through misfortune, of course. For it is not from happiness that opportunities arise for fates to change and paths to diverge but from within the realm of the tragic—that which leaves us scrambling for solid ground, overwhelmed and lost. *Caminante,* the poet now declaims from stage right. *Walk, for the path is made by walking.*

Mónica Clemente had been sent to Seville, far from the fields of her beloved *Crocus sativus,* upon the death of her father and, with that death, had begun travelling a path that would change the direction not only of her own life but that of our mapmaker as well.

Seville was the home of Don Ricardo Medina, her mother's cousin, who was in need at the time of her father's demise of what the English called a governess. Mónica's skills were not extraordinary—embroidery, simple crochet, a tune or two played on the piano—but she performed them with reasonable technical skill and the lack of enthusiasm that was expected then from a proper lady.

"How lucky you are," her aunt had told her, when she was offered a place in the home of Don Ricardo, "to have found a saviour, even one so far removed from La Mancha." And, saying this, her aunt had sniffed at her own words, stopping to peruse Mónica with a look that said she was clearly undeserving of such beneficence.

Mónica herself would come to believe that it had not been luck but fate that had guided her way to the great city, because fate was like a giant serpent that coiled itself around your neck and dragged you towards your destiny without mercy or restraint. Escaping it was as useless as trying to stem a tidal wave with a fingertip. It was fate that had seen fit to free her from the dismal life that awaited many in her position, an existence lived within the confines of a convent or, worse, in a marriage arranged in haste to an old man with oxen and land to spare but with the spirit of decay emanating from his bones and breath like the steam that rose up from the earth during the hottest days of summer.

Instead, Mónica had been sent here, to Seville, to a city brimming with life, a city bustling with possibilities, as far away from the quiet plains of La Mancha as she could imagine. And although she was thankful, there were times when the city overwhelmed her, when it seemed too large, when its heartbeat was too penetrating, and then she would bring her fingers up to her nose and summon the comforting memory of Bautista's saffron stews with their fifteen ingredients that blended and brewed for hours.

So it was, then, that Emilio and Mónica chanced upon one another inside a cathedral that sat on an ancient mosque, with its spectacular Gothic *retablo* carved with the forty-five scenes from the life of Christ, the Capitular with the magnificent domed ceiling mirrored in marble on the floor, paintings by Murillo, silver reliquaries and monstrances and the keys—above all, those tear-stained keys—handed over reluctantly in the thirteenth century by the Moors to the Castilian king, Fernando III, after they were forced to surrender their beloved city to him. There, every day, Emilio would linger as long as he could near the kneeling figure of Mónica Clemente, providing the English with every detail of the enormous cathedral so astounding it could only have been built by madmen, all the while staring at the young girl who never failed to materialize here, always at the same time, always alone, it seemed.

A Spaniard for sure, he thought, for she wore a proper lace *mantilla* upon her head and not one of those infernal rose bonnets favoured by the English. It was true, the young women from the good families of Seville were lately succumbing to such fashions— bonnets from England, cretonnes from Alsace, crinolines from Paris, *malakofs* they called them. But this, he knew, was a proper Spanish *señorita*. A bit long in the nose, a tad thin of lip, but a Spanish *señorita* nonetheless, *mantilla* on head, rosary beads in hand, prayers regularly offered to the virgin—*a woman,* Emilio supposed, *who would make a splendid wife one day.* And once his mother died—*and forgive me Lord, but let it be soon,* Emilio thought, now looking up at the roof by Borja—it would be a woman like this Emilio would be courting.

Ah, and there she was now, head bent, eyes closed.

"*Bueno, señores,*" Emilio said to his group, his eyes fixed on the young woman's face. "Let us now take a final walk around the cathedral to inspect its jewels in all their magnificence."

"What did he say?" an old man, exhausted already by Emilio's first frenetic run around the building, asked his wife. "Not another damned walk around the cathedral!" he added furiously, beneath his breath.

Ah, but the English. Let us just admit this one thing now, shall we? Among their greatest virtues are their impeccable manners. So the unhappy man circled and then circled again, breathing in the damn "jools" of this magnificent cathedral, never suspecting that the tall, hawk-nosed seminarian who was leading them about was inspecting a young girl with all of this to-ing and fro-ing, this *vamos*-ing and *venga*-ing.

In the meantime, oblivious to Emilio and the English in his charge, Mónica Clemente continued, head bent over rosary, to issue her prayers. *Who was she praying for?* Emilio wondered, eyes glued to her face. *Was it for a mother, ailing and near death? Perhaps her prayers were being said for a sickly brother. Pray God, let them not be meant for a suitor,* he now thought, and thinking this, suddenly stumbled.

Mónica Clemente, sweet of face yes, but not, as he would later find out, so sweet of tongue, was not praying for a father or a mother, a brother or, thank God, a suitor. Mónica Clemente was praying, as she did every day, in order that she be granted her most cherished desire. And what is this, you ask? Ah, in a million years you will never guess. For Mónica Clemente, thin of lip and long of nose but sweet of face nonetheless, was praying fervently that the wife of Don Ricardo Medina—Doña Fernanda—be sent to her death.

"And it would be better if it were sooner rather than later," she whispered between her many *Padre Nuestros,* her countless *Ave Marías.*

"And not without a little pain," she added, as an afterthought.

But this, *claro,* only if the good Lord Himself should think it best.

We listen to the woes of Doña Fernanda

Enter stage left now Doña Fernanda Olivares—the woman whose death Mónica prayed for so fervently—an imposing figure in possession of her own map, though not, it is true, a map any cartographer would easily make sense of. This map was a catalogue of treachery, one she created in the darkest hours of the night and which she brought into the light at dawn. *Mira*, she would whisper to herself, fingering the imaginary parchment, these are the places where the heart has withered bit by bit. In the corner is the house that lies west of the Calle San Vicente, home to many of Seville's booksellers and several women of ill repute. Moving east—the house of Doña Alicia first, and almost next to it, that of Doña Lucía. And then there is the city of Malaga, all sun-drenched and blue water, a dot so brimming with affronts that it threatens to spill into the sea and blur away the details of the parchment.

The dots that were scattered across this map were responsible for making Doña Fernanda a very unhappy woman, a fact she used like a shield, revealing it at opportune moments to gain the upper hand. She was—in Mónica's words—imperious, domineering and hard on the eyes, but Mónica had good cause to dislike her, so it is best, perhaps, to try to get at her through other means. What was true, because it had been passed on from generation to generation like a canker gnawing in the family mouth, was that Doña Fernanda had forever lamented having known only fourteen days of happiness in all of her life. For years, her family had waited for her to add one day to that count, but no *fiesta*, wedding or family celebration ever made an impression on her, and she died leaving those two weeks firmly imprinted in her children's minds.

What did make her happy (or at least less rancorous) were the visits of Don Pedro, her parish priest, a corpulent fellow with a knack for attracting all of the city's gossip, and a ferocious appetite for kidneys and stewed beef. Every weekday afternoon, at exactly half past three, Don Pedro would amble over to the house of Doña Fernanda, making sure that all of Seville knew where he was headed and the ceremony with which he would be received.

And what ceremony! The Seville of the time was not so much a city as a medieval court with rules of conduct that would have made even the most enamoured knight desist his courting in despair. Take the visiting hours as an example. Why was Don Pedro so insistent that he must arrive at the gates of the Medina house at no later than a quarter to four? The answer resided in the rules of etiquette that governed the lives of the *Sevillanos* of the time, for it was strictly held that all visits should occur between the hours of three and six, with the most formal visitors being received in the first hour, the semi-formal in the next and the most intimate arriving in the final hour between five and six.

Don Pedro had been visiting Doña Fernanda for a decade and should have graduated to the final visiting hour long before, had he himself not strenuously objected. Claiming the hour between three and four was the only part of his day with some time to spare, time to be provided "to you, of course, Doña Fernanda," he would say, hands on his chest, "to which I add all my attentiveness and my respect," at which point the corpulent priest would attempt, with some difficulty, to bow and kiss Doña Fernanda's hand, a hand that would be quickly retrieved before the cleric's flaccid lips ever once managed to raze the lady's clammy skin.

The master servant of the house, a certain Don Raimundo, who hated the Church and, more than the Church, all of the priests, never failed to rail against the pompous prelate in the privacy of the kitchen at the back of the house.

"That pious ass says he lacks the time to come visiting at a later hour," he would complain to the other servants of the house. "I'll tell you what he does with his time. The weasel spends it inside the bars of Triana, rubbing shoulders with the gypsies and thieves—drinking and laughing it up when he should be saying a Mass to save some poor bastard's soul from the pit of purgatory. It's just like a priest, isn't it? A bleeding wound on the corpse of Spain." *Ay sí, Amén* the servants would all respond with gusto, for Don Pedro had few admirers among the members of the group, a group who resented his daily visits, his disdaining gaze, his insistence on a cold drink of *agraz* and most especially, the special treatment he demanded for his hat.

Ah, his hat. In the whole history of Seville, nothing had ever generated more conversation than Don Pedro's black felt hat. It was an ordinary top hat, much like the ones worn by the men of the day, but it sat rather uneasily atop the priest's head, contrasting oddly with his clerical collar and his long, black cape. That he should be demanding special privileges for his hat—"a cushion no less," the master servant had guffawed to the cook, outraged, when first told of it, "That barrel of a priest is looking for a cushion for his hat"—

was unheard of. Raimundo himself could hardly believe it, would not have believed it, had he not heard it from Doña Fernanda's own mouth: "Raimundo, make sure Don Pedro's hat is placed on that chair cushion by the door," she had said.

"I beg your pardon," he had replied, earnestly confused, for many were the archaic customs in this land bottled for antiquarians, a land where one of its ancient kings—finding himself seated too close to the fire—preferred burning to death than breaking the rules of decorum by moving away from the fire or shouting for help. In this land of hierarchies, titles and entitlements, the worth of a man could indeed be determined by the treatment accorded to his hat.

But never had a cushion been reserved for the head covering of a simple priest!

Doña Fernanda had repeated her command on that day and had done so in such a way that the servant, no fool himself, knew that she too realized the idiocy of her request, that she hated giving the command nearly as much as the good servant hated receiving it, but that some things in life came at a steep price. What those things were, Raimundo could not even hazard a guess, but he could think no improper thoughts of her—not out of any respect, but because it seemed inconceivable that even a character as decrepit and despicable as Don Pedro could want anything improper with the lady of the house. And so Raimundo placated his ire by complaining unendingly about the situation to the servants under his command.

As the scene began, Don Pedro was arriving at a quarter to four, late for his customary appointment with Doña Fernanda. It was a hot day in Seville, hotter than usual for May and the unseasonable heat, coupled with Doña Fernanda's anxiety over the appearance of yet another dot on her imaginary map, had stewed inside of her to such an extent that by the time Don Pedro rolled in—not, in the end, more than ten minutes late—she had almost resolved to decline receiving him at all.

If only she didn't need him so.

It is tragic to be burdened with a lack of confidants on whom anxieties can be deposited and whose kind words can erase fears, those imagined and those real, but Doña Fernanda—with her curt demeanour and imperious ways—had managed to alienate everyone but the priest and *thank God for the sanctity of his robes*, she thought, for many were the secrets she shared with him, always in confessional tones, so that the sanctity of his own vow to secrecy would compel him to keep her words guarded deep inside his breast.

(It did not. Don Pedro did not consider Doña Fernanda's confessions to be received in his capacity as a priest but as a respected guest who—*ojo, señores*—was even offered a cushion for his hat. Indeed he poured fuel on many a good hostess's fire who—for the price of a paltry dish of garbanzos and beef—could learn of the goings-on inside the house of Don Ricardo Medina as if from the mouth of Doña Fernanda herself.)

What ailed Doña Fernanda on most occasions were those dots—markers of her husband's infidelities—and her husband's infidelities were the stuff of legend in Seville, a city well accustomed to legends of the sort because it was home, after all, to Carmen, the Barber and Don Giovanni himself.

Madamina, il catalogo è questo. One thousand and three and counting still.

It was yet another indiscretion that had the *señora* in a state on this day, that had her brimming with anxiety and despair, that hardened her to the many entreaties of Don Pedro to "please for-give me for being late" and "Señora, I am at your feet" and so on until he finally tired of entreating and she tired of hearing him beg.

("It is amazing, Rosita," he would tell his sister later, speaking of Doña Fernanda, "that our fair Seville ever produced a slab of stone such as this!")

"Give your hat to Raimundo," Doña Fernanda told the priest gruffly, "and sit down quickly, as we have little time and much to discuss."

"I am at your service, Señora, as always of course," Don Pedro replied with relief, for he would have hated not to have been for-given especially because this exchange had been conducted before the insufferable master servant of the house. The same servant had just smirked at him—*I am sure of this,* he would tell his sister later—as he placed the priest's hat on the cushion, bowing his way in such an exaggerated manner that Don Pedro knew for sure Raimundo was having a laugh at his expense. And though his blood boiled at the thought of the man's impertinence, he knew nothing could be said. Some exchanges are conducted so that only the parties involved recognize all the undertones. Doña Fernanda, blind to anything that did not affect her directly, would frankly not have cared had she perceived the injury in any case.

For the next hour the priest paid for his tardiness by having to sit there immobile (not even a drink of *agraz* was offered this time) as Doña Fernanda embarked upon one of her more vicious tirades— her waiting having made her mood all the more virulent—in which every bone of her husband's body was put at risk through the enumeration of an impressive array of threats, none, of course, which would ever be realized—this was nineteenth-century Spain after all, and Andalucía yet, where well-to-do men spend Sunday afternoons promenading with wives and children and the evenings with mistresses or whores inside the brothels of Granada and Seville.

So you see, a little indiscretion was not so bad, at least in the larger scheme of things.

Doña Fernanda, it is true, had been bearing the weight of her husband's many indiscretions quite some time—for it must be said now that she and Don Ricardo did not marry for love; such a luxury could ill be afforded by the more prominent families of the day. The trick was to marry into one's social circle and forever maintain a stiff *inglés* upper lip. But Doña Fernanda, a martyr till the end, had never maintained a stiff upper lip, *inglés* or otherwise.

"This time it is worse, Don Pedro, infinitely worse, for it is happening here, inside my own house. Of this I am sure. Ricardo has always hid his indiscretions badly but this one he is not even bothering to hide at all. *Virgen María Purísima*, the things I am forced to accept."

The governess. Don Pedro knew it had to be the governess—she was the only one young enough in the household to have attracted Don Ricardo's eye—a lecherous eye, that one, he would tell his friend Doña Ana later. How that eye ever found itself resting on Doña Fernanda's face was one of God's greater mysteries, although marriage was not made for the sins of the heart—even a simple priest like him was certain of that.

For the next hour he sat listening without interjecting anything other than the usual exclamations of *Oh* and *Ah*—the signs of outrage expected of him at the appropriate times, as Doña Fernanda vented her rage. "Oh, God, how difficult it is to have been born woman," she railed until, spent, she finally allowed him to excuse himself. It was almost five by then and he was to give a Mass to free from purgatory the soul of a certain Don Calixto, who had managed to sire six illegitimate daughters throughout his long life, the news of which was snaking its way along the streets of Seville.

"Then do not bother with the Mass, Don Pedro," Doña Fernanda told him, her nostrils pinched, her head held high, "for that man is not in purgatory, but in Hell roasting along with the rest of the world's libertines."

On his way out, Don Pedro made sure to take the insufferable servant aside and, far from the ears of Doña Fernanda, lecture him on proper conduct and the respect that should be granted to the priests who had taken the Sacrament of the Holy Orders: "For there is no greater Sacrament than that, you ignorant peasant—a sacrament that makes one responsible, lest you should forget, for seeking absolution for the miserable likes of you. But only, *oye bien,* when and if they like."

And with these words barely out of his lips the priest grabbed the hat from the servant's hands and turned to leave but not before being subjected to one last bow from Raimundo, a bow lower than any bow ever delivered the priest's way so that the servant's nose came to touch the floor and his ample behind rose high in the air saluting the heavens from where, it is supposed, God himself watched the scene unfold in silent repose.

On a stone bench, a seguiriya

By the time Emilio García and Mónica Clemente actually met, the young woman was four months' pregnant and desperate for Doña Fernanda's death. Yes, it is true, our heroine was caught in one of the most hackneyed situations in the books—unmarried, pregnant, an innocent Zerlina to Ricardo's Don Giovanni—seduced from a balcony into a bed not by a man's looks nor his charm, but by a spectacular dot on a Spanish map. For what Mónica Clemente fell in love with is a city and you, of all people, Abuela, knew well what Seville is capable of—she can bewitch, ensnare, overwhelm the senses with jasmine, roses and sun until you are weak at the knees and in love with love, whatever its guise, whatever its name.

Mónica Clemente, at this point just eighteen years old, was caught in a muddle of emotion—saffron memories, grief over her father's death, relief to find herself in Seville and not in some godforsaken convent up north, homesickness at times, elation at others, desperation, excitement, and the irrational fears that were seeded during this time and that would flourish and afflict her throughout her life. She was, in short, a small-town innocent adrift in a city whose dimensions were too large for her to fully comprehend—easy prey for the likes of Don Ricardo, who, let's face it, was used to dancing the tango with much fancier fish.

It is worth repeating that Mónica had not fallen in love with Don Ricardo's charisma nor with his looks—both of which he might once have had but of which he could boast no more. He was an old man now but still trapped inside the illusion that his charm had somehow outlived his youth. It had not. What Mónica had fallen in love with was what only he could provide: the chance to assume a position in Seville, to live in his house not as governess to his children but as his legitimate wife—with access to all a wife was privy to, his circle of friends, his home, every important nook and cranny of a city that had taken her heart by storm.

It did not occur to Mónica that even with the Doña dead, Don Ricardo would not marry her, that marriage was an arrangement made according to family name and family wealth and that she possessed neither. It did not occur to her that she was merely one of many—that this business of *Lá ci darem la mano* had been played out many times before and would be played out many times again. (It is curious indeed that only one illegitimate child is known of, given the many dalliances Don Ricardo engaged in during his long and sordid jaunt through life.)

It was at this point also that Emilio had finally resigned himself to a life lived among chalices and crosses—a speck of white in a long life of black, of Masses for the dead and baptisms for the newly arrived and the confessions uttered by old women harbouring tedious secrets of the heart.

His mother would not be dying in any foreseeable future—this much was clear. In truth, she seemed stronger than ever now that the time was fast approaching for her son to take his vows before God, and as that day neared, Emilio's spirits grew steadily worse.

It had not gone unnoticed. Yesterday it had been Don Pedro who appeared before him, issuing the stern warnings that were meant to separate those with a true calling from those who longed not for a union with God, but the guarantee of a warm meal and a roof over one's head. Don Pedro had put it clearly enough. A priest's work was the most important of all for he was an emissary of the Lord; he had the power to absolve sins; only he could exorcise evil spirits from the hearts of troubled men; he was the conduit that bound heaven to this sullen earth. "And, above all—listen well, my boy, for this is most important—because he has the power that is bestowed by the people themselves when they offer up their most penurious secrets in exchange for forgiveness from the Lord."

Emilio did not want to hear the penurious secrets of strangers. His heart was not in it. *To become a servant of God was never my wish.* Besides, he had his own penurious secrets—his desire, especially, that his mother die before he was forced to don the habit; his love for the tales of Sir Walter Scott, the blue flower of Novalis, the poetry of Wordsworth and Keats. At night, when his fellow seminarians pored over their St. Augustine and their St. Jerome, Emilio lost himself inside the exploits of English knights, and hung on to Byron's and Shelley's every ardent word of love.

You may ask how it is that we have come to know Emilio's dark thoughts with respect to his faith, and we will answer you that they have made their way to the map. There has never been a man in love with words who has not unburdened himself on paper, parchment, or in the most stringent circumstances, on the back of his aged hand. Emilio's words, exquisitely arranged because he had a sublime mind in addition to a generous heart, are represented symbolically on the parchment we hold in our hands. A lone figure at the top, dressed in seminarian black, holding onto a book of poetry, sadness pulling at the corners of his eyes.

Every afternoon he confessed his sins with the rest of the penitents, always stopping short of confessing his darkest truth—that he questioned the existence of God Himself. It was this, above all, that kept him from marching towards his fate with anything other than trepidation, and no infinite number of *Ave Marías* or *Pater Nosters* or times he ingested the body of the Lord—*in vitam eternam Amen*—or the deprivations he visited upon his body with the fasting and the all-night meditations, naked on a stone floor—none of these things did anything to erase the uneasiness from his soul. He felt imprisoned by his own doubt—could not rid himself of the questions that distanced him from God.

It was at this point that Emilio and Mónica met—the gods of symmetry rejoicing in their splendid machinations. Two people praying for a death in order to acquire a different life found each other inside a *temenos* of the most splendid kind. A gorgeous cathedral: roof by Borja, sculptures by Cornejo and Roldán, pillars by José de Arce, incense in almost obscene amounts.

Mónica Clemente, agitated from all the praying and the fears that were magnifying with time, got up to leave and managed, in her haste, to bump into Emilio as he returned from dispatching the last of the tourists he had been shepherding about. Looking up and seeing nothing but black, Mónica mistook the hapless Emilio for a man vested already with the power of God. She had a thought. Perhaps she must confess—it had been an awfully long time and she was asking God to grant her a favour. Something would have to be offered up in return.

Emilio, breathless from the simple act of being so close to the object of his desire, faltered and stammered when she looked up, smiled and told him, "I need to confess, *por favor.*" What was a besotted man to do? Tell her the truth and thus destroy the one chance to meet his lady love, for this was nineteenth-century Spain and decent young women did not engage in talk with men who were not their fathers, brothers or their parish priests? No, he thought, this was no time to be honest, not when fate had delivered up this chance, this one moment in which to reorient a life.

He took her to a nearby confessional—so emboldened by the opportunity that he did not bother to check to see if anyone had caught him playing the priest months short of the mark—and there he listened to every detail of the lady's deeds, every one of the lady's dark thoughts. And it was at that very moment that Emilio finally experienced a moment of spiritual truth, an epiphany if you like. Lady Serendipity beats on his door for the very first time—as two people, each in need of a quick death, met in darkness, one seeking absolution for sins of the heart and mind, the other, in the act of committing an even greater one.

Yet the time was not ripe for Emilio to reveal himself. Reasoning that a flustered young woman—one mired in such an ugly dilemma to boot—was unlikely to remember the brief glimpse she had of him before being ushered into the darkness of the confessional to unburden herself of her sins, he merely nodded his head like the best of them and offered up a smattering of the Catholic repertoire for her to repeat in prayer.

And then he waited. Emilio was more sophisticated than Mónica Clemente, who had been raised in a small town far from the danger and profligacy of a city such as Seville, and he knew with certainty that there would be no marriage to the *estimado* Don Ricardo Medina of the Medinas of Seville, and that the day was fast approaching when the child she carried would no longer be so easily concealed under long capes and carefully arranged shawls.

And as that day approached, Mónica's eyes, once star-struck with city love and the excitement of this new life so far from her simple home, began to dim. Don Ricardo was told of the child, between heartfelt sobs and pleas for help, and she, naïve as could be, actually expressed surprise when her devout lover recoiled from her in shock and did not, as she had hoped, embrace her in blissful delight.

"I know a family who can take you in, Mónica," he said, the smell of fear on his breath. He promised her help far from his home, far from Seville and far from his wife. "But you must leave the house before your situation can be perceived." He insisted, knowing that this affront would be more than Doña Fernanda would be prepared to allow. "In my own home!" she would scream. "Beneath my very nose!" And so on until she bellowed him out of the house and he found himself lying prostrate in the outskirts of Seville. His wife had lungs of steel and a voice as sharp as the blade of a Toledo sword and she would not tolerate news of an illegitimate child with anything less than an uncontainable rage.

"No, no," she had told him more than once. "Let all the other men in Seville dilly and dally till they're blue in the face. But you, Don Ricardo, would be wise to respect my family's good name."

Everything always began and ended with the family name. But what was a name if not four walls within which to imprison a husband: a stifling ten letters to strangle the life from a man full of it? He liked to look at his reflection and see the energy brimming from his gaze, liked to position himself in front of the mirror and witness the glow—still as strong as a young colt, he would think, ignoring the jowls that tugged at his face, his toothless smile, his ever-protruding girth. Oh no, the girl would not put an end to his conquests. He was no more in love with his young cousin than his own wife, would not let this young thing, silly in the extreme, he now thought, keep him from continuing to explore the mysterious contours of the city of his birth.

Oh Seville, from whose heart sprung Velázquez and Murillo, whose feet gave life to music, city of a thousand guitars, a thousand celebrated songs. City of lights and *fiestas* and the lament that unites death and life in one single moment of neverending passion and joy. A city that is not just a city but a burning bush, *mi amigo*— capable of transforming even the most severe Victorian gent into a passionate, emotional fool.

Beware at what point you choose to stop and live your life, Emilio cautions from the depths of his fabulous map. Take heed. For a city has a role to play in how things will unfold. How right he was then and how much truer it seems today, when the choices are endless and we find ourselves adrift on an ocean, swimming desperately from shore to shore in search of that one magic place to call home.

Emilio watched as the days passed and Mónica's agitation grew more marked, her face more peaked, watched as her every prayer was uttered with more vehemence, waited until the day she literally collapsed into the pew, and it was on that day, finally, that he knew the time had arrived to make his move.

He approached her as she was leaving the cathedral. "Señorita," he said, "you may not remember, but you asked for confession not too long ago from me."

"*Ay sí,*" she replied, not really remembering, but sufficiently disoriented to assent with a nod of the head.

"Could we speak over here?" he asked, motioning to a corner, private enough for a talk but public enough so as not to alarm the young woman, who was growing evermore confused. She had been instructed well by the nuns at the Convent of the Carmelitas, knew how to embroider on fine linen, could play the more popular pieces on a piano without the need of a score, had mastered the art of not infusing the playing with any unwomanly passion or verve. She could quote the poetry of the best poets from the Golden Age, knew the adventures of Don Quijote from beginning to end. And, despite her naïveté with respect to Don Ricardo, she knew a thing or two about priests as well. Knew that not all were as wholly dedicated to God as they claimed. Take Don Gustavo, the parish priest back home. He had at least four illegitimate children and a live-in help rumoured to be more lover than maid. So she was not entirely surprised that the young priest—who turned out not to be a priest but a seminarian masquerading as a man whose allegiance to God had already been pledged—was offering a solution to her plight.

"We need each other," he said.

Mónica coughed, lowered her eyes, and said nothing yet.

Emilio was careful not to scare her off with the weight of his true feelings. The girl was frightened and the girl was lost, he thought. Why tell her more than she needed to know?

"If we marry," he continued, "you will have a father for your child, and I, an excuse to abandon the cloth."

Still she said nothing. But she began to raise her eyes, furtively, stole a quick look at the awkward young man who was seeking, incomprehensibly enough, to make her his wife. His nose was prominent and his skin strangely sallow in a land awash with so much sun—but he was not an altogether repulsive man.

He was not cut from the same cloth as Don Ricardo, she could see that. And let us be clear, this bothered her more than she cared to admit. He had neither the bearing nor the clothes, could clearly not offer her the position she so coveted, a life lived among the luxuries she had grown accustomed to in a short time.

Dreams die hard if they die at all, and Mónica's dream of marriage to Don Ricardo was struggling to remain alive in the face of a certain ugly demise. Perhaps Doña Fernanda would still succumb to some mysterious disease, she thought. Perhaps she would disappear, would be magically transported to another place and time. Perhaps, *quizá*, perhaps.

Time was galloping. The walls were caving in.

During the next three weeks, Mónica appeared at the cathedral for her regular morning prayers, where she waited to meet with the seminarian on a bench close to the building's main doors. Here they sat, not too close but close enough, Emilio growing more determined as each day passed, Mónica's dreams dissolving, minute by minute, bit by bit.

Do you know, we ask our Abuela, the most powerful of all flamenco songs? The *seguiriya*, *sí*, but do we really have to ask this from a woman who lived and breathed for flamenco, for her memories of Seville, where the guitar is ascendant and the tap-tap of the dancer beats constantly, helping the city to keep time? The *seguiriya*, you say, *sí*, the most powerful gypsy lament, the one that tells of a tragic and bitter existence, sung in a rhythm that alternates between 3/4 and 6/8 time. It is a song worthy of the lament; for those who are not versed in the intricacies of the *cante jondo*, it is hard to discern where the *seguiriya* begins and where it ends.

When we think of Mónica on that bench—a cool spot to hide from the punishment of a too hot sun, a stone chair for a heart that is growing colder and wiser in equal time—it is the *seguiriya* we hear in the background. It is a song of despair never abandoned by the strumming of a guitar, a song awash in black tones and deep feeling, a song sung for all the dreams we had for ourselves, our hopes and expectations for a life that never delivered on its promise, that took our adolescent dreams and squashed them like a hammer beating on an overripe pear.

They married in the end, no one as happy with the outcome as the surprised, then relieved, and finally, indifferent Don Ricardo, who promptly forgot the whole affair until he was compelled to remember it many years later by a force of hand and a twist of fate.

We have always wondered about Don Ricardo, about men like him. Was he just a simple womanizer or a man more complicated than the details of his life can hope to reveal?

But history is like that. As hard to interpret as a map created by a culture whose traditions and mindset you know nothing about. It leaves only outcomes in its wake and very rarely evidence of the true feelings and motivations of those in whose hands events unfolded and whose actions had a role in shaping our destinies into what they are.

There was one victim who emerged seething from the marriage of Emilio and Mónica—Remedios, Emilio's Mass-mad mother. Bad enough to have lost her one chance at immortality, her one opportunity to have endless prayers said on her behalf, ensuring her prompt escape from the pit of purgatory into the glory of heaven guarded by St. Peter and his haloed help. Infinitely worse was the fact that her son, the seminarian, had impregnated a nobody from La Mancha, had been forced to make the girl his wife.

She never forgave him. Never saw her grandson who, as we

know, was not her grandson in any case. She lived for many years after that, in decent health and in want of nothing, her outrage at her son's betrayal providing ample fuel to keep her going well past her allotted days.

Inside a bookstore on the Calle San Vicente

Let us turn now to the maps of our childhoods. Therein we find the coordinates of happiness and loss, of innocence and half-remembered dreams. There, too, is the taste of the madeleine and the ever-present promise that hangs, forever suspended in mid-air. Intense sunsets, first-love and heartbreak, moments lived as if all subsequent ones are destined never to pass. The past merges into the present; the present subsumes into dreams of the future; the future is too nebulous and distant to be of use. Childhood is a dreamlike state, a vibrant map—and for too many lost souls, it is a lifelong curse.

Diego García Clemente, born on a warm Christmas Day, was blessed with a happy early childhood, at least. When Emilio married Mónica, he accepted not only her, but also her son, fully into his heart. "Only saints are born on Christmas Day," he said to Mónica. "Jesus, the boy Segundo, who once minded my mother's stables and was as good as freshly baked bread, and our own child, Diego."

Alas, Abuela, although you wished it otherwise, there would be no other portents that they were witnesses to a momentous birth. No wise men appeared; the trees in Seville did not suddenly burst into bloom; no star shone brightly in the East.

They would have other children, Mónica and Emilio, but all

would fail to survive past the early few months—victims of premature birth, disease or, as Mónica liked to put it, "of being wise to what the world would deliver and choosing to abandon it quickly." Despite Emilio's kindness, his generosity and his unconditional acceptance of Don Ricardo's bastard son, Mónica would never fully abandon her dream of reuniting with the Don himself, would never fully accept that this little life she had stumbled upon was the one she deserved and not punishment for having dared to dream. And this thought, insidious but deeply held, hardened her against what others in her position might have interpreted as her supreme good luck.

Instead, she retreated to that spot on her map that marked her past, only to be held captive there by the many if-onlys and the countless could-have-beens. Thus, her days as a convent girl, those days she had once decried for their brutality—the good sisters had taught her well but often with the backs of their hands—seen now from a vantage point skewed by regret, became her glory days, days of fresh air and the smell of the *azafrán*, and her present life in Seville, the city she had once loved, was now the jail that had, through force of circumstance, become her home.

So it was that she transformed the quiet town of her birth into a shrine, the boredom of the long days and the hard work harvesting the saffron forgotten in the wake of the blow that life had delivered her. Instead, what was now remembered was the town as it appeared on one day a year, dressed in its finest vestments to celebrate the festival of its patron saint, Saint Agatha, when the women congregated at the baker's house to cook and talk, their efforts infusing the town with the seductive smells of freshly baked cake.

So it is with the past—a state, a place the great St. Augustine spoke of as a spacious palace—a vast, immeasurable sanctuary.

Who really can plumb its depths?

Emilio was not held captive to his past in the least. On the contrary, his love for Mónica had armed him with the courage to embark upon a new life and he did so with relish and without regret. His Uncle Alfonso, owner of a bookstore in the Calle San Vicente, provided him with employment inside his shop, a shop visited increasingly by English travellers who wanted to learn more about Spain. They appreciated being guided by Emilio, whose English was respectable and whose enthusiasm for their own writers flattered and convinced them that they were being served by the very best.

By the time little Diego was one, he was spending most of the day inside the shop—the Librería Alfonso—hiding among the books, a happy prisoner of dust and ticks, mesmerized by the feel of heavy paper, the smell of glue and ink. There he would be taught how to read, first in Spanish and then, under the spell of Emilio's enthusiasms, in English, as it appeared in the poems of the Romantics. His knowledge of English was forever coloured with elegies and odes, things less useful than they were beautiful, and he came to share Emilio's belief that English was the language not of progress, as its native speakers believed, but the language of beauty and of life itself.

Uncle Alfonso, a lifelong bachelor and a man of many ill moods, never ceased to complain about the child. "There he is again, the scamp, eating the books," he would accuse, pointing a shaky finger his way. Emilio would respond by laughing and removing little Diego from the scene of the crime, bits of paper hanging still from the edges of his tiny mouth, screaming at the indignity of being moved until he could crawl back to his spot and resume his meal of words and rhymes.

In his more impatient moments, Uncle Alfonso would try to move the boy with the end of a broom, poking at him until Diego's screams filled the store and Emilio appeared to rescue him from the old man. But eventually Diego came to view the episodes with the broom as a game and, growing stronger as his aged great-uncle grew weaker, he would pull it from the old man's hands and swat it back at him until Alfonso's curses drained the store of all the fine poetry lodged inside.

"The boy belongs with his mother," he would tell Emilio, who would nod but keep Diego close by his side because there was always something amiss with Mónica. She was either weak because she was pregnant, mourning a dead baby when she was not, and with no energy whatsoever in-between all the births and all the deaths. It was all she could do to keep the house in a semblance of order and cook the occasional meal.

They lived above the store and below Uncle Alfonso, who hovered above them in a room in the attic, from which he shouted at them to be quiet, couldn't they see he was an old man, infirm and weak, and couldn't they be thankful, for it was he who had given them a roof to live under and bread to eat? And where was his meal? That's all he ever asked for, a meal and not a good one at that because Mónica of La Mancha had no talent in the kitchen and from what he could see, little talent to boast of when it came to everything else as well. What a shame to have been burdened with such a woman, Emilio, he would shout down at them. That you should have abandoned God for such a woman is more than a shame, it is an unpardonable sin.

Mónica, her body spent from pregnancy or childbirth, yes, but her lungs made of sterner stuff, would scream up to the attic, "*Cállate, viejo.* Be quiet for once, you silly fool." And then, bitter from having to deal with the old man upstairs, from having to live in three small, dark rooms with no fine linen, no kitchen help, nothing to compare to those hallowed days inside the house of Don Ricardo Medina, with its proper courtyard with decorative fountains and plenty of fresh air, she would turn her anger to Emilio.

"Patience, Mónica, patience," Emilio pleaded with her, though in truth he was the only one with patience, a patience he nurtured by escaping with Diego at every opportunity, to the store, to the street, hiding behind a book that he read by the dim light of a candle, retreating to any corner in search of a moment of quiet, a bit of peace.

It was to escape from the weight of Mónica's bitterness that Emilio dreamed up the idea of offering tours of the city to the English, for if they had expressed interest in the cathedral, how much more would they express for the city as a whole? "Because Seville is not only a city of oranges," he would tell Uncle Alfonso, "but a city dreamed of by Hercules and founded by none other than Julius Caesar himself—one, *oye,* of the greatest men to have ever lived." And then, to underscore this, he would embark upon reciting the well-known refrain:

Raised by Hercules,
Julius Caesar fortified me,
with high walls and towers,
I was conquered for the king
of heaven by Garcí Pérez de Vargas

to which Uncle Alfonso would respond by rolling his eyes and saying, "That, *sobrino,* is a load of rot, but if it pleases you and brings in the English money, so be it."

The tours began slowly at first, but their popularity grew because Emilio not only spoke English but he was also a good story-teller and always knew what to leave out and what to tell. It was his theory that the English people, from whose minds sprang such glorious poetry, had of late been prone to a certain surliness born of industry and that for this condition, stories of love were the only cure. And so along with the tales of the Romans and the Visigoths and eight centuries of Arab rule, he never failed to tell them of Pedro I's unrequited passion for Doña María Fernández Coronel, who suffered immeasurably at the hands of this cruel king, so desperate to have her that he imprisoned her husband and had him tortured to death. Inside the kitchens of the Convent of Santa Clara, the poor woman rid herself of Pedro's advances by throwing boiling oil over her face. Emilio would tell his group, his eyes raised upwards, passion in his breath, that, thus disfigured, she became venerated for her chastity and her mummified body lay in the choir of the Convent of Santa Inés.

The English liked the story well enough but preferred visiting the great Álcazar and the Giralda to perusing the remains of a virtuous woman disfigured by the obsessions of an ancient Spanish king. In any case, stories of love did not inflame their industrious hearts as Emilio had hoped, but reminded them instead of the unruly passions of the Spanish—and especially the Andalusians— who were responsible for keeping their country mired in the brackish waters of tradition, ignorance and economic despair. A city concerned only with the carnal pleasures of love could not hope to ascend the world's stage, could not expect to lift itself from its lethargic existence of sleep and song. City of a thousand roses, yes. City of heat and light, that too. But also the city that lost a continent, lest you should ever forget.

And as if to underscore their suspicions, Emilio would then trot the tourists over to the Plaza de los Refinadores to show them the bust of Don Juan Tenorio himself, which astounded the English even more because their busts and statues were of weighty persons like Shakespeare and the great Elizabeth I and not of fictitious libertines.

Ah, but the Spanish—and the Andalusians, above all. Oh dear, oh well. No, no please, Don Emilio, do go on.

These tours would not be worth a mention had they not turned out to be especially important to the history that followed, and more than the history, the means to depict it as well. It was through these tours that Diego stumbled upon the two obsessions that would define his life, driving him like an ancient conquistador across an ocean and into the arms of a spectacular New World— the twin obsessions that have weaved their way through the generations of this family like a hereditary virus capable of infecting even those of us who sit here so far removed from the coordinates of Diego's own life.

The vector for this virus chanced upon them during one of Emilio's English tours. His name was Mr. Raleigh and he appeared in their lives when Diego was just nine years old—armed to the teeth with copies of ancient maps and eager to share the stories they told, stories so full of wonder, so brimming with the steps and missteps of the human race that their mere mention today never fails to bring a chill to our spines.

Little Diego, enamoured already of the books that lined the walls of the Librería Alfonso, found himself battling a greater obsession yet, just like Pedro I, but not for a woman, no, no woman was worthy of a passion such as this. The maps that

Mr. Raleigh traded were not just beautiful, they were much more than that—their brilliance truly did shame the stars, the stories they told more majestic than the words of Lope de Vega and the delusions of Don Quijote combined. The maps made Diego nervous, anxious to possess them, jealous of those men, like el Señor Raleigh, who had the means to travel the world in search of these ancient treasures and who, upon finding them, could make them theirs.

It was here, in one of Mr. Raleigh's maps, that Diego first saw the country that would eventually beckon him forth.

"Mexico—did I tell you how Charles V first learned about the nature of Spain's distant colony?"

"No, Señor Raleigh. Please do tell."

"Very well, then. An envoy of Hernan Cortés appeared at the Spanish court and when asked by Charles V to describe what the new land was like, he picked up a sheet of paper, crumpled it into a ball and then unfolded it in his palm saying, *it is like this, sire.* "

Sire, it is like this. A paper, twisted and creased, a land with unkempt borders but, when straightened and flattened, capable still of piercing the skin.

He had an intuition then—would remember it much later on—that this crumpled paper would be his future too.

In the meantime, Diego's father was sinking every day further under the weight of all his unfulfilled dreams.

Poor Emilio. The brighter a man's light, the darker the shadow, and Mónica's ill moods had done their work on him. He had been nodding apologetically for much too long. His head felt weary from all that movement, his heart heavy from the love that had once changed his life but was now siphoning it from his very bones.

Could she not be quiet for just one moment? Something was always wrong: the house was too dark, the city too lit up. It was too hot, at times it seemed dreadfully cold. There was no money in books, no money to buy a new *mantilla*, not a *real* to spare with which to buy Diego some proper shoes. How long was she supposed to live like this? Nothing in her past had prepared her for the disappointments that visited day after day with no respite visible on the horizon, no light left to guide her way through the dark.

"You hear that, Emilio?" Uncle Alfonso would shout from his attic, interrupting Mónica's litany of complaints. "This is what you get for your ridiculous love of English words. That's right, my son. Congratulate yourself, for you've managed to find a proper Shakespearean shrew!"

And then the arguing would begin in earnest. "The old man, that sick and useless old man," she would scream at Emilio, as if Emilio had suddenly lost his hearing, and Uncle Alfonso would shout back, "More useless than the *señorita* of La Mancha? Impossible!" And the night would continue like this, one shouting up the stairway, the other down, both cursing and reproaching, both indifferent to what Emilio thought or felt, both oblivious when he quietly slipped through their venom and went downstairs to the store for a bit of quiet, some peace of mind. And there, in the corner, crouched tightly as if he were attempting to disappear, was Diego—a fugitive too of the war of words upstairs, book in hand. When he caught sight of Emilio, his hands flew up in the air as if to say, there they go. There they go again.

It was hard for Emilio not to resent the child at times, though it always sickened him later, his resentment, because he did love Diego. The child's enthusiasms were his own. He was the only bright light existing in his universe, next to his tours and his books.

But it was hard to bear the fact that Mónica could carry Don Ricardo's child without incident, could give birth to this boisterous, happy boy and not manage to supply him, Emilio, the man who had sacrificed himself for her (that's how he came to see it, as a sacrifice) with a child of his own flesh and blood capable of surviving beyond the first three weeks.

Not even the English poets could now bring him relief. His days were too long and too full to permit himself the luxury of reading any of the books he sold. At least he could still depend on the friendship of those who, like el Señor Raleigh, brought some much needed light into his world. The Englishman stopped by the bookstore often, where he entertained Emilio and little Diego with his magnificent maps and his towering tales of the New World.

"Did I tell you how truly admirable your Columbus was?"

El Señor Raleigh always referred to Columbus as "your Columbus," a statement that flattered Emilio and Diego both, though they knew it was not Columbus who belonged to them but his discovery of the New World. Yet, it was a fine discovery and it pleased them enormously that an Englishman should remember that it was indeed "theirs."

"The Spanish *conquistadores* were indeed a fanciful lot. Upon returning to Spain, they told of the extraordinary sights to be found in the New World—whales with breasts, flying fish, and beaches covered not with sand but pearls. The mermaids were a disappointment though. They had imagined extraordinary creatures and were dismayed when they failed to be as beautiful as their imaginations had conceived them to be. Columbus himself believed in the existence of Saint Bernard's Island, where the daughters of Atlas guarded a luscious garden filled with golden apples.

"They were men in search of mythical cities. Some they found and some remained trapped in their imaginations for all time— the seven cities of Cíbola, for example. Have you never heard tell of this?"

Emilio knew the story well enough but he encouraged its telling for Diego's sake.

"Around those fanciful times, legend had it that during the Moorish invasion of Spain, seven bishops and their congregations had sailed west and founded seven great cities of gold in the New World. These cities were known as the seven cities of Cíbola.

"Many men planned expeditions to find these fabled cities, but it was Francisco de Coronado who ventured into the American Southwest in 1540 in search of them. He did not find them in the end, but the dream of their discovery nurtured the aspirations of many other men in the centuries that followed."

El Señor Raleigh lowered his voice to a whisper. "There is a rumour in Madrid that a map exists of the seven cities of Cíbola, drawn by the one man who made it there but took the secret with him to his grave. That man was an Andalusian and it is thought that his map is in the possession of one of the booksellers of Seville. Is it you, Don Emilio?" he asked with a chuckle.

"Ah, if only I were in possession of such a map! How much easier it would be to live my life. No, it is not I, Señor Raleigh. Regrettably, it is not I. Nor anyone that I have ever come into contact with."

For years, Diego would be haunted by the thought of that map. More than years—for that map, the thought of that map, inflamed Diego's imagination, haunting him throughout his life. Who was that Andalusian, who was that bookseller and what of the seven cities of Cíbola? Were they indeed made of gold? Did they boast the most beautiful mermaids in the world? Were they the cities where one could find the key to eternal life?

Diego's own mind was fanciful. He had read the dreams of those who had gone before him and was convinced that his future lay there. On the other side of the ocean, in a world not only new but golden, not only alive but overflowing with life. How he longed to travel the yellow waters of the Guadalquivir until they deposited him in the vast ocean, to ride the waves like Phaeton in his golden carriage as he dragged the sun across the sky.

Ah, but you, Abuela, who lived so long, know more than anyone how the world sags under the weight of our intentions. How our dreams, once realized, are dreams no longer. Dreams and night-mares—two sides of the same coin; he who dreams of knights will live to see them transformed into monsters in the morning.

In the meantime, under the cover of darkness, Emilio had stumbled upon the tiny spark that would ignite his life for one brief moment before the curtains fell on his spot on the stage. A song. A dance. A lament worthy of the name, where voices carry for eter-nity and ruptured hearts find a way, through the intensity of the *jaleo,* to mend.

To his shame, it was a tourist who alerted him fully to this glory, a foreigner who arrived intent on imbibing Andalucía's riches inside the confines of a dimly lit café, for these were the great days of the *cafés cantantes* in Seville. Oh, how your eyes would once shine, Abuela, when describing these days, how you seemed to float back in time as if you had been there yourself witnessing the rebirth of flamenco inside those rooms lit by oil and paraffin lamps.

In those days, a man by the name of Silverio Franconneti, half-Italian, half-Spanish, but with the spirit of the gypsies coursing through his blood, opened the Café de Silverio on the calle del

Rosario, with a view to waking his countrymen up. He opened the doors in order to stoke the passion that lay dormant in their bones, to unearth the unuttered howls that clouded minds in a land filled with so much sun. He opened the doors to music that soaked the organs with quicksilver and found its way right to the pit of the soul. He opened the doors so as to sing, his voice as powerful an instrument as there ever was—a mixture, in the words of the great poet of flamenco, García Lorca, of Italian honey and lemon from Andalusian soil—a man who knew all the songs and sang them until those who listened wept in despair and begged him to stop.

Inside the Café de Silverio—a Sevillian patio with a fountain in the centre, Moorish columns, multicoloured tiles and the sacred platform, the *tablao,* from where guitarists, dancers and singers conducted their incomparable Mass at the front—Emilio sat night after night until the amber voices of the singers insinuated themselves into his blood, displacing the hallowed words of the English poets with the sighs of the *seguiriyas* and the howls of the *soléas*.

There, on that sacred stage, the singers intoned and declaimed what he himself could not, the frustrations, the deceptions, the ache that surged from the weight of all life's unfulfilled promises, an existence where there were only scant minutes of happiness, scattered pages where one had expected more substantial tomes. It was as if the singer and he were strings tuned to the same pitch, and when one was plucked, the other could not help but vibrate sympathetically to the touch. It was as if something had been unearthed from that part of himself that had once seen the potential in everything, that had been able to fashion dreams from specks, universes from three lines of a poem.

Inside the café, a cup of wine in his hand, his eyes heavy from the sounds, the smells, the view of a dancer's bare leg as a foot came down furiously on the floor, Emilio felt himself transported to a kingdom outside of space and time. *Olé*, he whispered at first, unable just yet to let the word rise forcefully from its birthing place in the pit of his gut.

(Was he aware, we ask ourselves, that the mathematical proportion of the distances between the planets from the Sun out to Saturn is exactly that of the notes on a guitar string? And if he did know, did he attribute this relationship to the ethereal nature of the music, to its capacity for invoking the heights of heaven and the depths of hell below? Alas, this we will never know.)

He now arrived back home in the early hours of the morning—the hours of indecency, Mónica called them, for she was afraid of this new Emilio, this stranger who arrived humming to himself, eyes lost inside mysterious landscapes, sour wine emanating from skin and breath. She was afraid that she was losing her grip on her husband, that he had gone the way many others have before and since, was spending the little they had on pleasures she abhorred. Above all, it enraged her that he was siphoning resources from their already inadequate stocks.

"You have turned out as rotten as the rest," she spat at him when he stumbled in, uncaring, tired, needing only the comfort of silence and a partial night's rest. And so he would climb into bed alongside her and offer her his back, falling into sleep almost immediately, leaving Mónica to nurse her bitterness and reproaches until the morning light announced the day and then Emilio would slip away quickly again, leaving her with all of her unexpressed rage stored corrosively inside.

She thought: *How has this come to pass? How has this respectable*

*man, once a servant of God, managed to degenerate into this lamentable
state? How has he come to wander so perilously down this shameful path?*

She blamed it on the old man on top. Uncle Alfonso in his attic
with his miserly ways and his venomous tongue. She was sure that
the old man was hoarding the profits from the bookstore, that
there was much more to be had than the old swindler would
admit, that he meant to keep them like this, dressed in rags, living
from hand to mouth like peasants, beholden to him, when he gave
them so little and he himself had so much. She was convinced that
this, above all else, was driving Emilio into the arms of disgrace,
driving him into the darkest hours of the night in search of respite
from the unappeasable sorrows that plagued him in the harsh light
of day.

She cried, full of pity for herself, not yet thirty years old and an
old woman already, with little to look forward to—nothing but the
endless drudgery of cook, clean and mend. And the unbearable
sun to contend with, and the smells of Seville, the burning charcoal, the horse manure, the grease and the sweat. And the noises,
the infernal conflagration of noises, yells, barks, the sobbing of
children, the clanging of church bells. When would it all stop, dear
God, when would the misery end? She brought her fingers up to
her nose then and summoned the scent of the fifteen ingredients
from her aunt's stew, the memory of a distant childhood, uncom-
plicated, secure.

And Emilio thought: *How lucky I am to find myself in this city filled
with life, this city that bears witness to* el compás, *to the beat that makes
all music ring truthfully, ring loud, ring straight through to the heart.* He
thought this because it was night, because darkness had descended
and the voices would soon cease to utter mere words and be over-
taken by song instead and the pain would rise to the surface then,

would be experienced and then expunged. He had, for the first time in his life, found a way to balance body and spirit, to cope with the disappointments of the morning by receding with the singers into the underworld.

Estoy viviendo en el mundo
Con la esperanza perdida.
No es menester que me entierren
Porque estoy enterrao en via.

(I am living in the world
with no hope to speak of.
Don't bother to bury me
for I am buried alive already.)

Emilio thought: *There is much in the world left to me.* The bejewelled night, the endless river of song, the hope I carry in my heart for Diego, the brightest star in the heavens, my beloved son.

And Mónica thought: *There is much in the world to despair of.* The sorrowful days, the smells and the noise, the fear I hold in my heart for Diego, fruit of my one true love, my only son.

In the meantime, Diego himself, now eleven years old—lost until then in a world circumscribed by books and maps, a sanctuary in which to hide from his mother's bitterness, the ill moods of his Great-uncle Alfonso, the unhappiness that radiated from his father's eyes, all the disappointments that seeped from their hearts and into the very walls of the house—was moments away from placing another piece in the puzzle that would become his life, moments from adding bits of earth and sky to a hitherto uncharted bit of his map.

It was around this time that a book arrived at the Librería Alfonso for el Señor Raleigh. The Englishman had recently settled in Seville, hoping the climate would soothe the aches in his aged bones and that the proximity to the Archives of the Indies—the impressive building that housed the history of the Discoveries—would satisfy the unquenchable curiosity that continued to course through his blood.

The arrival of this book marked the moment that Diego Clemente left all childish things behind. Herewith, he would embark on the journey that would begin right there, as a single bacterium that lodged itself in his mind, a fantasy, a boy's delusion that, like the delusions of small and great men alike, would provide the spark to send him across an ocean and deposit him into the arms of the *Mondo Novus,* the glorious New World.

What book was this you ask? Ah, in a million years you would never guess. For it was none other than one of the volumes of the famed octavo edition of Audubon's *Birds of America,* published in 1842, hand-coloured and magnificent even if plates had been removed here and there so that he could no longer admire the Brewer's Black-bird nor the Crimson-Throated Purple Finch. But there were treasures to be had, in any case. There, in all their natural splendour, were the Cape May Wood Warbler, the Burrowing Day Owl, the Louisiana Tanager, the homely but comforting Brown Finch.

Diego hid the book inside the floorboards where he kept the three precious items that provided him with comfort when all upstairs was awash with regret and loss—a tin horn, a glass marble and a book of Becquer's poetry, ragged and well worn but magical, he thought, a salve against the injustices inflicted by those who claimed to love him most.

And now this, an infinitely more precious book. He failed, in his ignorance, to appreciate how precious it actually was, but the boy had his own barometer to gauge the things of the world and the monetary value of the book would not have impressed him had he known it. Instead, he waded carefully through page after page of the beautiful birds—here a Scarlet Tanager gliding, his plumage resplendent, while the less colourful female perched tranquilly on a branch below. Over there a duck, the Greater Scaup, with its pale blue bill and its perfectly webbed feet. And more, so many more, it seemed to him unbelievable that these creatures could even exist. Were they not just a madman's fancy, the delusions of an artist tired with God's inventions and determined to dip into the well of creation for himself?

And the boy wondered, is it possible, if they do indeed exist, that these birds, tiny and delicate as they seem, is it possible that they can cross lines of latitude and longitude so easily, that they can travel vast expanses of a land I can only envision in my dreams? He located their path on his atlas, traced a line from north to south across a great continent, from the broad shoulders in Canada to the end of the tail that was Mexico, and he thought, *there on that line, on that grid, lies my future,* though its shape eluded him just then, the particulars still nebulous at that point in time. But the days would pass, the months would fly and the moment of departure would arrive; the details would work themselves out.

It was one of the first signs of Diego Clemente's ability to refashion his world, to reimagine it so that it would never fail to live up to his dreams, and it began there, with the images of birds that, until he sighted them with his own eyes, he would find difficult to believe were real.

Before he handed the book over to el Señor Raleigh, he dedicated himself to copying the images of each bird onto paper, using a simple charcoal pencil to draw its outline, committing the colourful markings to memory, so that years later he would be able to identify many a bird from the memory of a masked eye, a yellow band at the end of a tail, a pair of pink legs and feet.

He gave the book back to its rightful owner, fearful after three months of hoarding it that he would be found out, that el Señor Raleigh, who had always been so kind, would think ill of him suddenly, would detect the covetousness that resided inside his heart and he would be left bereft, not only of a precious book but also of the respect of a man he considered a mentor and friend. But if the older man suspected Diego's crime, he kept his suspicions to himself. What was more, he shared the book eagerly with Diego, bringing it by the bookshop, where the two spent many moments perusing the specimens contained therein.

Not too many years passed before fate began its work in paving the road for the realization of Diego's dream. Suddenly, it seemed, dramatically, it happened, in a wink of an eye, in a flash, with no time to make sense of it, no time to mourn, no time to adjust. Just ten days after his fourteenth birthday—the glorious fourteen, el Señor Raleigh proclaimed, the dawn of a truly golden age—Diego watched in horror as Emilio was commended, within a single turbulent day, to his eternal rest.

It was Diego who found him lying flat on the floor of the Librería Alfonso, feverish and writhing in pain. It was as if all the disappointment that had seeped through Emilio's veins, all of the venomous words that had fallen from Mónica's tongue, Remedios's orders and later her disdain, it was as if all these things had coalesced in Emilio's gallbladder until it was too much and the beleaguered organ poisoned him to death.

Diego held Emilio's hand throughout all of it, hoping against hope that the fever would break, oblivious to Mónica's shrieks, Mónica's laments. For what would become of them now, good God? Had she not already weathered enough? Had she not suffered more indignities than the good Job? What was she to do in this wretched city with no husband to protect her, no way to survive without a man to fend for them, without a place to live?

Uncle Alfonso, old, ill-humoured, tired of life, yes, but genuinely fond of his nephew, genuinely distressed by Diego's despair, yelled back at her, "*Mujer,* if there was ever a need for peace it is now, woman. Can't you see that Emilio lies close to death?" And old as he was, weak and withered as he felt, he dragged the hysterical Mónica upstairs to give his nephew the silence he needed for rest.

Diego did not record Emilio's last words, and he leaves to our imagination his feelings, the despair he surely felt as he watched his beloved father fade. But in the half-light of the early morning, a dim and tenuous light, we are sure we can see them—a boy lying over the dying body of the man he has loved deeply, while his father tries desperately to ward off the pain and offer a few consoling words.

Upstairs a woman wept, engulfed by her fears, wallowing in her misfortune but torn by her equally strong feelings of love— because she did love him, make no mistake. Love is an unruly emotion, few parameters can limit it: There are as many ways to love as there are ways to meet your death and she had loved, not well perhaps, but loved in the only way she could.

Upstairs, too, an old man grimaced, keeping his emotions in check, tired, distressed with the machinations of the world. Is this how it all ends, *Dios mío,* he asked, are we mere instruments to be played at the whims of the gods?

A month would pass after Emilio's death before Mónica conceived her plan.

And then a new dot would be added to an ancient map and another wound would be administered just as others were beginning to mend.

Sorry her lot

If our philosophers are right, then we must accept their assurances that the bad can only lead to the good, that everything on the ascent is descending at the same time, that tragedy has its purpose and that events transpire as they do because there is a plan, though the shape of it eludes us and the end remains a mystery until the moment it arrives, blowing in like an unpredicted hurricane, strewing the pieces of our little lives about.

Emilio's death opened its own doors. Mónica—once drowning in self-pity, a victim of regret and all the wretched disappointments in the world—was sharply awakened, one could say *rudely,* given the circumstances, but awakened she was and she now grew docile in equal measure to the anger that had possessed her before. Up above her in the attic, counting time with frail fingers and a stale cup of wine, was Uncle Alfonso, revelling in his newfound power, for Mónica would not dare let an errant word escape from her lips now, he surmised correctly. No, *señor,* not one complaint would readily roll from that wicked tongue.

Instead—"Could I get you something, Don Alfonso?"—she would ask, her once unhappily pursed lips unzipped, the sarcasm of old displaced by the considerable weight of her fear.

Uncle Alfonso did not press his luck too eagerly. Old age had its own handicaps—a boulder around a frail neck, you said of it once, Abuela—and old Alfonso was not eager to be abandoned, to be left on his own to face the encroaching frailties that emerged with the passing of time. A weak leg, a cloudy eye, a shaky hand.

Finally, there was silence—a charged silence to be sure, for the air was wound as tight as the string of a guitar. It was impossible to guess when one of them would snap from the tension, when the veneer of civility would be abandoned and the war of words resumed. But in the immediate aftermath of Emilio's death, silence filled the house and Diego was thankful for it, wondered often how much his father would have appreciated this sudden ceasefire, how much he would have enjoyed a peaceful home.

The English kept coming to the store, though the tours were cancelled, Diego being too young for the task. In any case, his knowledge of English was still poor and he had no desire to be trotting about Seville with a group of foreigners bent on a bit of culture after a morning of hunting in the Andalusian countryside; he could not but feel badly for all those dead bustards, the deer, the red-legged partridges and the wild boars.

Without Emilio, the bookshop fared even worse than before. They were reduced to selling the standards of old—the French and Spanish dictionaries of Nuñez de Taboada, the *Arte de la Lengua Arábica* of Pedro de Alcalá, paper made of linen, which pleased the Englishmen who were used to the inferior product sold in their own country, paper fashioned from cotton rags.

Uncle Alfonso rarely descended from the attic to help mind the store—there was no need for it, he reasoned; his own life was sure to end any day, his rheumatic legs were a torture and he could no longer boast of the sharp wits that had once astounded those who knew him—many of whom were now long dead.

It was easy to grow used to the silence that had emerged in the aftermath of Emilio's death and hard to recall what all the fuss had been about during all those years of recrimination and strife. Silence such as this was bliss, a pocket of heaven in an often-wretched earth. *Sí señor,* we should have arrived here long ago, Uncle Alfonso told himself, happily almost. But then he would find himself looking into the eyes of *la señorita de La Mancha,* and looking into those eyes he would see that for all the amiability that now spilled from her once too-tight lips, those eyes were painting a much different picture instead.

You have won for now, old man, they were saying, *but it won't always be like this.*

Mónica had a plan. It had entered her head even before Emilio had breathed his last—a guilty sin, a sacrilegious thought weaving its way through her grief, but a welcome solution nonetheless to the sudden tragic turn of events.

Without Emilio there would be no reason to hide the truth from the boy, to continue misleading him about who his father really was. The time had arrived for Diego to learn that he was not the son of a humble bookseller but of a man of means—that he carried the proof of it in his name, Diego—the name of Don Ricardo's own beloved father. It was the only request Don Ricardo had ever made with respect to the boy and one she honoured, ignoring Emilio's dismay and the fact, too, that Don Ricardo already had a son named Diego, named, *claro,* of course, also for his beloved *papá.*

"There is nothing in a name," she told Emilio when Emilio, timorous and bookish yes, but capable of feeling the slightest injury in the core of his being, mouthed his objection to this. "A name means nothing in the end," she had argued then, but deep down she felt quite the opposite to be the case. The name Diego would connect her son to Don Ricardo, would keep the flames of her hope alive. Perhaps there could still be a marriage in the end. Perhaps Doña Fernanda would finally succumb and things would be put in their proper place—Diego would be returned to the home that should have been his from the start.

What would happen to Emilio she had not considered at that time. She never envisaged his death—she dreamed only half-truths and half-dreams where the barriers to fulfillment merely melted away. It was a dream that had nurtured and comforted her through all those years with Emilio, all those miscarriages, the stillbirths and the two-week-old deaths. It was a thought that had steeled her against the onslaught of the old man and his broom sitting up in the attic, composing the next aria to spice up the opera between them.

She did not reveal the secret just yet. Instead, after years of unwilling neglect (she would justify her indifference up till then by telling herself that Diego had been inseparable from Emilio, that only now, in his absence, could she begin to forge a relationship with her son), she began to hold Diego for the very first time, began to kiss him as if he were not a young man of fourteen but a baby of no more than one. All those wasted years, she told him. All that lost time.

And to lead him into the story that would irretrievably, irrevocably change his life, she began by telling him not of Don Ricardo, as you would imagine, but of her nostalgia for the smell, the taste, the feel of a purple plant.

Saffron. In Spanish, Monica's beloved *azafrán.*

"From the Arabic, Mamá," Diego told her when she embarked upon the story. "To be yellow—*za'fran.*"

"Very interesting, *hijo*," she replied. "But not so important to the tale I'm about to tell."

Ah, but how fine things were once, she lamented. How miserable she was without the taste of a *paella* that could boast of a generous quantity of the spice—part flower, part bitter herb. Once this had been the world she had inhabited—a governess in a beautiful home where no *paella* or winter stew was deprived of the colour and the taste of saffron because that was a house of means, a house that did not have to resort to substitutions—the vanilla and rose water that often masqueraded as the real thing in inferior homes.

The price of an ounce of *azafrán* was equal, even then, to an ounce of gold.

"But even before that, much before that," she told him, "the taste of saffron saturated everything in my life."

This was how the recipes for the famous stews of Mónica's aunt, Bautista, came to land in our own hands. Because for months before Diego was told of the truth, he was forced to hear the lengthy descriptions of the ingredients that went into the dishes that had consumed Mónica's early life. It was an expiation for her, perhaps—we all need, it is true, to revisit that point on the map where things began—but it was baffling to Diego, who could not understand why his mother needed so desperately to tell these stories, who battled the pleasure he felt in his mother's arms, the embraces she had neglected to give him as a child that were offered so freely now, and his embarrassment, "Mamá, *por favor*, I am not a child," he would say when she reached out to embrace him, reached out to touch the skin that had sorely missed a mother's touch until now.

A child no longer a child but longing, at times—as we all do—to remain one for life.

Of all Mónica's memories, the ones that would persist with Diego would be her stories of the great harvests that took place in mid-October before the chill set in, and that would culminate with the Feast of the Rose—a celebration that contained the essential ingredients of any good Spanish *fiesta*—the food, the music, the games and the unusual number of unruly drunks who sang until all hours of the morning, songs in honour of their beloved mothers or cherished sweethearts and sometimes, as in the case of Ignacio Aguirre, a neighbour and not totally sane of mind, songs in honour of a much-beloved goat.

"The work would start at dawn," she would begin, "and when the men, women and children congregated in the fields to commence the task of picking the flowers before the sun rose and burned them with its rays, the excitement was palpable in the air as if they were there not to work but for a pagan celebration in honour of those flowers with their miraculous stems. In the afternoon the work would continue as the petals were separated from the threads—an arduous task—for even the most experienced man would find it hard to strip one thousand of these small flowers in one hour and it takes thousands of them to make just thirty grams of *azafrán*. In the evenings, the stems would be placed to dry over horsehair sieves warmed above tepid, half-spent coals.

"My father—may he rest in peace, he has been dead so long now—had the means to pay workers to do the harvesting for him but that did not save us from lending a hand, and we cooked all day to keep the workers well fed and content. Oh, but those were wonderful days! It is easy to forget the work and to remember only the colours—the mauve not-quite-purple of the flowers, the deep yellow-red of the stems; and the taste too of the newly produced saffron which brought to life one of Aunt Bautista's splendid stews. I can smell them, *hijo*," she would say then, and saying it would bring her red, hardened fingers up to her nose in an effort to recapture the moment, as if the taste of those stews rested still on her tongue.

There would be a point to Mónica's stories, though it would take her some time to make it as she meandered around a hundred digressions and as many laments, but Diego would come to learn that Mónica's memories exacted their own price, for none was offered without the expectation of receiving something in return. And the price, in this case, would be akin to blood—though not what courses through our veins, but the metaphorical stuff that links one generation to another, the one that links father to son.

"Because there is a reason to recall all of these memories, my son," she told him, just when he was beginning to despair that the secret she hinted at would never be revealed. And the point to all of these bucolic harvest-memories and her happy time as governess in one of the grandest houses in Seville was this: "I miss the spice that once grew freely at my back door; the spice only the rich can afford while the rest of us wade in rose water dreaming of the taste. The *azafrán* that is not only spice but medicine, one that has saved many a good woman from suffering the pain of miscarriages and stillbirths and babies dead too soon to be properly mourned.

"Because there is no greater tragedy than this, Diego—listen well and never forget it, my son: To have savoured something so potent only to see yourself deprived of it for the rest of your life."

And before he had time to digest the meaning of it, before he had time to understand the direction, the tenor of the tale, Mónica quickly sat him down and without emotion or remorse, told the young man every detail of his parentage, leaving out nothing—

providing no proper preamble, for how can you jump from saffron to a secret of such magnitude?

The woman was a *bruta,* no doubt about it; we will soon see just how much of a *bruta* she really was.

Diego did not react to the news in the way she expected. He did not ask for more information than he had already received—did not want to hear about the colour of his father's eyes, his manner of walking or his many peculiar likes and dislikes. Thinking about it later, Mónica realized that she was relieved, that she could not remember the colour of Don Ricardo's eyes, his manner of walking or any of his peculiar likes or dislikes. That when she remembered him she thought only of the silk of his waistcoat, the green velvet of his breeches with the filigree buttons, the deep blue suit he often boasted of, made by Utrilla himself in Madrid—"the greatest tailor who has ever lived."

As soon as he could, Diego left the house to recreate all the walks taken with Emilio, because it was clear to him that Emilio was the only father he would ever admit despite his mother's stories—stories that convinced him only that there was something amiss with her head, that perhaps Uncle Alfonso was right, she was indeed a *loca* and what a martyr his father had been to have put up with this. What a saint, he said out loud, suppressing the onslaught of tears.

He walked to the cathedral first, entered it as his father had done, with respect and awe, not for God, Emilio had once told him secretly, but for the wondrous artisans who had fashioned this monument from stone. From there, he made his way across to the Patio de los Naranjos, a peek at the Giralda, and then run, run, run to the banks of the Guadalquivir, where the Torre del Oro stood, a resplendent monument of gold.

All the while, inside his head, he could hear Emilio's voice chatting to the English.

It was Seville that first heard of the New World, that witnessed the arrival of Columbus himself on Palm Sunday in 1493. He had returned from his voyage of discovery in triumph and with a few other things besides. A suite of plants, exotic birds and the few Indians whose likes had never been seen in Europe and whose sad faces stunned those ladies who peeked at them from behind their tortoiseshell fans.

In Seville, Diego Velázquez was born—perhaps the best painter Spain gave to the world. Here, too, the first words of our national masterpiece, Don Quijote, *were written by the great Cervantes, while a prisoner in the Carce Real.*

Eventually Diego stopped in front of the Archives of the Indies, his favourite spot in all Seville.

Hijo, he heard Emilio call out to him, *will you never tire of the reams of paper, the exuberant scrawls of a bunch of explorers eager to tell of their exploits, more invented than real?*

Diego was not hungry for the reams of paper but for the memory of a map.

El Señor Raleigh had taken him there once. "To look upon one of the best maps of all time," he had said to him in his tentative Spanish, with its soft *r*'s and lightness of tone. Juan de la Cosa's *Mappa Mundi*—"astounding," el Señor Raleigh had declared, in English this time. And after the *Mappa Mundi*, the maps of the *Relaciones Geográficas* commissioned by Philip II—"a madman" to the English, "a man made of more complex stuff than could ever be unearthed" to the Spanish—a king, nevertheless, who had dreamed of revealing the invisible to the naked eye.

Diego stood outside for almost an hour, accompanied by his memories—the maps, Emilio's tours of the city, el Señor Raleigh's musings on life and Philip II. Had the king been a simple madman or had he been indeed a man of more complexity than history could ever hope to discern? He stood there, as if transported, but really just a confused bony child aching for certainty, aching to have his father back—Emilio and his stories of love, Emilio and his jumbled, not-quite-right English rhymes.

He went home then. Mónica was waiting for him, and remorse now tumbled from her lips—"I should not have told you about him. I should have taken the secret with me to the grave." All night she apologized like this, chastising herself, cursing at their bad luck in losing Emilio so early, could fate have been crueller to them? Her words of regret and reproach were uttered quietly. There was no need for Uncle Alfonso to know any of this. "No, no, *hijo*," she cautioned him, fear in her voice. "Uncle Alfonso would waste no time throwing us out onto the street."

In the morning—after a night of tossing and turning for Diego, a surprisingly solid rest for his mother—the point of her stories came to land, finally, at his feet.

"Not now, *ahora no,* not yet," Mónica told him, as she fed him his favourite breakfast of hot chocolate and sweet bread made by the Carmelite nuns, "but soon, very soon, Diego, you will go to the house of Don Ricardo Medina and demand to be received in the manner that you deserve."

Later, when he thought back to that day, Diego would recall that he had not liked the thought of this. He had not liked it one bit.

The house on the other side of the world

The "soon" arrived sooner than he imagined, sooner than he would have chosen if it had been offered up as a choice.

What madness was coursing through Mónica's mind when she conjured up the idea of a meeting between father and son? History did not record it. History—Diego—recorded only the lengths to which Mónica went to find him the right attire for the occasion, the right attire being as essential in Spain a century ago as it still seems to be today.

With the skills she was taught by the nuns, she sewed breeches of black velvet—"not the finest velvet, not fine at all," she told him, "but no one will notice in the dim light of the parlour inside Don Ricardo's house." She sewed also a vest of blue cashmere with black stripes and added the coral buttons she had acquired in exchange for a slim bracelet given to her long ago by the Don himself.

And when she deemed him suitably attired, she turned her attention to ridding Diego of all of his Emilio-inspired fantasies—the maps, all talk of American birds, the views of Seville as seen from the perspective of a tour guide—"Por favor, Diego," she cautioned him, "just remember that no one cares about Columbus. And that the Mappa Mundi whatever of Juan whoever is just a piece of parchment. What matters, Diego, is who you know, the homes where you are received, the treatment accorded to your hat."

Diego nodded, thought again that his mother might be a little mad.

She moved on to the issue of language. In this case, Emilio's beloved English.

"Members of Don Ricardo's circle do not pepper their phrases with English but with the glorious words of the Italians and the French. Look here," she instructed and then proceeded to mouth the one or two French words she had heard Don Ricardo utter, using the same exaggerated mannerisms that had marked all of the Don's phrases and that had given him that pompous air that amused his servants and irritated his wife to no end.

There was more. Lessons on how to kiss a lady's hand, on how to treat the help that answered the door, on what words are to be used in a note if the gentleman of the house happened to be out and a note was required. He learned too how important it was to be the first to applaud at the opera (though he would never attend an opera in Seville or indeed, anywhere else, "But you never know, *hijo*," his mother told him, "knowledge like this seeps through the very skin"); the importance of good form on a horse and the authors that gentlemen of a certain kind are expected to read: Paul de Kock, d'Alencourt, Voltaire and Sir Walter Scott.

Mónica had, of course, never read any of these books, had never been to the opera or any other public performance of any kind. But she had been seduced by Don Ricardo's talk of these things, had been taken in by his meticulous renditions of the minutiae of upper-class life: the words, the dress, the food, and yes, even, silly girl, the colourful descriptions of the love affairs that all gentlemen like the Don were expected to have.

Mónica had but one thought in her head. She wanted something more *ya,* now, *ahora,* do you hear me? she screams across the ocean, her voice still crystal clear even though more than a century has passed. For I was not born to live like this, she is yelling, I was not born to sew breeches, I was not born to be deprived of a flower that once grew freely at my door. I was not born to serve an old man in an attic, whom I despise and fear.

All that time, as Emilio and Diego traipsed across Seville with their tourists in tow, Emilio rattling off this fact and that, Diego trying to make himself useful, offering up oranges, water and fans to keep the heat from injuring sensitive English heads, Mónica had been busy with a little rattling of her own.

Seville was not so big that you couldn't find out things, that you didn't know a servant who knew another servant who knew the master of Don Ricardo's house. Oh and how eager too they were to share the goings-on inside the houses they served, for make no mistake about it, there is not a servant in the world who doesn't resent those whom they serve, no matter how well they are treated—no matter the little extras given to them from the pantry of a spacious kitchen, the well-intentioned offer of second-hand clothes. Between a man and his superior there can only be resentment travelling along one route—from below to above, from the shoes that the servant polishes in the morning to the hair he brushes from his master's coat in the afternoon. And there is no better cure for resentment, no better way to assuage it when it rears its ugly head than to spread the news that a master wants kept hidden—the battles, the embarrassments, the secrets guarded fiercely inside each and every home.

This was how Mónica had come to learn of the disappointment Don Ricardo felt with the other Diego—his eldest and only legitimate son, whose bad fame was legendary in Seville. This was how she had come to learn of the elder Diego's addiction to gambling and of his drinking, a weakness that had exuded from his chin when he was younger, a weakness that had grown more pronounced until chin melded into neck. That was how she arrived at the idea that her Diego must be offered up as a substitute, thinking—ever the strategist, ever the fashioner of ridiculous dreams—that Don Ricardo could not but welcome this worthy young man. Heir to his father's strong jaw and his hawkish nose, but most of all, worthy of the name given to him—he was a young man capable of being the New World whereas all the other Diego could be was the Old—dilapidation, waste, a land buckling from the weight of its own decay, desperate for the fresh air that arrived with the discovery of every unknown land. Let any *conquistador* tell you just how fresh.

In the meantime, lost in adolescent fantasies culled from ancient books and maps, Diego too was thinking of a new world—not a world fashioned by *conquistadores* but one that arose from the dusty realms of a seventh-century mind. Diego was a dreamer at heart, heir through his mother's line to the illusions that had once captivated another Manchegan, the Don of all Dons—Don Quijote himself, who with nag and squire rode out one day to set the world right.

Can you guess what Diego was thinking? No? We will tell you then. The young man was meditating on the notion of Paradise. Spain's very own Isidore of Seville had been the first to place it on a map, the first to describe it from its many fruit trees to the firewall that enclosed it to the glorious temperatures that could be enjoyed inside. That was how one man, theologian, archbishop and encyclopedist (as if the previous two weren't enough) perpetuated a myth that would persist throughout the Middle Ages in the form of a seductive dot.

Paradise, east of the land of spices, the land of incense, the source of morning light. What would Isidore have made of us, so eager to sail west, far from the source of paradise, away from the rising light?

Diego told his mother about Isidore of Seville, of spices and incense and the light that beckoned from the east. Mónica, usually quick to dismiss such stories—"*Hijo,*" she would exclaim, "this sounds like one more tale from that Señor Raleigh and tell me, why has he troubled your head with such things?"—surprised him this time by asking to hear more about this Isidore and the paradise that had appeared, until the fourteenth century, in every medieval map as a destination in the farthest reaches of Asia, a beacon, a promised land.

When he had told her everything he knew, his mother screamed out in delight, "There you have it, Diego. Your father's house lies also to the east. *Sí, sí!* Think of it as a sort of paradise of your very own and so it is. A grand house with a grand courtyard and help to spare. And like paradise it holds a spice more precious than any other," she told him, referring once again to her beloved *azafrán.*

Poor Diego was so taken aback by his mother's unexpected reaction to their very own Isidore that he did not have the heart to tell her that the paradise that appeared on those maps had never been found.

The day arrived and in his breeches of velvet not-so-fine-but-it-will-do, in his vest with the coral buttons and the black stripes, he stood before his mother as she inspected him for lint and bad posture, combed his hair, rubbed an imaginary spot from his well-scrubbed face, all the while fretting over one thought—would he be found worthy of Don Ricardo's approval, would he be found worthy of being Don Ricardo's son?

Skinny Diego, all eyes and limbs, had only one desire in mind and that was to keep his mother's love. His trip along the east, towards an Eden of its own kind, a house with a grand courtyard, a house with servants and *paella* made with good-as-gold *azafrán*, was important to him only in equal measure to the happiness it would bring to his not completely right-in-the-head Mamá.

So it is that he found himself arriving at his destination almost by accident, travelling through the streets of Seville in a haze— water offered by water-sellers, oranges peddled by boys much younger than he; *Eh niño,* a gypsy woman screamed out to him, *Where are you going dressed in such finery on a hot day like this?*

Later he would remember none of it, not the water-sellers, not the oranges, not the taunt of the gypsy nor the furious bells of the cathedral that rang in honour of a dead man's soul. He would forget that day's heat, beating on his back and on the top of his head, the sounds that erupted around him, the screams, the laughter, the mournful song of the blind man who sat on a street corner with an outstretched hand, the beauty of the courtyards glimpsed during his interminable walk, step after step, heart in his hand.

It was Master Raimundo, the same servant who had once bowed disrespectfully to the busybody cleric, Don Pedro, who answered the bell when Diego rang it and in ringing it realized at that moment that there was no turning back, that if Emilio were observing from high above, then *Please forgive me,* he thought, *I want nothing from this Father, not riches, not acceptance, certainly not love.*

We can only imagine, sitting here all these years and years later with the benefit of hindsight, how different things would have been at that very moment if Diego Clemente had obeyed his most powerful instinct, which was to run back to his humble home.

Instead he stayed, found himself staring at the coat of arms painted on the blue tile that surrounded a door made of Oxford oak, found himself responding to the question of "Who goes there?" which rang out from beyond the door, in a voice an octave higher than its usual tone—found himself saying what was expected of him, "a person of peace," as he waited breathlessly for Raimundo to shuffle over and let him in.

The servant did not know the young man who appeared before him, but he suspected that he was related in some way to a gambling debt of the other Diego and, suspecting this, immediately began to shake. Inside that house, visiting Don Ricardo at that very moment, was none other than a Duke. There was no title more important in all of Spain aside from the king himself and it had taken years and years of effort on Don Ricardo's part to coax this man to his door. The servant knew Don Ricardo would be less than pleased at being interrupted by this—a collector of yet another debt foisted upon him by his failure of a son. And being less than pleased, Don Ricardo would take it out on Raimundo, for having the temerity to allow this young man inside, for daring to excuse himself when an excuse was demanded and finally for just existing because his mere existence could not but affront Don Ricardo in that angered state. But what could the good servant do? He feared the scandal the young man could create even more than the severe reprimand he was sure to receive from the Don.

"Look here, could you not come back some other time?" he asked the young man anxiously. But no, he could not, this was a matter of great importance Raimundo was told, and it could not wait for another time nor, Diego thought to himself, could he face the prospect of the long trek across Seville to visit this house once more.

There was nothing to be done. Raimundo escorted the young man through the courtyard, as grand as his mother had described it with its porcelain tiles and its glorious fountain and the potted flowers on every corner. *Do you see them, Diego?* he heard his mother ask, such beauty, such symmetry, such perfect pitch. He wandered through a hall whose walls seemed to buckle under the weight of the many engravings of saints and ebony crosses and the portraits of family ancestors, with their thin lips and imperious gazes, trying all the while to quell the volcanic rumblings in his stomach, the sense of foreboding that had lodged itself in his knees.

He was escorted then to the withdrawing room, the parlour where all visitors were received, where he listened still in a haze as his name was called out—Don Diego Clemente, he heard. He watched nervously as three men, dressed in grand clothes, cigars in hand, turned to look at him quizzically, then dismissively, for a young man dressed in such clothes could not be deserving of too much respect, they communicated to him with their eyes; a man dressed like that was perhaps not even worthy of being referred to as a "Don."

"I come on a private matter," he said, addressing the room in general, for he did not know which of the three was his father, could not even venture a guess, and as he said these words he noticed, for the first time, the woman who sat on the sofa, a sour-faced lady dressed in black, none other than Doña Fernanda herself.

The three men who stood before him—the Duke, Don Ricardo and Don Eusebio Villareal—had been discussing matters of great importance, judging from their flushed faces, their conspiratorial tones, the last traces of their *madre mías* and their many *Por Dioses*.

No, it was not politics that occupied these weighty minds, nor the scientific discoveries taking the continent by storm. While other Europeans of their ilk threw themselves into industry, made daring excursions and invented machines that would revolutionize the world, here were these men—Spain, scant years away from losing her last colony, of becoming the backwater of Europe, the nation of last resort—yes, while their nation wilted away, Spanish men of means gathered in each other's salons dressed in grand clothes to fritter away the hours with gossip, idle chatter, cigars in mouth, snuff up the nose.

Don Ricardo, eager to impress the Duke and surmising, as Raimundo had, that this visit could only be related to the gambling debts of his son—the scoundrel, a crooked branch on an otherwise healthy tree, he thought—immediately excused himself before his guests and informed Raimundo that he would take this visit in the parlour at the back.

They walked there in silence, Don Ricardo leading the way, Raimundo cursing his luck for being born a servant, for finding himself there at that very time, knowing that he would be reprimanded severely once the Duke had left, wanting to wring the neck of this young man who had appeared so inopportunely on the one day when everything was to be perfect—when all had been cautioned and groomed and prepared in honour of the bloody Duke.

"Just my luck," he repeated to himself, under his breath, "just my cursed luck."

Once in the back parlour, Raimundo was dismissed—in a cutting tone, he thought, retiring to the kitchen to fret—and Diego was left standing, Don Ricardo making sure to cut the visit short by not even offering the guest the dignity of a seat.

"Is this about my son?" Don Ricardo began, "because if it is, then this is not the time to discuss such matters. These matters, you must know, are to be resolved in the early hours of the afternoon."

"No, this is not about your son," Diego began and then added quickly, "although in a way it is about a son."

"Speak clearly," Don Ricardo ordered now, his patience already spent, his thoughts on the Duke, what would the Duke make of this visit, the Duke was not impervious to the gossip that his son generated so generously about the town. What would the Duke tell the others in his circle about this moment of infamy inside Don Ricardo's house? Oh, to be saddled with such a son! At times he could not bear the thought of it. At times he wished his son forever gone.

Diego spoke clearly then. He told him that his mother's name was Mónica Clemente and when Don Ricardo's face failed to register even a hint of recognition, as if he had never even met her— *the bastard,* Diego would write in his journal later, *the rotten bastard who abandoned my mother to her fate*—he added, "your cousin from La Mancha, the woman who left your house fifteen years ago in disgrace." And then, yes, oh yes, the name registered and he finally conjured up her face, relief washing over him for a fleeting moment, relief that this was not about Diego and his gambling, until it occurred to him, in horror, that this visit was perhaps even worse than one to do with an unpaid debt.

"I am her son, your son," Diego said now, "named Diego after your father, sir. Just as you requested of my mother back then."

Don Ricardo's eyes opened wide; he inhaled deeply, attempting to curb the fear that surged immediately in his chest. For inside the withdrawing room with its grand furniture and its doilies of

Belgian lace, sat not only the Duke of Olivares but worse, much worse, his own wife, Doña Fernanda, who had not mellowed in the slightest with the passing of time. He could picture the outcome of all of this now, his wife exploding at the news of this misbegotten son arriving at their doorstep with the Duke. Yes, he could hear her words, could feel her fingernails clawing already at his eyes, could feel the weight of her rage on his aged skin. *Madre mía*, it would be the end of him, this son, he thought, cursing, like Raimundo before him, the ill luck that had brought this young man here, to his door at this very time, on this very day.

"What do you want? What do you intend with this visit, in the name of God? Can you not see that I am a busy man?" Don Ricardo asked, his frustration and fear rising so that his voice sounded choked, his eyes bulging perceptibly from his face.

Like a sea bream, Diego thought, *dead on a plate.*

"I want nothing, sir," he answered quietly, "but to look just once upon the man who is supposed to have fathered me and then be on my way."

Don Ricardo, relieved then furious again, his anger building in response to what he perceived as insolence in the tone of the young man's voice, now walked over to him, stopped for what seemed an interminable moment and suddenly and with remarkable force, slapped Diego hard across the face.

"Then do not leave without learning the most important lesson a father can impart," he said, spitting out the words at the shocked young man. "This is how life is. Unfair in the extreme. Take stock of this so that the next time you will be prepared for what it delivers and have no reason to be caught unawares." And with these words he called out to Raimundo, ordered him to show Diego to the door, telling him in no uncertain terms that no more visitors would be allowed in that day, and that words were still pending between them.

Just you wait, his eyes were saying, *just you wait*.

As Diego walked west, away from that house, away from the man who had imprinted his hand forever on his face, he could think of one thing only—how to avoid passing the humiliation onto his mother, how to keep the sting of Don Ricardo's ire from extending across the city to slap not one but two faces. He had surmised correctly that his mother had lived for this moment, had placed all her hope on this man—all arrogance and pomposity—and that what had been struck was not only his face but his mother's last remaining dream. God only knew the full extent of it, but he knew the matter must be kept quiet, the secret guarded close to the chest.

He told her little of his encounter. He said only that Don Ricardo had been courteous but understandably there was the issue of his wife. And what a fine young man he had turned out to be, he had said, so well dressed, such good posture, such education in his speech, such dignity in his bearing. He asked that Diego pass on his warmest regards and his heartfelt congratulations for raising a good son, which was not so easy in these troubled times. But, really, there was no question of another visit—his wife and children would simply not understand.

Poor Mónica! How her composure crumbled, how the light disappeared from her once-eager eyes.

For Diego it was a question of putting the episode behind him as if it had not occurred at all. He thought with the innocence of a child that it was possible to erase what one did not fully like or comprehend. But Don Ricardo's slap had buried itself already inside the marrow of his bones, merging inextricably with the pain of losing Emilio until both affronts became one, driving him unconsciously and mercilessly from that day on.

And it was on that very day, after his mother had retired with her disappointment to her bed, that in the deepest hours of the night Diego picked up a quill and put the first strokes on the wondrous map we now hold in our hands.

Time passed then, the days, the months and the years, first crawling and then, as he grew older, picking up the pace. He continued to sell books—some months many, some fewer and often none at all. He continued to learn the names and markings of his beloved birds, venturing on occasion into the surrounding countryside to observe the European and African specimens during migration, accompanying an increasingly frail Señor Raleigh, who shared Diego's love of these birds. He continued to hone his skills, drawing the birds with evermore precision, nurturing the artistic talent that would eventually help to pave the road to his dreams.

As time passed, things changed for those around him as well. Great-uncle Alfonso, reduced for ten long years to an attic room, with hardly a spot of fresh air and no view to console him, no cathedral spire, no glimpse of the great Alcázar, deteriorated further, until he was a shell of his former self. All was quiet now except for the sounds of the occasional reveller outside and the soft footsteps of his nephew's wife below him as she travelled the hallways like a ghost. And as Great-uncle Alfonso's health deteriorated, Mónica's did as well, and for every moan the old man uttered, she delivered a cough in return.

Typhus, a doctor told her son, the scourge of the age and no remedies discovered yet to save the day. And what did it matter in the end? Mónica, first bitter, then hopeful, then finally resigned to her fate, had lost the thing that had once armed her with the strength to carry on—the expectation that things would somehow change. In the mirror of an aged armoire she watched her body shrink, her shoulders stoop, her head jut forward until it seemed to Diego that she resembled one of his beloved birds, flitting through life as if lost in a dream, grounded no longer by the routine that had once given her existence meaning, descending into the lower vocal ranges step by step. She soon grew too weak to emerge from her bed except for short periods at a time and this suited her well; she preferred to be cocooned under the covers, remembering her childhood days, her invented memories of simple meals transformed into feasts and the singing and the dancing and the celebrations that seemed larger, more resplendent to her as each day passed and she grew weaker beneath the weight of embroidered sheets.

Upstairs, an old man remembered as well. He remembered those days when la Señorita Mónica had climbed the stairs to the attic to serve him with flaring nostrils and tight lips. He remembered her spirit, the fervently issued attacks, the insults that had once travelled through the stairs and had provided them both with the spark, the desire to live. The sound of Mónica's coughing seemed to him to be a harbinger of his own looming death and he took to striking his cane against the floor in hopes that it would somehow anger the *señorita* below into warding off the black-hooded intruder bent on sucking the marrow from their respective bones.

"*Venga, muchacha,*" he would shout, his voice weakened by age. "Time to get up, to walk about. *Arriba, sí, arriba!*" And then, tap, tap, tap, he would strike with his cane, hoping the noise would raise her from the stupor into which she had fallen and which had banished her forever from his sight.

And so they lived. The old man incapable of making his way down, Mónica in no condition to climb up. Their lives were reduced by their respective physical infirmities into a duet of tap, tap and cough, tap, cough, tap, tap, tap, cough, cough. Only the appearance of Diego three times a day to tend to their needs provided respite for the endless silence, the weight of their long days.

The old man would attempt to engage his great-nephew in the only way he knew how, with complaints, recriminations, and then later—because Diego, like Emilio, refused to be drawn into the old man's ill moods—exaggerated sighs of despair.

"Are we selling anything of late, *sobrino?*" the old man would ask Diego, caring little for the response but eager to keep him there for as long as he could.

"The same titles of old," the young man would respond in that gentle voice, the voice of a warm afternoon that always reminded Uncle Alfonso of the young man's father, gone so many years now but still sorely missed.

"And how is your mother faring these days?" the old man would ask next, this time eager for the young man's response.

"Some days better, some less well, *tío*. It is getting harder and harder for her to get out of bed."

"Ah, well, that is the way it is with disease. It leaves you helpless like this, decaying inside a bed, eager to see the last of your sorry days." *Still, there is hope,* the old man would add, referring to Mónica's condition, surprising Diego, who could remember the many years his uncle had sworn up and down the narrow stairs, the many times he had threatened her from the safety of an attic room. And now his concern seemed genuine. Was it possible that the old man had grown, unbelievably enough, to care for the woman for whom he had once only insults and scorn?

"We all grow soft with age," el Señor Raleigh had once said, referring to himself, explaining his diminished interest in traversing the spaces of the earth that had once been his life's quest. Now there were infinitely more important things to be experienced. A good night's rest, the taste of a well-cooked meal, the view of an ancient cathedral on a late afternoon as the sun transformed stone into gold.

In the evenings, Diego would sit by his mother's bed, sharing with her the details of the map that had by now become his greatest creation, a parchment full of symbols and grids and land masses drawn over time, so that some lines had been erased here and there and some newly added as experience and knowledge required. He spoke to her of Ptolemy's *Geografía*, of its errors, "the Mediterranean hanging down like a bad dream, Mamá. See here," and he would turn her face towards him so that she could see for herself the error in a reproduction he held in his hands.

Mónica would attempt to focus on the book, her body tired but her eyes eager to take in whatever she could of her son's world. "*Sí, hijo,* I see what you mean," she would whisper, fighting the discomfort that even a tiny amount of light brought to her eyes. Encouraged, Diego would speak then of the famous Portuguese prince, Henry the Navigator, how the great man—a king's third son destined for obscurity by order of birth—had managed to outshine his brothers, creating his own splendid court peopled by the best cartographers, astronomers, shipbuilders and navigators of the age, working in tandem to fulfill the prince's goal of exploring every corner of the earth.

"And let us not forget Columbus," Diego added, enthused, "the man who once sailed across a formidable ocean and found land on the other side, this in spite of so many gross miscalculations on his part, from the circumference of the earth to his estimations of the length of a degree of longitude itself."

Mónica listened between laboured breaths. And when she could no longer conquer the torpor that invaded her bones, when she could no longer focus on her son's enthusiasms, his love of this obscure world of discoveries and maps that seemed like a foreign language to her but which lit up his face so warmly, so intensely—when her illness succeeded in defeating her and the lethargy crept over her body and shut her eyes—then Diego would pack up his books and speak to his mother of his other love, the birds that had been his companions since that day he had discovered their existence between the covers of Audubon's great book. He spoke to her of birds he had never seen but had been able to sketch from his dreams. Birds that appeared in the work that had sparked his interest first and all the birds that followed, the ones that had escaped from the pages of the other books in el Señor Raleigh's collection, the titles of which he recited to his mother as if he were singing her a lullaby—Ray and Willughby's *Ornithologia*, Albin's *Natural History of Birds*, and Catesby's *Natural History of Carolina*. And then he described the birds themselves—Ray and Willughby's splendid Black Stork, Albin's earnest Barn Owl and Catesby's Crested Titmouse perching on honeysuckle.

And he spoke of other birds as well, the ones that appeared now only in men's memories, the ones like the Dodo, banished forever from the earth.

In her half-sleep Mónica would smile at her son's enthusiasms, her eyelids shut but her mind staying with him as long as she could and she wondered on more than one occasion, hearing the way Diego's interests suffused the room with warmth, if blood accounted for anything in the end. For she could see traces only of

Emilio in her son's demeanour, in his habits, his obsessions, in the way he pushed his hair impatiently from his eyes. She searched in vain for a hint of Don Ricardo, but his image too had faded in her mind, was now only a figment that appeared distorted in her dreams—like the Dodo, she thought, a bird gone forever, leaving nothing but a ghostly imprint behind.

She slept. On and off, in fits and starts, between cough and tap, she slept, opening her eyes less and less, but welcoming her son forward with a turn of her face and a weak nod of her head.

One afternoon, when her breathing seemed more laboured than usual, it was Uncle Alfonso who called the young man upstairs, a frantic call for help as if he were standing on the edge of a great abyss and needed to be rescued from himself.

"Take me down to see her," the old man ordered, tapping his cane against the floor with even greater insistence, all of his strength dedicated to this one wish, the desire to close the distance that lay between them and take in her face one final time.

As light as a pile of feathers, Diego thought as he carried the old man down the narrow stairs and into the room where his mother lay on a bed, ashen-faced and quiet, seemingly lost to the world.

He worried for a moment that the old man had come in search of one final battle, one last heated exchange, but he quickly put the worry aside, reasoning that neither had the strength nor the will to do much harm to the other at that point in time. In any case it was not words that the old man wanted but to take one final look at la Señorita Mónica, lying quietly on her embroidered sheets, a wisp of what she had been—*just like me,* the old man thought as he reached out to cover her hand with his, bowing towards her like a priest, listening as she fought for each breath. And then it was as if the strength had been suctioned from his own breast and he motioned to Diego to carry him upwards again, his face devoid of emotion except for the occasional gasp of pain that emerged from his chest.

She was buried three days later in her one good dress, with her lace *mantilla* on her head and the gold chain given to her by her father lying between her breasts, with few people in attendance—Diego, el Señor Raleigh, and a few of the neighbourhood women who appeared at every funeral, ever mindful that it could be their turn next. She was buried without fanfare or music and with none but her own son's tears shed.

We are mere travellers on this earth, the priest said. *We wait only to ascend to heaven, where our prayers will be answered and our everlasting life will commence. Amén* then, Diego thought, exhausted from so many consecutive nights of little rest.

Once his mother had been buried, he wandered the streets of Seville, gay on that day as they always are, flowers in abundance, lemons and oranges perfuming the air, the cramped, stone-cobbled streets resplendent then as they are today. He wandered unperturbed by the sight of those astoundingly beautiful façades. Renaissance, Gothic, *Mudéjar,* whatever you like—you are wandering in a city of contrasts, of hidden courtyards, exuberant gardens, a city unconditionally alive. A city brimming with life, yes, let us not forget this now; the music continued to play and over there a woman twirled in her beautiful gown, a rose in her hair. And if he were to cross the Guadalquivir and head into Triana he would have occasion to hear the claps of the flamenco dancers, the strumming of guitars, the *gritos* from the audience, *Olé! Bonita! Eso es!*

Diego wandered like this, through dazzling streets, without direction or a plan until he found himself standing, incomprehensibly, before the gates of Don Ricardo Medina's house. *What am I doing here?* he asked himself, shocked that his feet would have taken him there of all places, on this very day, his mother freshly buried and an old man waiting anxiously for his return so he himself could die in peace. What in heaven's name had possessed him, arriving at the gates of the grand home his mother had once so desired be opened to them, but which loomed before him now as closed and foreboding as before?

And then, just moments later, the doors did open suddenly, willed by his mother from the grave, Diego thought in the confusion of the moment as he watched a man emerge—the other Diego as it turned out—he of the short neck and the weak chin, who stopped only to give the young man a dismissive look, ignorant of the fact that they were related by blood.

"Excuse me," Diego said, bowing his head towards his half-brother ever so slightly, scurrying away quickly before further words could be exchanged.

Seven days passed and it was Great-uncle Alfonso's turn to leave the worm-worn, blasted earth, the misery of existence, the wretched farce of having to act like life mattered and how could it matter when you were like him, stuck in an attic, with no hope of getting down, no hope of watching life unfold. It was only fitting that he should last one more week, it seemed to him—one week more of life than la Señorita Mónica and it was in fact her death that armed him with the anger needed to continue living seven days more than his fill.

"You had to get there first. Always getting the upper hand on things. Always getting your way," he said to the wall, his voice a whisper, his words marred by bitterness and regret.

And so it was that at the age of twenty-five, Diego Clemente found himself completely alone in the world, save for the man who had been lingering in the shadows, emerging only to guide the young Diego towards his greater destiny, a destiny where nothing was certain yet, neither the ground that he would walk on nor the direction he would turn.

It was now el Señor Raleigh's turn to take center stage. Almost eighty but still vibrant, a bass blessed with the timbre of God himself, a man with the demeanor of a wizard, the evidence of a life well lived on his face, he urged Diego to take a seat. He was about to sing of important things—he would tell of the Age of Discovery and of oceans traversed, those conscious and those as yet unlit. He would speak in metaphors, with mysterious words, his passion igniting the exposition until it would be impossible for Diego to tear his eyes from the older man's face. He would sing of the future. "Diego, *sí*, the future, your future, for when one door closes another one opens, when one fire dies another one ignites close by," and to prove this point completely, the old man now unfurled the map he held in his hands.

"Here, my friend, lies an opportunity the likes of which you have never seen." He traced a line that began at the banks of the Guadalquivir, crossed an ocean and stopped at the tail of a great and wondrous beast. "America," he said, "the *Mondo Novus,* the great behemoth, that breathtaking, unpredictable New World.

"Sit, sit," he insisted. "I am about to speak of a beautiful part of this world, a region of Mexico known as the Yucatán, the southeastern point of this vast and varied nation that once was known as New Spain."

Together they traced with their fingers the outline of this land, mythical, mysterious, a still-uncharted dot on Diego's personal map. Here he learned its true dimensions for the first time, traced its contours, imbibed its borders and in his mind inhaled the air that lay waiting on the other side. The tail of North America, a limestone shelf, the dwelling of the ancient Maya who built pyramids that today awe us still. A mythical land, let us not forget this, for it is entirely possible that something can exist in reality and still assume a very different shape in our minds. And the birds, ah the birds, Diego—look here, el Señor Raleigh had clearly saved the best for last.

"The birds, Diego, how can I possibly hope to describe the birds? Birds with tails that will bewitch you, birds of a thousand colours and beaks of every shape and mien. Birds the likes of which you have never seen before and which will thrill you to the core of your being."

And once he had finished describing the area's wonders, once he had filled Diego's mind with a thirst he had not recognized was his but which now seemed unquenchable, el Señor Raleigh moved in for the kill.

"There is an American, Diego, a very clever man, a man full of passion, a dear friend who has been living in the region attempting to catalogue the area's birds for the American Biological Survey— a man by the name of Edward Nelson, who is in need of an assistant, as it turns out. I have written to him about you, told him of your talent with paint and brush and he is eager, Diego, that you should join him in that region to help him with his monumental task."

It would take some months before Diego could set out, armed with a modest sum of money he derived from the sale of the house and store, armed with the enthusiasm of those who have traversed the ocean before—immigrants of all shapes and beliefs, eager to leave their memories, their disappointments behind.

He would learn all that he could in Seville about the land that was to become his home but there was much he could not hope to know. He learned, for example, about the dimensions of the Yucatán Peninsula, could see the land delineated clearly on one of his beloved maps, found himself tracing the shoreline of the peninsula with an eager finger, from the edge that bordered the dull aquamarine of the Gulf of Mexico on the west and north, to the sparkling blue Caribbean Sea to the east. He tried to imagine the porous limestone that covered the peninsula, and the underground rivers and natural wells that provided water for this scorched region of the earth. He found himself planning his every move before leaving Spanish shores, found himself envisioning how the whole of his life would unfold, weighing this possibility and that without having first had the decency to crouch down and kiss Mexican soil.

But then it is the curse of the immigrant, is it not? To forever be placing a foot on land unseen, forging a life's path from faraway, guided by dreams of what will be, ignorant still of the power of what will soon be left behind.

Yes, Diego was hungry for the land that had now rooted itself in his dreams and he ventured forward towards his fate with determination and few regrets.

So it is that we turn our gaze westward now, across an ocean, towards the doorstep of Mexico, on the eve of 1909, as eager as Diego to open the door and walk in.

ACT TWO

In a Mérida square

Let us now take a moment to revisit the map.

Inside an imposing monastery cradled by the verdant mountains near Madrid, an aging Spanish king is attempting to chart a future for the empire he holds firmly under his command. It is 1588 and Philip II is just moments away from launching the ill-fated Armada against the English and their Protestant God. But on this day the king is thinking not of his future conquests, or of the military strategies that are to be adopted in the coming naval assault. Seated in the library of the El Escorial monastery, beneath a ceiling covered in the sumptuous frescoes painted by Zuccaro, Tibaldi and Cambiaso, surrounded by the finest collection of Arabic writing in the world, King Philip is at this moment thinking not of future wars, but of his desire to know the dimension of his realm.

Is an empire real if you cannot see it? This is the question that torments him most. He has read the exploits of the *conquistadores*, has heard the stories of those men who had ventured forth into the New World, but what are its dimensions, how does it feel, look and smell? He wants, *needs* to unearth all the nooks and corners that belong to Spain, to make his realm visible to himself and to the world. Almost a century earlier, his own great-grandparents,

Ferdinand and Isabella, had travelled through their fragmented realm with the intent of claiming with their presence what rightfully belonged to them. But things are no longer the same. The Spanish realm is no longer confined to a land traversable by horse and carriage. Now it is an empire stretching across an ocean that takes upwards of three months to cross and embracing the Low Countries, with France in between, as hostile a barrier as any midnight ocean ever was.

Philip thinks once more of summoning his cartographers to his side to demand they explain why it is they cannot unearth the dimensions of this new land. The king does not wish to hear of the difficulties they have encountered in undertaking such a task. None of his cartographers have set foot on these distant shores; none of them have witnessed for themselves the colour and feel of the land, the sound the waves make as they crash into these coasts. Instead, they have sent questionnaires with sailors and merchants, hoping to amass the information they need from these men who travel to the New World and back.

So far, the questionnaires have yielded little information that could be put to use in the creation of a master map. The local officials who fill them out rely on the native population to help them navigate the intricacies of the local space—*indios* who speak only Otomi, Cuicatec and Nahuatl. Moreover, these men have their own understanding of physical space, have found their own ways to map their surroundings, one that does not use the Euclidian or Albertian projections of the Europeans to make sense of space.

And so the king waits in vain. The years pass, one cartographer dies, another is put in charge of the master map upon the first's death. Information trickles in, bit by excruciating bit—descriptions of the flora and fauna, sketches of hills and valleys, innumerable and often exotic symbols that confuse those who try to make sense of them back in Spain. Sadly, Philip's eyes will never feast on an accurate drawing of the vastness of his realm. Instead, he will be a witness to the disaster that is about to befall him. The Armada. The beginning of the end for the most vast empire the world had yet seen.

And now we turn our eyes towards another map, the one drawn more than three hundred years later by Diego Clemente—the score to this opera, which begins anew on the other side of the world. Tracing a line with a finger we begin where Diego embarked and then move slowly west—from the Old World to the New—across the once-indomitable Atlantic Ocean until we arrive at the spectacular Mexican city of Veracruz. We note the symbol that marks the spot on the map, marvel at how different everything already looks. In Veracruz the muted yellows and pinks of Diego's native Spain have become ardent oranges and reds: the colour of tropical fruit—the spiky green grooves of the *guanábana*, the yellow flesh of the black *zapote*, the vibrant red of the *pitaya* fruit. What was once lively is more vibrant still; the strokes of Diego's brush are bolder, proof of how the New World has intoxicated him with colour and sound and, as we shall soon see, with his first glimpse of true love.

Although he would stay only a day, it was here, on the seductive shores of Veracruz, that Mexico first entered Diego's body, weaving its way through until it had thoroughly saturated liver, stomach and heart, until it reduced him to a pitiful wreck, an awe-struck boy all drool and nerves trembling at the sight of this astounding land, a land that had existed only in his imagination but which seemed infinitely more magnificent in the flesh.

Though it would eventually drive him to his knees, the truth of the matter was that the country first entered Diego Clemente's unsuspecting body by way of his nose. For the rest of his days he would insist on this, swear that he had smelled the country before he had ever placed a foot on her soil. That in the steamship, with the outline of land still blurry and his eyes tightly closed, a melody of scents led by mango, vanilla and red rose had drifted over him, beckoning him irresistibly forward towards his new home.

Those who heard his claim called him a *fantasioso*—a weaver of fantasies—because *vamos hombre,* they guffawed, do you not know that the city of Jalapa is too far from the port of Veracruz to have provided you with its floral scent, that mangoes do not grow by the side of the sea, nor do vanilla beans sprout from musty wharves? But Diego Clemente would insist on his fragrant memories, like all madmen insist on their skewed perceptions of things. Later, he would add to these first memories only a single heartfelt lament, and that was that he had not encountered one of those mermaids who had once lured his ancestors to the New World— men bent on conquests of gold, yes, but equally bent on seducing those wondrous beings, said to possess green hair and large eyes and capable of stripping men of their souls with just one note of their singular songs. There had been no mermaids waiting on the coasts of Veracruz, he would admit and, admitting it, would lose himself inside one of the stories told by el Señor Raleigh. This time, it was the one about Martin Behaim's *Erdapfel,* the world's oldest existing terrestrial globe where the only mermaids to be found appeared near the Cape Verde Islands, far from the then-as-yet-undiscovered Mexican shores. No, there were no mermaids, he would say shaking his head, but he would insist—just as improbably—on having been greeted by that melody of mango, vanilla and red rose.

But it is time now to move from the program notes and onto the stage, time to abandon the reminiscing about kings long dead, for the curtain is rising and the tempo of the music is slowing, signalling to all that the action is to commence once again.

Applaud now, *señores*, applaud, for we have arrived in the Yucatán Peninsula, the eastern point of the Mexican tail, bounded to the east by the azure waters of the Caribbean Sea and to the west by the Gulf of Mexico, shores that once witnessed the arrival of Hernán Cortés, the first Spanish *conquistador*. A land of limestone and *cenotes,* of hidden jungle cities fashioned from engraved rock, a world of windmills and cacti and birds of every hue and call. Magnificent, in a word, and to prove it, just look, for before us now lies Mérida's Plaza Mayor, the city's main square, polished and spectacular as if time has not weathered the sacred rock of the cathedral nor the enormous *ceiba* trees that provide much-needed shade during the hottest hours of the day.

We feast on the contrast of colours—the resplendent white of the stone, the brilliant blue of the sky, the intense green of the tufted laurel trees that stand erect in the windless, midday sun. We watch mesmerized as the women, dressed in their pastel muslin dresses and their English hats trimmed with Belgian lace, promenade counterclockwise around the square, stealing furtive looks at the young men who promenade in the opposite direction, laughing as they inspect the young women with open, confident stares.

On the outside benches of the square sit the town's officials—on the west side, the mayor in his white suit and Panama hat and, sitting next to him, the judge and the chief politicians discussing the day's events and the news that travels to their city, belatedly, they complain, from Mexico City and abroad. Across from them, on the other side of the square, sit the local *hacendados,* the henequen barons who have transformed this once sleepy city into one of the most astounding in the whole of the world. Keep moving now, for as you make your way farther, into the centre, the light changes and so does the colour of the faces that have congregated there on this glorious Sunday in December 1909. On the first inside ring are the *mestizos*, those who can claim both Mayan and Spanish blood; respectable, yes, but men and women who can boast of few of the privileges accorded to those with the white faces who encircle them on the square. Move into the centre itself and you will find those who can boast of even less, the pure-blood Mayans, the women dressed in their beautiful *huipils*, the men dignified in their *guayaberas* and matching white pants.

Notice now the cleanliness of the square, how everything shines, the stately street lamps that will be lit at sunset, the elegance of the *calesas*, the horse-drawn carriages that wait nearby.

And the sounds! What is Mexico without music, without mariachis and *rancheras* and even the waltzes and polkas borrowed from other cultures, which take on an added effervescence here, becoming not so much music of palaces but of longing and of life? On the east side of the square, a band is playing such music to scattered applause. Talk and laughter fill the air as well, a din punctuated by the occasional *poom* of a firecracker that is set off by a young child to the delight of his friends and the censorious look of an unmarried aunt, tight-lipped, who watches out of the corner of her eye.

Now look more closely still, for there are other things you should notice as well. Those things that will have grave consequences for how this story will play out in the end. Like over there, stage left, for instance—notice those young men dressed in black with the look of romantic poets, their frames emaciated, their faces pale, intellectuals oblivious to the revelry and the celebration that is taking place all around them as they discuss *sotto voce* the sorry state of the country under the shade of a generous palm. Remember them, keep them ready in a corner of your mind, for they are not as much "fifth business" as harbingers of the change that is in the air already, waiting, suspended, for the explosion that will take place in Mexico City almost a year from this day.

But for now all is perfection: the heat which has not yet reached the opprobrious levels that will make breathing difficult in two or three months' time; the beauty of the women, which has not wilted in the midday sun; the confidence with which the portly men inhale the smoke from their fine Cuban cigars; the cigars that arrive in those cedar boxes that the less-privileged sons of the region, those who toil in the fields from dawn until dark, find and hoard—the perfect toy that opens and closes and retains for years the perfume of the wood and the tobacco it once sheltered inside. Yes, for now, things could not be better, for it is a Sunday and the Mass has just been heard and the midday meal of four courses will follow and then a game of billiards for the men, an afternoon of gossip for the women, who will sit in the splendid gardens of their haciendas arranging the marriages between their various daughters and sons.

Into this idyllic scene strolls our hero, Diego Clemente, traipsing about the square as if lost in a dream. *Can you believe it,* he is asking himself, *can you believe you have finally arrived?* It is true—he has to pinch himself now and then, incredulous at his own good fortune, at the feast that lies before his eyes, this magnificent square, this perfect day, the astounding beauty of the many birds that grace the sky.

By one of the benches he stops to take in the scene in wonder, a wonder that bestows upon him the look of a poet lost in a reverie of rhythm and words. A look of wonder that announces to all that he is a newcomer; *a handsome one*, some of the young ladies whisper to each other, giggling as they promenade around the square performing their Sunday ritual of walk and talk, the ritual they wait for impatiently all week while trapped inside the confines of their fine haciendas under the watchful gaze of a suspicious mother or a bored aunt.

Lost in his thoughts, Diego is entirely oblivious to the curious stares that appraise him, is wholly unaware that the people here are assessing him as he walks. He would be surprised to learn that they know already that he is a foreigner—that they can tell by his manner of dress, by the length of his hair, by the absence on his face of a moustache that is de rigueur for the Mexican men of the time, a tribute to the nation's leader of thirty-three years, Porfirio Díaz, the dictator who rules this country from the distant capital with an iron will and a ruthless heart.

Snippets of conversations drift up as Diego weaves his way slowly through the square.

"Do you remember, *compadre*," an old man is asking another as he waves a cigar into the air, "that day the phonograph arrived?"

"*Cómo no?*" the other man replies, laughter in his eyes. "Of course, I remember. It was on the doorsteps of the Teatro de San Carlos. The owner of the machine had put up a sign that read, 'The latest invention by Edison. Here is a machine that can speak, sing, laugh and cry!' You had to put a little tube made of gutta-percha in your ear to hear the music and there we were, lining up like the English, waiting for our turn to stick that tube in our ears and listen to the music of the stars!"

"'What things the *gringos* invent,' the people said," the first man says, laughing.

"Sí, *compadre*. And they were right. The things they invent! Music boxes, telegraphs, electric lights. Soon they'll have us flying to the moon!" And then they both laugh, savouring their memories underneath that wonderful midday sky.

The bells of the cathedral—it is the oldest cathedral in the whole of the New World, Diego will be told many times in the days to come, because regional pride knows no limits here as it knows no bounds anywhere else in the world—the magnificent bells begin to toll, sounding out the hours, reminding Diego of the reason he finds himself here on this day, in this country so far from his native Spain.

In mere moments he is to finally meet Edward Nelson, the esteemed American researcher from the Biological Survey who in just twelve years has managed to collect more than thirty thousand specimens of Mexican mammals and birds. It is because of this extraordinary Mr. Nelson that Diego has made the journey to Mexico, hoping to work with the man who has already assumed legendary dimensions in his mind. El Señor Raleigh arranged it all back in Spain, writing to Mr. Nelson on Diego's behalf, lauding the young man's abilities—his impressive skills with quill and brush, his intelligent eye, the photographic memory that permits him to remember the exact colour of a patch on a bird he has glimpsed for the most fleeting moment as it flew from a treetop into the open sky.

Just the assistant I need, Mr. Nelson had responded, *and that he understands and speaks some English will make it so much easier to get things done.*

Yes, indeed, Diego is very eager to meet this Edward Nelson. He has pored through the papers that the esteemed naturalist forwarded to el Señor Raleigh recounting his adventures in the Arctic and Mexico, has marvelled at the sheer energy of the man. Above all, he is in awe of Nelson's accomplishments, especially in light of his humble beginnings—why, he is the son of a seamstress and a butcher—a man with no formal higher education, a one-lunger to boot, reduced to ill health by a bout of tuberculosis twenty years back. And yet. This man, born with no advantages, no social connections, nothing but an insatiable curiosity that seems to know no linguistic, climactic or scientific bounds, this man has collected biological information and recorded ethnological observations that are entirely new to the world. He has pioneered into the Yosemite Valley, traversed the whole of Mexico, even the most remote and unreachable areas, has even, and in spite of his poor health, ascended its twelve highest peaks, oblivious to any obstacle in his quest to catalogue every species of mammal and bird. Only the New World could offer a man such opportunities, Diego thinks and, thinking this, cannot help but let a bitter note seep in for he has not yet forgotten the closed doors of Don Ricardo's house, the slap that had been crudely imprinted on his face.

Inside the cathedral he is greeted by the smells of incense and burnt wax, the scent of baptisms and burials, of all that has been lost and all that is still as yet unlived. He thinks then of his beloved father, of the days when Emilio had wandered through Seville's cathedral with a group of English tourists in tow, aware of their derision for all things Spanish, the incense, the virgin, the women who lay prostrate on the cathedral floor, supplicating and praying to God. He tries to imagine what his father would have made of this country, of this cathedral with its limestone walls erected from the ruins of an ancient Mayan temple, the miraculous Christ of the Blisters, subjected to a trial by fire but still hanging there scarred and magnificent, serving as inspiration to all those who pray to him from below.

Lost in his memories, Diego does not at first feel the hand that comes to rest on his shoulder, does not at first hear his name being spoken out by a heavy, unfamiliar voice.

"Don Diego Clemente?"

The voice grows more insistent, repeating the name until it finally coaxes him out of his memories and into the world.

When Diego finally looks up, he finds before him one of the most peculiar-looking men he has ever seen, a man who stands no more than four and a half feet tall and appears twice as wide. Piercing eyes and a wide nose dominate his face and a generous smile reveals two missing front teeth. The man's appearance seems all the more strange due to the manner in which he is dressed, which consists of a bright orange *guayabera* and green breeches that would suit a man a head taller than he. Is it possible, Diego thinks, that this is the esteemed Mr. Nelson? That this ill-matched, odd-looking man standing there before him smiling like a simple-minded court jester is the great American naturalist, the man who has accomplished such magnificent feats? It is true—Diego knows this better than anyone—a man's appearance should not matter, clothes do not make the man in any part of the world. Still.

"Mr. Nelson?" Diego asks, a note of uncertainty suffusing his tone.

"Mr. Nelson!" the man replies breaking immediately into a loud, high-pitched laugh. "Mr. Nelson!" he says again, slapping his leg and putting his other hand upon his chest, oblivious to the confusion that is passing over Diego's face.

"Oh, that is funny indeed," he says, once he has calmed himself and wiped the tears of laughter from his eyes. "You must excuse me, Señor. No, no, of course I am not Mr. Nelson. How could you imagine such a thing?" And then the man breaks into laughter once more, stopping himself this time after only a moment, looking nervously about him as if he has suddenly remembered the sanctity of the space on which they stand.

"I wonder what Mr. Nelson would make of your confusion?" he says, lowering his voice a notch. "Oh, he would like it, I am sure he would!"

The man brings himself up to his full height now, manages to adopt a dignified air despite the clothes he wears, the missing teeth, the hair that is strewn about in all directions as if he has been knocked about by a ravaging wind.

"I know you were expecting *el patrón*—that is, Mr. Nelson himself—but he was called away suddenly on an urgent matter and asked that I attend to you today. I hope that this will not prove inconvenient for you, Señor."

The peculiar man now bows ever so slightly Diego's way, "I am Mr. Nelson's assistant, well—" his hand shoots up in the air, "he calls me an *assistant*. In actual fact, I am more of a servant but the *patrón* does not like this word. Perhaps it means something indecent to the Americans, who knows? But an assistant he has made me and I am happy to be one to be sure, for better to be an assistant, I say, than to be shamefully unemployed.

"And what do you think of our magnificent cathedral, Don Diego? Is it not as grand as those on your side of the world?"

It is, Diego tells him as much, marvelling at the energy exuded by this short man whose face seems a collage of the multitude of nations that have come together to form this nation—Maya and Spanish, above all, but hints of others like the French who arrived in Mexico, among other reasons, to fight something as improbable as a Pastry War. Yes, indeed, how preposterous it seems to Diego now that he could have ever mistaken this odd-looking man for the great American naturalist himself.

"I have been instructed to take you through our city, to show you both the beauty and the squalor because even though you may not see it here, there is squalor to spare. We can stop at a cantina to eat and I will answer any question you have for me and I am sure you will have many, this being the first time in our region. And a more beautiful region you will be hard-pressed to find, do you not think, Señor?" The little man is pointing the way to the door already, as if wishing to embark immediately upon the task that has been entrusted to him by his *patrón*.

"Wait, wait," Diego calls out to the man, attempting to detain him before he begins to make his way out. "Please, I am in no great hurry and besides we have not even been properly introduced. I don't even know your name."

"My name? My name? But of course, *claro*, imagine, I haven't even told you my name." At this the little man breaks into that high-pitched laugh once again, placing his hand over his belly as if he finds the matter the most humorous in the world. He abruptly stops laughing after a moment and assumes a serious demeanour, bowing slowly towards Diego once more, "My name is Very Useful, Señor, here to serve you, no, no, to *assist* you in all of your needs."

"Very Useful? No one names his child Very Useful! You are surely having a laugh at my expense."

"No, Señor, I am not," he replies, a hint of injury entering his tone. He lowers his voice now as if what he is about to tell Diego next is a secret that has, until this moment, never been revealed. "My parents named me Very Useful because they believed a man was only as good as his name and, being humble, with no family name of any consequence to offer and finding themselves saddled with a boy of such a stature, and, let us admit it, this unappealing face, they determined that my only salvation resided in being given an appropriate name. Imagine, with another body and another face I might have been named Very Handsome or, better yet, Carlos Miguel. With wealth in abundance I would have undoubtedly ended up as Very Good Catch or Luis Ángel. But alas, such is life and Very Useful has until now, I must tell you, served me quite well."

"*Bueno, bueno,*" Diego says, happy to accept the man's story even if he is having a laugh at his expense, "Should I call you Very or Useful then?"

"Aaahhhh, do not jest with me, Señor. You must call me Very Useful because the Very without the Useful could belong to anything. Just think of it, Very could be used to modify such names as Hateful or Perverse or Incompetent or worse yet, Useless, and then, pray tell me, where would I end? And Useful without the Very is just useful, not much to separate me from all those hungry men who wander the city in search of a meal and a place to rest our heads."

Mr. Nelson's assistant takes Diego by the arm, "Let us begin our journey then, Don Diego, for I am eager to ensure that your first experience of our city is a most memorable one."

As they walk towards the door, another laugh rings out, a feminine one this time, a laugh that is musical, joyous, intensely alive. The two men turn towards the laugh and find the young woman to whom it belongs; she is still laughing, ignoring the look of dismay that is being directed her way by the female companion standing at her side.

Diego Clemente—lover of birds and maps, hitherto too lost in his interior world, since his father's death too burdened with the responsibilities of a bookstore, an ill mother and an aged uncle in the attic to attend to—a young man old before his time, unable to think the carefree thoughts of his contemporaries, burdened, so burdened until now—finds himself suddenly frozen to the spot as if what stands before him is not a young lady at all but a rare species of bird.

The young woman looks up then, meets Diego's eyes boldly, playfully, graces him with her spectacular smile.

"Who?" The word escapes unbidden from beneath Diego's very breath.

Now it is Very Useful's turn to laugh. "Ah, Señor, I see you have located one of Mérida's treasures already." He pauses momentously before announcing her name. "La Señorita Sofia Duarte," and then watches as Diego's eyes follow the young woman, who has finally been silenced by her chaperone and is now being guided reluctantly out the door. "But do not worry, Diego, do not worry. You will see that young lady again. You will have a chance to be introduced to her quite soon, in fact, for she too has a role to play."

Very Useful now grabs Diego's arm and guides him forward, forcefully this time. "There are other things to see," he assures him, "other things that will delight and surprise you. Buildings and monuments and statues and people of every shape and size." And with these words they too are out the door, leaving behind the Christ of the Blisters, the painting of Tutul Xiú, the richness of the decorations that adorn the cathedral still but which will be stripped six years hence during *la noche triste,* the sad night when a long and tumultuous Revolution finally arrives in earnest to this corner of the world.

*

Sofía.

How cruel this opera that dares to wait until the second act to introduce the lead soprano, that dares to keep the diva hidden from view until this point in time. As young children we would insist on her immediate appearance, would demand her presence before us on the stage from the very first act, only to be reminded that patience was a virtue, that things could not be rushed before their time, that there was a score to follow and that no alterations could be made to the map. This was not a story that began in medias res, we were told. This was an opera with a beginning, a middle and an end.

Still, our enthusiasm for her knew no bounds. We took turns imagining her from the descriptions provided, the large hazel eyes, the black hair, the tiny frame that exuded such strength, the hearty laugh that shook her body so completely for she seemed, above all, to be indecently, enthusiastically alive. And the voice! A voice that was both feminine and masculine at the same time, a voice that hinted of mountains and forests, a voice that seemed to be rooted in the very earth itself.

But we shall see more of her later. Very Useful is quite right. For now you must register one thing and one thing only. She has noticed Diego Clemente, she has met his eyes boldly and there is much in that gaze that requires interpretation, for a gaze is not merely a gaze in this world. In this world such a look is, without a doubt, an invitation to dance.

*

Later Diego and Very Useful share a meal of *cochinito pibil*, pork wrapped in banana leaves served with a sauce that sets Diego's unaccustomed lips on fire. He insists that it is delicious, even as his eyes burn and he is driven to down glass after glass of *agua de lima* to help him survive the onslaught of the *achiote* and the other spices that add the heat. Very Useful laughs as he watches Diego's eyes water, "*Hombre*, do they not use chilies in your native country then?" he asks.

"Of course," Diego replies, "of course, but not like these, nothing as bold as these, nothing that brings tears to your eyes. But the food is delicious," he hastens to add, worried that Very Useful might interpret his battle with the *pibil* sauce as evidence that he is not enjoying his meal, indeed that he is not enjoying sitting there, in a cantina three blocks from the cathedral, imbibing the sights and smells of this beautiful city on this glorious Sunday afternoon.

They speak then not of birds but of a magical plant, a plant known to scientists such as Mr. Nelson as *Agave fourcroydes*—henequen to those who export the rope made from it to the Americans, at a profit that has allowed this city to become so spectacular by 1909. Just that fall, an American photographer by the name of Ronald Stewart had arrived in the Yucatán on the invitation of one of the area's *hacendados* to document the miracle that transformed this former backwater into one of the wealthiest regions in the whole of the New World.

At this point the New World is no longer so new—four hundred years and counting—but the city of Mérida, founded by the great Montejo in 1542, once a town of dust and soot, once a nonentity like all the rest, has arisen from its lethargy in the early years of the twentieth century to become the jewel in the Mexican crown, its streets paved with macadam, at night resplendent, illuminated by the magic of electric lamps. Those who arrive here marvel at this apparition, a city of pink and blue cubes, a city with a touch of the East at its heart but thoroughly modern with its street railways, its traffic police, its uniformed firefighters, its quaint hotels with their interior courtyards and oriental tile floors.

All over the city there is evidence of the henequen boom, a boom so spectacular, in fact, that the rich are often at a loss as to how to part with profits so large their imaginations have ceased to make sense of them. Hundreds of automobiles, sailboats and even luxury yachts are purchased even though there are no lakes, no rivers and few roads to navigate outside of Mérida's carefully numbered streets. The finest specimens of English cattle are imported only to perish in the heat. Women lace up in the bone-crushing corsets that are all the rage in Europe, encouraged by the visiting teams of Parisian *modistes*. Mansions of marble and glass appear along Mérida's Paseo de la Reforma, glowing testimonials to the talent of the Italian architects who arrive to give form to the lofty aspirations of the city's nouveaux riches. Along the coast, in the city of Progreso, once nothing but a mosquito-infested swamp, luxurious residences sprout up along the port's beach wall. Enormous warehouses are built to shelter the raw fibre, and even the American consulate makes an appearance, attempting to be near the hustle and bustle of an increasingly bois-terous port.

And to think that all of this, Very Useful marvels—the majestic houses, the modern streets, a city of flowers and courtyards and light—that all this has been built entirely on the back of a cactus-like, grey-and-blue plant.

Agave fourcroydes. Henequen. "Did you know, Diego, that the word *agave* means noble? And that it is a type of lily rather than the cactus it so resembles, which confuses even those in the know about plants?"

"But how does one grow rich off such a thing?" Diego asks, per-plexed. "Did not the men who ventured forth into this country come in search of something much more resplendent, something more tangible—let's just say it now without mincing words or retreating into metaphors. Did those who landed here not come in search of gold?"

"Ah, dear Diego, it is true, they did, for gold was once the coin of the age. But there are other times and other coins and in the Yucatán today, the coin is not gold but green. The *Agave fourcroydes* may be a spiny plant, a plant of no importance to the naked eye, but it provides the raw material for rope, cables and riggings for clipper ships as well as the twine needed on American farms. So Mr. Nelson tells me, you understand," Very Useful adds. "Yes, Diego, this cactus-like plant is at the same time both green and gold. *Oro verde* we call it. Glorious green gold."

Later, Diego will remind himself of one inescapable truth— everything depends on your place on the map. *Ah, poor Mexico,* as the dictator himself had once said, *so close to the United States, so far from God.* For the henequen magnates, those who have enriched themselves beyond their wildest reckoning during the heyday of this green gold, the United States is perhaps not close enough. Because were it not for the fact that one of the greatest economic powers on earth—one growing greater with each passing decade, each passing day—were it not for the fact that this Goliath lies panting so close to the North, the henequen boom would have been not a boom but a hiccup, a meaningless blip in a history told no more.

Although he is eager to hear more about this plant, Diego does not ask any more questions on that day. There is so much to learn, so much to discover and Very Useful has moved on to other things in any case, a description of the different chilies, undisputable truths learned on the knee of a Mayan grandmother, the habits and peculiarities of their *patrón,* Mr. Nelson, who is a little *despistado* now and then, a little lost in his own world but nothing too serious, eh? Very Useful rushes to assure him. Nothing that cannot be anticipated with a bit of quick thinking, some manoeuvring behind closed doors.

After their meal and a short rest, they make their way through the streets of Mérida, which are becoming alive with music and talk now that the midday meal has been consumed and the *siesta* ended; the late afternoon is full of promise as everyone prepares for the evening promenade around the square.

By the cathedral, the two men stop once again. Very Useful points to the doors.

"There are things, Don Diego," he says, "that only a native son knows about the city he calls his home. After all, only one born and bred in a town can truly know all its corners, can know all its quirks, and I am a native indeed, have exhausted its streets, have lived its dramas since childhood, have loved it as if it were a member of my own family, loved it even before it was buffed and polished by the henequen boom, love still its patches of roughness here and there that do not detract in any way from the perfection of the whole."

Yes, there are many things he knows, the things one knows from spending one's life in the same city, living in the same house, the same street. The names of the better barbers, the location of the houses of ill repute, the merchants that are honest and those that have proven themselves thieves. And other things too, so many other things, the things rarely spoken of by tour guides who care only for monuments and stories from a distant history too far removed to longer be of any use.

"Over there," Very Useful begins, pointing to the cathedral, "is where the bishop's ghost appears at midnight. Yes, right there, look, look, *sí*, over there. All of the locals know about it, have seen the movements of that ghost with their two *ojitos*, their very own eyes. Me? No, I have not seen him myself but I can imagine it because I have seen other ghosts roaming through the streets in my time. They say the bishop begins his travels at the vestibule of the cathedral, slides through the mural of the Sagrario and leaves by the Mariana door until he disappears inside the patio of the Church of San Juan de Dios. Who knows what memories drive that poor man through murals and sacred doors? There is a lot that is mysterious, Don Diego, there is a lot that we don't know, despite Mr. Nelson's science, despite the dawn of this new century of talking boxes and electric lights.

"And speaking of electric lights, I must tell you of the extraordinary day they arrived right here, not so long ago. The governor and the mayor had called upon us to gather at the Plaza de Armas to witness this miracle of light. Well, it was only natural, we rushed to the spot, bursting with excitement, our hearts in our hands. The owner of the electric plant was a tall German, notorious in our town for his love of beer and his bald head that shone spectacularly in the dark. On that day, he had climbed onto a platform and had spoken to us of the miracle of science. 'With this science we can do anything,' he said, 'illuminate the streets, speak to people oceans away, we can even, Señores, find the key to eternal life itself.' Well, we were impressed, of course we were. The things the man says, we marvelled to each other. Could they be true? And then, just as if he had heard us, the German raised a glass ball that had been attached to a stick up in the air and, with a nod to the governor, the ball was magically lit up.

"Over here, the barrio del Maine, yes, not the most polished, most respectable part of town but one that belongs to us anyway, for it cannot all be good can it, Don Diego? Light without shadow is impossible, though men will try to achieve it until the end of their days. The *barrio* takes up only eight or nine blocks, after all, not much space in a town such as Mérida, which has plenty of streets for the respectable people to claim for themselves. At this hour, of course, this area is deserted, it is the late afternoon. The *fiesta* begins here once night descends. Cantinas are opened then, the drunken troubadors appear and the women head out into the streets, dressed in their suggestive garments and smelling of cheap oils imported from God knows where. Everything reeks suddenly of decadence, of *pulque* and despair. But you cannot deny they are having a good time of it, despite the misery, despite the fistfights and the screaming, yes, despite all these things, here too there is the sound of laughter and celebration and life.

"And there are other equally colourful sections of Mérida as well. The Turks live in the Italian *barrio* and sell their lace, silks, buttons, thimbles, perfumes and such things in stalls in the Mercado García Rejón or out of suitcases they place right on the floor. And by the calle del Comercio live the Chinese who sell their own wares—fans, fireworks, silks, chenilles, and so on. And of course there are the Koreans, the Lebanese and the French, each with their own habits, their own peculiarities, their own wares. My father, may he rest in peace, once sold his own goods by their side, pots, pans, trinkets made in the villages that were prized by a certain type of lady here in town.

"As you can see, Diego," Very Useful says, finishing his detour through the alleys and byways of Mérida's life by extending his arms far and wide, "we have everything imaginable in this town, ghosts, spices, electric lights, fireworks on occasion and plenty of whores to keep you warm during the odd chilly night."

They take a seat on one of the benches of the Plaza Mayor where all is awash once again with studied elegance, the women dressed in their evening suits, hats abandoned now that the sun has set, hair elegantly coiffed, diamonds glittering as they are waved strategically about.

They sit there in silence watching the people promenade, the young girls giggling, the young men emboldened by the encroaching dark, the occasional secret love letter exchanged quickly as they circle each other, performing the mating dance that has its own sacred rituals, its own secret songs.

In the half-light of the encroaching evening Diego searches the crowd intently, taking in the details now, when he had earlier noticed only the whole. He is searching for the face of one young woman, though he would have perhaps denied he was doing so, so unconscious is he of his motives, so unused is he to lying in wait for a species that does not travel through treetops. But for all of his searching—the attention he brings to the matter is as if he is attempting to identify a type of kestrel, robin or hawk—the young woman remains hidden from view, lost in the throng like a warbler, who, having seduced the birdwatcher with the trills of its mating call, melts into the foliage, oblivious to the anxiety of those who long to catch a glimpse of it from below.

*

Just four blocks away, Sofia Duarte is sitting inside the courtyard of her home, staring into the garden of orchids, hibiscus, lilies, Copas de Oro and Birds of Paradise. She is dressed already for Domingo in Mérida, the Sunday evening festivities that have begun nearby at the Plaza Mayor. For the moment, though, she is savouring the few precious seconds she has to herself, a few moments without the well-intentioned advice of her aunt, the censuring looks of her grandmother, or the tiring prattle of her mother, who, God forgive me, Sofia thinks, could bore even the most selfless saint with her talk. Only her father and two younger brothers seem reasonable to her. Only they seem to be immune to the hysterical interactions of the women of the house, their bickering, their attempts to dominate each other, the ongoing battles that course through their conversation like an underground river, always on the verge of spilling over, always on the verge of crossing the boundary from a barely contained skirmish into a full-fledged war.

There is only one thing that brings the three women together in fact, and that is their shared obsession with arranging a marriage for Sofia, who, at twenty-two, is in the gravest danger of soon being considered past her prime. In the afternoons, from the window of her bedroom, Sofia can hear the women plotting in the courtyard as they embroider and sew.

"What about Felipe Navarro," her aunt typically begins, "you know, the eldest son of Octavio Navarro? He seems a worthy young man, educated in New York I hear, and as decent as you can hope to find."

"Felipe Navarro? What nonsense you speak!" Sofia's grandmother responds in that gruff voice of hers, the voice, Sofia thinks, of an aging Mother Superior burdened with a convent of rebellious nuns. "The boy is a half-wit. The family has made it appear otherwise, of course they have. They are not as stupid as they seem. I hear this supposed New York education was an invention of theirs. I hear the boy spent two years locked up in a room so we would all think he had gone north and so they could later foist him upon one of the decent families of Mérida such as ours." Here her grandmother snorts. Although Sofia cannot see her, she can picture her perfectly, sitting there with her lips twisted into a frown, arms crossed, dressed as always in her mourning clothes for her dead husband, Sofia's Abuelito, a man whom her grandmother had driven to the grave years ago with her nagging and complaints.

Now Sofia's mother descends into the fray, "I think," she begins, her voice sounding muffled—she must have a piece of string between her lips, Sofia thinks, must have paused to arrange her needle and thread—"I think," she continues, "that the problem here is not this Felipe the half-wit but Sofia herself. The girl has found fault with every boy we have suggested, has not one good thing to say about any of the town's eligible men."

"Of course! And whose fault is that? Yours, *claro!*" Sofia's grandmother barks back, seeing the perfect opportunity to attack her daughter-in-law and not hesitating for a moment to close in for the kill. "You have given that girl too free a rein, Gabriela. I have told you so before and I will tell you so again. Why, she spends her days at her father's bookstore, doing all sorts of things my Christian mind dares not even entertain. She has no discipline, is even a bit unfeminine, if you ask me. A shame, such a waste of a girl. A disappointment to be sure."

"Doña Laura, really, I must protest," her mother responds, injured by this assault perhaps, but not, Sofia thinks wryly, left bereft of words. "It is your son who insists on taking her there. I have on many occasions told him it is inappropriate, that a girl must not be seen anywhere but inside the family bosom, the Church or the evening promenade, but it has proved useless. You know your son. He will listen to no one but himself."

Harrumph. The old woman is silent for the moment though Sofia can feel her displeasure weaving itself through the garden of orchids, lilies and Birds of Paradise, weaving, weaving, until it arrives at the spot where Sofia herself is hidden beneath the window of her room.

"*Bueno, bueno.*" Her Aunt Marta now jumps in, trying to clear the air between her sister and Doña Laura before they erupt into a war of words. "We must concentrate on finding the right boy, *señoras*, the right boy will make all the difference in the end."

The right boy. Sofia smiles to herself. There is no right boy in this town, they are all very wrong in fact, each in their own individual and insufferable way. Of course there are some decent boys, Joaquín Sánchez for example or Raúl González—both kind, *divertidos*, good for a walk around the square or an insipid conversation when their families come together at a *fiesta* or a dance, but they were not the men you married, for God's sake. No, there is not one man in the whole of Mérida who has yet caught her attention, made her catch her breath, insinuated himself even for a moment into her Virgen de Guadalupe heart.

She thinks back suddenly to that morning, inside the cathedral after Mass. She is sure that the young man who had met her eyes was none other than Diego Clemente, the Spanish assistant Mr. Nelson has been waiting for to prepare his catalogue on the birds of the Yucatán. What other stranger would Very Useful be meeting there at that time? Mr. Nelson had spoken to her father about the young man, said he was quite talented with the brush, was just the person he needed to help him now that his American assistant, Mr. Goldman, had left to continue their scientific studies in Panama and farther south.

How Sofia envies these men, how she laments having been born a woman, stuck in this house listening to the insane plots of her mother, grandmother and aunt, women who have nothing but needle and thread, nothing but the household to tend to, marriage plots to hatch. Had she been born a man she would be able to travel with Mr. Nelson across the whole of Mexico, sleep under the rumblings of an erupting volcano, wade knee-deep through the mud to take a picture of a rare duck, travel by mule and canoe through dirt roads and clear lakes collecting valuable skins and specimens that would be put on display and admired by the whole of the world. She would write books, travel to the Arctic and live among the Eskimo like Mr. Nelson once had. How she admires the American naturalist, his wisdom, his gentleness, the great distances he has travelled, the passion with which he approaches his work. Yes, it is indeed a shame to have been born a woman, Sofia thinks again, stuck in this town with nothing to look forward to but a Sunday evening walk.

And now Mr. Nelson's new assistant has arrived! She is both jealous of this Spanish newcomer as well as intrigued, although she must be very careful, she reminds herself, for her interest has already been perceived. It was her aunt who had witnessed the quick exchange of looks between Sofia and Diego that morning, an exchange that lasted only seconds but that had upset her aunt in the extreme.

"Brazen," she had called it, when they had stepped outside, "the kind of behaviour that sets tongues wagging, *niña,* the kind that ruins a reputation for life."

Once they had left the cathedral, Aunt Marta had not wasted a moment before sitting Sofia down to remind her about the rules of courtship, speaking to her much as if she were still a *quinceañera,* a green, silly fifteen-year-old girl.

"It is not really your fault, *hijita,* you have merely not paid attention to the way things are done. Sit here, sit here, and I will tell you how to get the thing done right."

Sofia had sat down, resignation in her smile.

"The first assault, Sofia, is done with the eyes," *la tía* had begun, knitting needles in hand, shawl as always on her back, a barely contained excitement coursing through her tone. "The eyes reveal what lies deep in the gut, anyone can tell you that, and if a man is interested he will make sure to look at you in just the right way, a well-considered raise of the eyebrow if you like, at which point—listen carefully now—at which point it is very important that you do not respond in kind. Why? Because you risk being immediately dismissed as a *cualquiera*—a woman without morals, a woman who, admittedly, does hold a certain attraction for a man but one he will certainly never consider in any serious way, for who would want to be married to such a woman? Only a charlatan and a fool, I tell you, and you are not in the market for such a man.

"Are you understanding me so far, *hijita*?" Aunt Marta had asked, galloping ahead without bothering to wait for a reply.

"Very well then, let us continue. If you were to receive such a look and were content to be in reception of such a look and had assured yourself by way of many discreet inquiries that the man was serious and decent and, above all, sane, and if you had also assured yourself that he belonged to a family that was worthy of you in every way, then and only then could you begin to consider returning the look, but *ojo!*—without rushing in all eyes ablaze as if you meant to start a revolution with those lashes of yours. No, *hijita*. Decorum. Calculation. Patience. The man will wait. He will suffer. He will imagine he is in the deepest recesses of hell and he should be kept there burning until one is good and ready to rescue him with the demurest of smiles, with the most fleeting of gazes. Then and only then can the courting begin in earnest and then, wait—never, eh, never too far from the reaches of a chaperone. For should things sour, assurances will most certainly be required from a future suitor that the courting never progressed to other avenues we will not even dignify here by naming."

"*Bueno, tía*, is that all then?" Sofia had asked, biting her bottom lip to keep from bursting into laughter at what was obviously a very serious attempt to instruct her on what she already knew, what she had known since she was old enough to promenade with family and friends along the Plaza Mayor, circling and then circling again around that square with its tufted laurel trees where the dance of the eyebrow was played out every Sunday night among Mérida's young women and men and the not-so-young as well.

Sofia had listened quietly out of respect for her aunt, who, although a little odd, a little antiquated in her ways, had a good heart, was full of noble intentions even if they often missed their mark. The poor woman was, in any case, usually not allowed to say much of anything in the company of the other women who ruled the house and Sofia was eager to let her talk. Compared to her mother and to her grandmother, especially, her aunt was a diamond in the rough. A bit teary, a bit superstitious, a bit sad, her life left largely unlived, condemned to be of service to a married sister who was much flightier, far less deserving of a fine husband and children than she herself was. And to be saddled with her sister's mother-in-law to boot. Well! Yes, Sofia thinks, that alone could make the woman a saint! But then one cannot choose one's destiny, one cannot rearrange the world to one's taste. And even if Aunt Marta must suffer the company of Doña Laura, Sofia and the boys make the whole experience worthwhile for her in the end.

Later, inside the safety of her bedroom, Sofia had shared the story with her friend Patricia, imitating her aunt with her knitting needles and her shawl, delivering the same speech complete with the emphatic admonitions, the pleas for decorum, the dance of the eyes. But Patricia was more interested in hearing about the Spaniard that had precipitated this lecture, wanted to know from Sofia just who he was and what her intentions with respect to him were.

"My intentions? My intentions?" Sofia laughed. "Why, to hate him with all of my heart. Yes, to hate him because of his great good luck. Just think, he will be allowed to travel about the region with Mr. Nelson, observing birds while I remain here, stuck in Mérida with only my books to console me and those three women to drive me slowly and irremediably mad. Yes, I shall dislike him on principle although, to be sure," she stopped then, winked broadly at Patricia, adopted a saucy smile, "the *canijo* Spaniard does have lovely eyes."

Patricia shrieked, shook her hands up and down. She was all excitement for her friend until she suddenly remembered something, stopped her joyful shaking and adopted a more sober note.

"What about Carlos Blanco Torres, *amiga?* What are you going to do about him?"

Sofia screwed her face up in displeasure, brought her finger to her lips, "Shush, Patricia, shush. You know that I don't want to hear about that fool!" She covered her ears with her hands like she used to do when they were both children and she wanted to block out the world. "It is not my fault that ostrich wants something with me. I did not invite his hairy eye my way; I never wanted it at all. I have not once responded to that intense gaze of his, his habit of bursting into song. Ugh! I can only hope he tires of it all soon before the three madwomen of Mérida learn of it and force that fool upon me, arias, moustache and all."

"*Bueno,* Sofia," Patricia said, sniffing loudly as if she felt suddenly aggrieved. "He *is* the eldest son of one of the most esteemed families in the region. Imagine the life you would have as his wife. Trips to Europe, the best box at the theatre, more diamonds than you have fingers, the French *modistes* at your beck and call."

"*Por Dios*, Patricia!" Sofia exclaimed. "The man is delirious with love for only himself. Look at the way he preens before everyone at the square." Here she got up, walked up and down the room stiffly, held her nose high in the air, imitating the hapless young man. "ARGGGGHHH!" she screamed, then pushed both Patricia and herself onto the bed, where they both exploded into a fit of laughter. Oh, how good life was sometimes, how easy it was to put worries aside in the company of a good friend.

"*Bueno, bueno*," Patricia, said, still laughing as they continued to lie there, side by side on the bed. "But we're not exactly young anymore you know. Girls are getting married all around us and here we are, not even a *pretendiente* but your Carlos in sight."

"Maybe," Sofia answered, "but I am sure I will never marry Carlos Blanco Torres no matter how old or how desperate I become. Even if I had sores up and down my body and smelled like an old mare I would not marry him. Even if I knew that marrying him would guarantee the very existence of the world. No, no, never, never, never! ARGGGGHHHHH!" she screamed again, rolling herself and her friend now onto the floor, where they both exploded into a fit of laughter once more.

"*Niñas?*" a gruff voice called from outside, bringing their laughter to an abrupt end. Sofia covered Patricia's mouth with her hands, whispered to her to be quiet as she rose from the floor by the bed.

"*Niñas?* What is going on in there, *niñas?*" The gruff voice demanded once again.

"Nothing, Abuelita, nothing," Sofia replied, running to stand behind the closed door. "We were laughing about something we saw earlier today. I am so sorry to have disturbed you. We will try to be more quiet, Abuela, I swear."

Harrumph came the reply and then Sofia waited, listened immobile to the shuffling of her grandmother's feet as she slowly walked away.

"I bet she was standing there by the door the whole time listening to us talk—the old cow!" Sofia whispered to her friend. She knew her grandmother was not above spying by the doors, listening to private conversations, trying to butt in where she was not needed or required, trying to dig up information to be used at a later point in time.

Sofia thinks now of her own hiding place beneath the window of her room, the spot from which she spies on the three women as they chatter and sew, but does not feel a hint of remorse. That is different, she quickly tells herself, a very different kettle of fish indeed. After all, it is Sofia they are trying to marry off to some godforsaken fool, Sofia they want to sacrifice at the matrimonial altar and she must be prepared, must be watchful in order to ward off each coming assault.

Two birds

Less than a kilometre away from Mérida a meeting is getting underway between the chief researcher of the Biological Survey of the United States Department of Agriculture, Edward Nelson, and one Victor Blanco, at one time the governor of the Yucatán, back in the days before the region had been split in two to make way for the southern state of Quintana Roo. Though his days as governor now lie in the past, Don Victor still possesses one of the largest henequen plantations in the whole of the Yucatán—over five thousand hectares of land with almost two thousand men, women and children under his command. With its own railway tracks, a chapel, a guesthouse that can accommodate more than fifty people at a time and the cultivated gardens that have given the hacienda the nickname of La pequeña Versailles, the plantation is almost a city in itself—a city, what is more, that boasts the latest inventions available in the grandest cities in the world: electric lights, washrooms with running water, large telephones that are used to call those on the other side of the vast hacienda or to conduct business with the henequen buyers up North. Whatever Don Victor desires he orders from all corners of the globe: tapestries from the Middle East, pianos from Germany, fine china from

Limoges, the purest *azafrán* from La Mancha to use generously in the *paellas* that are cooked up in honour of his Spanish past.

Yes, Don Victor has only one worry of any serious note: Carlos, his eldest son, a young man who has shown little aptitude for anything but an obsession with the opera, a love that has often taken him to London and New York in search of a production of the latest work by a favourite composer or the opportunity to see and hear a beloved tenor or soprano in the flesh. Yes, the boy seems intent on only one other thing aside from this—thwarting any number of fine marriages his mother has suggested and he has vigorously opposed. What a disappointment the young man was! A *pelele,* a clown, with no clear direction, no ambitions, no plans of any kind. No interest in the henequen business either, no time for anything, in fact, that is not music and balls and being measured for those fussy English suits that are hideously unsuited to the tropics and which make him sweat in the most unbecoming of ways.

But today he will think no more of this disappointment of a son who is, in any case, back in their house in Mérida, a mansion with marble walls, gold fixtures and a grand ballroom to entertain the very best Mexican families with multicourse meals and dancing until dawn. The house that has placed him fully inside the ranks of the Divine Caste, those five or six families who reign over every aspect of Yucatecan life, and to which all others bow in respect.

Yes, for the moment he will put all thoughts of his miserable son to one side as he receives this Mr. Nelson, a naturalist, he has been told, a man who had spent more than a decade traversing the whole of Mexico classifying mammals and birds. The meeting had been requested months ago, but Don Victor is an extremely busy man, so much to do, so many matters before him and he has never, in any case, been above making others wait for his time. So much the better if that man is a *gringo,* and better yet, *perfecto* in fact, if it is a *gringo* with no power in the henequen trade.

But first things first. This is Mexico and in Mexico business is always preceded by a bit of walk and talk, a drink or two, an entire meal if the visit demands it though no meal has been offered here because this Mr. Nelson does not merit such attention even if he is the chief researcher of the United States Biological this-and-that. The American will have to content himself with an offer of tea or a cold drink, some pastries at most, after which—*so sorry, Mr. Nelson, but so many things to do, so many people to see*—he will be politely shown the door.

They take a tour of the grounds of the hacienda first—through the carefully polished gardens maintained by a team of Korean gardeners who spend their days pruning plants and trees into marvellous shapes. Inside the immense central house itself they walk through parlour after parlour—the music room with its grand piano, the billiards and games room, the library resplendent with row upon row of leather-bound books, formal sitting rooms of various sizes and shapes, a dining room with a table that seats more than fifty people, the office where Don Victor discusses matters of importance and that features a glass window from Tiffany's in the shape of a magnificent Scarlet Macaw. "Astounding," Edward Nelson declares, when faced with the resplendent glass bird, "astounding, to be sure." But not, he thinks matter-of-factly as he turns away, nearly as astounding as those parrots of flesh and blood.

The tour is capped by a visit to the adjoining factory where the henequen is processed by the latest steam-powered machines—*motors made in Germany but the machine designed here by one of our own*—and then a walk to the warehouse where the fibre is stored and transported to the coast on the train tracks that begin right there by the building's back doors.

It is an impressive operation, and Nelson is seeing only an infinitesimal part of the whole. "You understand, the grounds are too large for us to cover much in just one day, let alone in one short hour," Don Victor explains apologetically because he has, throughout the course of the tour, begun to take a liking to this gentle, unassuming man.

Nelson nods, nods as he has nodded during their journey through rooms full of Italian furniture, beautiful oriental rugs, fine oil paintings and marble statues of every size. Nods as he did when Don Victor stopped to point out his sizeable collection of antique guns from the days of Maximilian and further back even, guns from the days when Mexico was still New Spain. Nelson nods as he has nodded absent-mindedly through all of it, attempting to show the right amount of appreciation for things that do not, in truth, impress him at all.

Don Victor is reassured by the American's polite veneer, by his absent-mindedness, by the way in which he focuses on Don Victor's every word, his manner reassuring his host that he has not made a mistake in allowing him in. For these are not the best of times to be traipsing about the hacienda with a curious foreigner in tow. Talk of revolution has been floating around in Mexico City and just two short months ago a group of insurgents had been thwarted right there in Mérida, caught with thirty-three sticks of dynamite and an ill-conceived plan and sent off to prison to rot for the rest of their lives. Yes, it pays to be careful these days especially around the Americans, forever passing judgment on the Mexicans, forever looking down at them with their hawkish eyes, ready to pounce on their southern neighbours in the name of liberty, democracy and many other such useless, self-serving words.

But this man is different, Don Victor thinks. He is all gentleness, all grace. The American has the ability to make a man like Don Victor think himself an authority on things that are foreign to his understanding, like the natural world that is Nelson's own area of concern.

Don Victor now brings the tour to a halt. "A cup of tea, Señor Nelson?" Don Victor asks and then, noting the way the American is dabbing at the sweat on his forehead with a handkerchief, adds, "A cold drink, perhaps?"

The handkerchief, Don Victor notes, is clean and pressed. It has to be admitted, this Nelson is quite elegant in his way, his appearance nothing like what Don Victor imagined of a man who spends his days roaming through forests and wading through streams.

They sit down inside Don Victor's luxurious office, where a team of servants mills about them with tea, hot chocolate, cold drinks of various kinds and European pastries made by the hacienda's very own French chef, an ill-humoured man by the name of Monsieur Jacques who is forever casting aspersions on the quality of the local materials he is given to perform his very important work.

"Cigar?" Don Victor asks, opening an engraved silver cigar box he has on his desk and offering it to the American, who shakes his head politely as he downs a glass of *limonada* instead.

Perhaps he is not yet used to the heat, Don Victor thinks. Had he not heard the man had spent years in the frigid Arctic? The Yucatán would seem like hell itself in comparison to the temperatures in such a northern climate. But then again, what in the *demonios* did one do in a place like the Arctic? Only the English and the Americans seem determined to head to such northern latitudes. And good riddance too, Don Victor, thinks. With the American attention turned northwards, perhaps they would for once leave Mexico to her own devices.

"This is not the most salubrious of climates, Mr. Nelson," Don Victor says. "Many a person finds it hard to accustom himself to this whorish heat. But have you not lived here for many years now?"

"Yes, I have," Mr. Nelson responds, his Spanish soft, his voice as gentle as a bubbling stream. "Yes, I have," he says again. "But my health is sometimes not the best and today is one of those days, I am afraid." He brings the handkerchief up then and gently wipes the sweat from his face.

"More *limonada?*" Don Victor asks, motioning to a young girl who appears immediately and quietly fills Nelson's glass.

A momentary silence follows as Don Victor smokes his cigar and Nelson drinks another glass of the *limonada*, hoping to calm the furious beating of his heart. From outside, the various sounds of the hacienda filter in—the humming of a thousand insects, the tink, tink of piano keys, the sharp voice of a music teacher, and, in the distance, the ever-present rumblings of the machinery that processes the henequen uninterrupted from morning until night.

How to proceed? Nelson has had time to think about this, has plotted his approach carefully, but now that he has the man before him, he knows no amount of flattery (which he is no good at anyway) and no arguments in the name of science may suffice. If the rumours Nelson has heard are true, Don Victor is in possession of one of the most valuable things in the world, but can they really be true? Even now, sitting so close to the man, having been given a small tour of the massive wealth that is under his command, Nelson finds it hard to believe. And because he is no good at small talk, has never bothered to learn the rules that govern high society, does not know how to engage this man on his own turf, Nelson jumps in now and begins to laud the area's birds—the motmots, the ibises, the hummingbirds, the owls and the terns. "So many precious birds," Nelson says. "Do your people know how truly lucky they are to live under this extraordinary piece of the sky?"

Don Victor nods in reply. Though he has only a passing interest in the area's birds himself, he is most pleased at a foreigner travelling from so far to admire the beauty of his region of the earth.

Nelson now asks him about his own collection, "I have heard, Don Victor, that you have one of the most splendid private aviaries in the whole of Mexico."

"Well, yes, one could say so, I suppose. But I am sure that a man who has spent his life studying birds in the wild could hardly be interested in whatever birds I may have locked up in a cage in the back, no?"

"On the contrary, Don Victor. I am interested in birds of all types and in all situations—in cages, in treetops, out in the open sky."

"Very well then, Mr. Nelson. Come to think of it, I would be very interested in your opinion of my collection, in fact."

They walk in silence past the cultured gardens to the aviary at the back that does indeed contain a collection of spectacular birds—a variety of toucans, macaws, hummingbirds, kingfishers, finches and even some species native to Africa that Nelson has never seen, such as a pair each of Lilac-Breasted Rollers and Bronze-Winged Manikins.

"Astounding," he says, staring up as the birds fly and swoop and land, and Don Victor is struck by how the naturalist's eyes have suddenly ignited, how he has stopped sweating, how he seems lost suddenly in a state of reverie, much like a mystic standing in the presence of God. Is this how passion infects the body, invades the heart? Don Victor thinks, for he has never felt captive to such a strong emotion himself. He has seen his share of dramas and disappointments, to be sure, but he does not have a consuming life obsession, feels some envy suddenly for this unassuming man who stands before him, his eyes searching the room in delight.

And yet despite all of this, Don Victor has the feeling that Nelson is still searching for something else, looking, looking around as if there is something missing from his collection of birds.

Nelson walks slowly from one corner of the large aviary to the other, through the tropical foliage, the trees and even the little stream that runs in the centre, the names of the birds tumbling easily from his mouth. A Black-Crested Coquette, a Common Woodnymph, an Aztec Thrush, two Blue-Headed Euphonias. He circles and circles, looking into the air, following a bird until it comes to land on a perch and yet searching, it seems to Don Victor, for something else still.

But what? The *hacendado*'s curiosity has now reached its peak. He searches the air with his own eyes and then observes in amazement as Nelson comes to a sudden and dramatic halt, watches as the American inhales deeply and then holds his breath. The colour has drained from Nelson's face and yet he continues to say nothing, standing there immobile as if frozen to the spot.

Like a petrified tree, Don Victor thinks, a tall, shiny pole.

The American is staring at a large cage that houses two pigeons— "Pigeons, Mr. Nelson?" Don Victor asks, astounded that this man seems so deeply impressed by a common species of bird when all around him there are infinitely more exotic, more interesting varieties to be observed.

Nelson does not respond. He is watching the birds intently, taking in every detail, disbelief clouding his eyes. He is assessing their size, their shape—like Mourning Doves, he thinks, but infinitely more elegant, more graceful with their pointed tails, their beautiful curved necks and heads, those red, red eyes that seem so startling, the bills a pure black, the legs and feet a pinkish red. The male flaps his wings then, as if knowing he is on display, and begins building, building until he flies up into the air and circles the cage, once, twice, three times, returning then to land on his perch before commencing the exercise once again. Nelson watches in amazement, thinking he has never seen a more elegant bird. He continues to stand there immobile for another minute as if the world around him has suddenly disappeared.

"My God," Nelson finally says, almost beneath his breath. "My God."

"Mr. Nelson?" Don Victor asks now, intrigued beyond compare. "Is something the matter, Mr. Nelson?"

Is something the matter? Nelson repeats to himself. Is something the matter? Before him are the birds that confirm irrefutably the rumour he heard but could not, until this moment, believe could be true. Don Victor, owner of acres and acres of land and lord of the thousands of souls who work it until they succumb from the heat, the impossibly brutal work, the conditions that would not be suitable for the lowest of creatures, Don Victor has in his possession two of the world's most precious birds—the *Ectopistes migratorius*—a pair of Passenger Pigeons, at a time when the species is on the verge of disappearing from the very face of the earth.

Nelson tries to think on his feet, collect himself, cook up a plan. It is imperative, he tells himself, that he somehow leave the hacienda with these birds in hand. But how?

"Where did you find these birds, Don Victor?" he asks, biding for time.

"From a compatriot of yours, as a matter of fact. He assured me that, although pigeons, they were extremely rare and so I purchased them at a considerable price, taking him at his word. The rarer something is, the more precious it seems to be, is that not so?" Don Victor asks, smiling broadly now, for he has been wanting to confirm just how valuable these birds really are and they had to be very rare indeed if a scientist of Nelson's stature could be reduced to such a state of disbelief.

"Don Victor, this type of pigeon is not only rare, it is almost virtually extinct. At present there are only two other birds of this kind that we know of still alive. They are sitting in the Cincinnati Zoo, where enormous efforts have been made to make them reproduce.

"Martha and George," Nelson says after a pause.

"I beg your pardon?" Don Victor asks.

"Martha and George are the names of those two birds."

"Oh, I see, I see. Named after the Washingtons, I suppose? Clever, yes, very clever. Wait, wait," Don Victor says, waving his hand dramatically about. "You know, I have a thought, Mr. Nelson. I have a thought." He walks over to where the naturalist is standing and draws pensively on his half-smoked cigar.

"I never bothered to name my birds, but now, hearing the story of those Cincinnati pigeons, I think I will baptize my own. Yes, yes. What do you think then, Mr. Nelson, about naming them La Malinche and Hernán Cortés?" Don Victor asks, all enthusiasm now that he has confirmed the value of the birds that stare at them from the inside of a cage.

"May I ask, Don Victor, that you consider selling them to me so that I could send them back to the people in Cincinnati? Perhaps there is a chance they can get them to mate and the species can yet be safe." It is a tiny chance, Nelson knows it, but hope has rushed in and filled his heart.

"Ah, Mr. Nelson, as you can see, I have all the money I need in the world. But these birds, well, as you yourself say, these birds are more precious than gold itself. One cannot easily part with something that precious, can one? I do hope you understand."

"Of course, Don Victor, of course," Nelson replies, quietly, careful to keep the disappointment from infecting his tone. Nelson can feel his heart in his stomach, beating with a low, painful thud.

"Wait," Don Victor now says.

Can it be true, Nelson asks himself, could this man have possibly had a change of heart?

"I will promise you one thing, Mr. Nelson," Don Victor says, all sincerity and warmth. "The birds will be yours because you have asked me for them and I rarely deny the wishes of important men."

Nelson's heart skips a beat, his eyes open wide.

"Yes, Mr. Nelson," Don Victor continues, smiling a generous smile, "I hear you have amassed an enormous amount of information about our area's mammals. That you are even trying to put together a guide of some type for the birds of the Yucatán? Is that not so?" Nelson nods silently and lets him go on. "Well, how can I not help a man who has shown such interest in our region? Who is such a champion of our piece of the sky. No, no, Mr. Nelson, I promise right here and now that the skins of these rare Passenger Pigeons will be delivered to you and only you, promptly after they have died."

And now the visit is over. Don Victor is pointing the way to the door, politely, of course; he has taken a liking to this man and wants to be liked in return. But the time is passing, there is much work waiting for him inside his study at the front of the house. They walk to the gates of the hacienda together, in silence, Nelson so lost in thought that he barely remembers to thank his host for his time, Don Victor smiling broadly, his mind already on other things.

*

A Turquoise-Browed Motmot with the green crown and broad turquoise eyebrow stripe; an Aztec Parakeet with the blue in the wing and the olive-brown throat and breast; a Violaceous Trogon with its dark eye and yellow eye ring; a Ferruginous Pygmy Owl with those black patches that resemble eyes at the back of the head. . . .

Later, in the early-evening hours as day transforms into night, Nelson tries, with binoculars and notebook, to bring order back into his life. It is a habit he picked up many years ago. To counter the bleakness of the world he tries to find consolation in the splendid variety of birds. Yes, there is much to be grateful for, he thinks after an hour spent like this, as much to celebrate at least as there is to deplore.

Two Black-Cowled Orioles, one Golden-Fronted Woodpecker, a Vermilion Flycatcher and, by a laurel tree, a Crane Hawk peering up at him with a bright red eye.

Such beauty, he tells himself, so many heavenly creatures in the air and yet—and yet one cannot hope to avoid the stinking rot on the ground. So much to admire up above and yet, and yet so very much left to despair about. He feels weary but it is not the heat that now braces his heart but the weight of an incalculable futility, a futility egged on by memories he has thought long banished but which have now come flooding back.

One stands out—a sweltering summer day in 1865 when his grandfather had taken him to a carnival where he had feasted on all of the sights, smells and sounds. He had always been a serious boy, a boy who had assumed the demeanour of a young man early on, who spent his free time wandering the fields and streams near his grandfather's house, collecting specimens and learning as much as he could about birds, mammals and plants. But on that day, in that festival of lights and candy and carnival rides, it was as if he had suddenly rediscovered the delights to be found in being a child. His joy had been too short-lived because on the edge of the fairgrounds they had stumbled by accident upon a most horrific scene—a shooting match involving the very birds he had so desperately hoped Don Victor would hand over.

Grandfather and grandson had stood side by side, silently watching as dozens of Passenger Pigeons were released into the air one at a time, bleeding and crippled, mutilated in the most horrific of ways by the organizers who hoped the bird's injuries would add more spring to their flight. The boy could hardly believe the macabre spectacle that was taking place to the cheers and enthusiasm of the hundreds who watched as blood and feathers showered from the sky. Even now, after forty-five years had passed and his eyes had seen more darkness than light, even now the memory could make him weary, his life's work seem meaningless in the face of the agony he had seen in those birds' eyes. An eternity, he thinks, an eternity will not suffice to erase that image from his mind.

He thinks then of a marvellous trip he had taken with his assistant, Edward Goldman, to Acapulco in December 1899, travelling through the spectacular mountains of Michoacán and Guerrero on mule and horseback, collecting specimens as they made their way to the port. Their native guides had warned them to be on their guard for a group of bandits that were roaming the area, accosting those who travelled along the country's dirt roads. They are a strange sort, these bandits, they had said, laughing—listen, can you believe? Not only do they rob their victims, but they also strip them of their clothing, leaving them to reach their destinations stark naked, their bodies shivering in the cold. "How odd human nature sometimes seems," Goldman had mused on hearing this extraordinary tale. Madness, Nelson had thought to himself then, it was the kind of madness that was all too often unleashed upon the world.

He recalls something else about that same trip, a much more pleasant memory now: crossing Lake Chapala on December 24th and spending a blessed Christmas Day among the birds, listening as the shrill calls of the geese pierced the air, making music from wind, flap and call. And it was just days later when, camped in a forest of oaks and pines near a patch of giant blue-flowered sage, he heard the most entrancing birdsong yet, the vesper song of a Gray-Breasted Robin that delivered such an exquisite melody the naturalist had been left almost breathless. Even the camp guide, a native of the region, as unemotional and stolid a man as they came, had felt his heart pierced by that bird. He had been lighting the campfire when the robin began to sing and he had stopped to listen, his head cocked, his eyes closed.

"Just listen to that bird," he had exclaimed afterwards in a hushed voice. "Just listen to that bird."

Up above him now, a dozen Plain Chachalacas begin to sing, at first only one and then all the others joining in, their raucous calls fading slowly until another songbird picks up the melody from where the Chachalacas' song ends.

Soon, these memories will be all that he has left. At fifty-four, he knows the time has arrived to return permanently to the United States, to abandon his fieldwork and retire to a desk. There is research to catalogue, speeches to be made, books to write. The time has arrived for others to do the fieldwork, others with more passion in their bones, more spring in their stride, those who, like Diego Clemente, still have the unlimited buoyancy of youth on their side. Even now, though, after so many years, having crossed so many lakes, mountains and streams, having slept at the foot of vol-canoes and made the journey through the thickest ice near Bering Strait, even now, Nelson cannot rid himself of his thirst, cannot help but pine for his youth, for that younger self who thought noth-ing of braving the extremes of cold and heat to collect a skin, to observe a bird in full flight, to listen to the story of a shaman and then record it so that it would be preserved for all time.

He has chosen for his last field project the writing of a bird guide to the Yucatán Peninsula, an area that boasts some of Mexico's most spectacular birds. If we are to save our feathered friends, he had said in a speech delivered to the American Ornithological Union just two years earlier, we must allow others to feast on what we ourselves have always enjoyed, the enormous variety and beauty of the world's birds. He spoke to them of Harriet Lawrence Hemenway and her cousin, Minna B. Hall, the ladies who had founded the Massachusetts Audubon Society and who had organ-ized tea parties to urge almost a thousand women to abstain from wearing bird feathers in their hats. Audubon societies were now sprouting up everywhere; bird watching was becoming more pop-ular every day. Soon, Nelson had said in that speech, hope filling his heart, men will be more interested in looking at than shooting at our many fine species of birds.

A Green Jay flits by now, revealing a black throat patch and a violet-blue crown. Another one sings in the background, hidden from view, emitting a series of raspy, scolding notes at first, a more comforting parakeet-like chatter later as if he has been soothed by the wind.

Madness, Nelson thinks to himself again, it is madness that keeps mucking things up. He thinks back to his visit with Don Victor, the cage with the two priceless birds, and then thinks of the henequen, the factory, the workers who toil on the land like slaves. Just last month another American, a journalist by the name of John Kenneth Turner, had arrived in Mérida, eager to uncover the shameful secret that cast a shadow over this land. The two Americans had met to share their impressions, their news. The journalist had spoken with passion, with vehemence, with disgust. "This is a story with a sordid history, Mr. Nelson, a history that goes back hundreds of years, a history that has ensured the continued enslavement of the Maya decades after the liberation of their counterparts in the plantations of our own American south."

Nelson had thought of his father then, a butcher by profession, killed fighting for the Union Army in the dying days of the American Civil War.

"Yes, what we have here is slavery, sir," Turner had repeated. "You cannot call it by any other name."

Nelson had travelled through the region extensively, knew the petty officials, mingled with many of the *hacendados* and locals, who kept him informed of how things worked in the Yucatán, how things should be seen or not seen. He could not in good faith argue with the journalist because he too had been a witness to the injustices that were being committed, he too had heard things that filled him with despair.

The *Agave fourcroydes* was a difficult plant. It required constant weeding and, once planted, did not yield its gold until seven years had passed. In that infernal heat, with the mosquitoes and horse-flies hovering over them, with nettles stinging their feet and the plant's prickly spines piercing their hands, the workers on the henequen estates resembled not men but stone statues weathered by time.

"Make no mistake about it, Mr. Nelson," Turner had continued that day, passion in his eyes, "without slaves, without the benefit of those who weed from dawn to dusk, bound to the hacienda like sap to a tree, bound to their *patrones*, the masters who rule them with an iron grip and ensure their compliance with beatings, liquor and the most insidious of things yet, the running debt—a debt that even death cannot hope to erase—without the work of these men and women, the *hacendados* would not be able to extract even a drop of gold from those green leaves."

The journalist's rage intensified; his eyes lit up.

"The slaves of the Yucatán get no money, Mr. Nelson. They are half starved. They are worked almost to death. They are beaten. If they are sick they must still work. There are no schools for the chil-dren, no physicians to help the ailing, no justice to protect them from a master, if he chooses to beat them to death."

Oh, but we have to beat them, a corpulent henequen magnate interrupts from stage left. *Their very nature demands it, requires it even, to help them stay on a straight and narrow path.*

"And there is more," Turner continued, "so much more.

"The slave rises at four in the morning and the work ends only after it is too dark to see. Each man is given a certain number of leaves to cut or plants to clean, numbers too hard to meet without the help of wife and children. At the age of twelve, a child is declared an adult and given his own two thousand leaves to cut. As nourishment, a slave is given one meal a day consisting of two corn tortillas, a cup of boiled beans and a bowl of putrid fish.

"They die unbearable deaths in an unbearable heat.

"But why worry, *amigo,* when labour is cheap? When one dies, another appears courtesy of the nation's leader, our very own American-backed Presidente Díaz, who, eager to push the Yaqui Indians off the land in the north, offers up men and women for a mere sixty-five dollars a head.

"Never mind the fact that wives and husbands are forcibly separated, ripped from each other's arms, their children given to others, their families dispersed for all time. Never mind the fact that they cannot easily tolerate the heat of the Yucatán, that they are used to a more forgiving clime, have lived for centuries in a more temperate part of the land. Never mind that two-thirds of them die a year after they arrive. President Porfirio Díaz has issued an order to deport every Yaqui man, woman or child immediately to the Yucatán."

The journalist stopped talking then and released a drawn-out breath. When he resumed, his voice had grown quieter, his bearing had softened, he no longer seemed so enraged.

"We are powerless to do anything here, Mr. Nelson, it is not our nation, not our fight. But it is time, I think, to wake those in our own country up to the situation they are helping to create by purchasing the fibre made from this infernal plant."

Nelson had listened in silence to Turner's story, the story that would be published abroad the following year to the rage of the henequen magnates, who knew, at the very least, that some things were best kept hidden, that some things would never be understood. Nelson had listened in silence because he knew that there was some work that was best left to others, best left to the reformers like Turner who sought to set the world to rights with paper and pen.

"I am here to observe, Mr. Turner," the naturalist had said, "to catalogue nature's bounty without opinion or judgment interfering in any way."

"And I, sir, am here to record," the journalist had replied, "to be a witness to the injustices being committed and bring the news back to the world."

It is madness, madness all, Nelson says to himself now, thinking of the fate of the Passenger Pigeon that once thundered over American skies and that was now mere moments from following the course of the Dodo and the Labrador Duck. Gone—them and so many more—vanished due to man's stupidity, man's unquenchable greed. Yes, madness rules the world as it has from the very first—a madness that allows for the destruction of a species, the decimation of a people through incalculable abuse and so many other abhorrent things, so many that the human imagination could not hope to cope with the enormity of the burden, could not hope to assimilate all the despair.

Time, he hopes, will find a cure. The only way to survive it now is thus—with field glasses pointed to where one can catch a glimpse of the tiny lights of perfection that roam the sky—here a Pygmy Kingfisher, there a Caribbean Dove, a Ferruginous Pygmy Owl perched on a branch above.

Nelson looks up now and the light begins to fade from his face, fading, fading until darkness turns to pitch black and no form can be discerned on the stage.

In a Mérida bookstore

The Librería Maya, founded by Sofía's grandfather, Miguel Duarte, before his much-lamented passing years ago, sits just three blocks to the east of the great cathedral, a location he had chosen carefully so that he could be serenaded by the ringing of the church bells as they called people to worship, or celebrated the life of a saint or tolled for a dearly departed soul. Sofía's own father, Roberto, had fallen in love with the cathedral bells as a child and had made it his business later on to learn all there was to know about the ringer's art. By the time he was twenty-one he had travelled the length of the Yucatán, visiting churches big and small where, with the approval of the verger, he would lovingly inspect the bells, gauging their weight, their tonal quality, how difficult or easy they were to handle, how each of them sounded in their different vestments of mourning, celebration and prayer call.

We are men tormented by an insatiable need to know, old Miguel had commented as he watched his son pack his bags, ready to embark on one of his improbable journeys, but he had ushered him off gladly, knowing full well that while today it was the church bells that called out to him, tomorrow it would surely be something else—marine history, mapmaking techniques of the seventeenth century, the mythologies of the native Indians, the scientific classification of the region's wonderful birds. There was no subject too small for the Duarte imagination; no day passed that did not present an opportunity to become obsessed with a new area of concern. It was a curiosity that had filtered down through the generations like a hereditary virus and whose latest victim was none other than our lead soprano herself.

And there she is now, inside the bookstore, dressed in a fetching pale pink dress, seated at an ebony escritoire, gazing at a favourite book. All around her, in shelves that rise upwards of twelve feet, are the leather-bound books that arrive monthly from London, Paris, New York and Madrid, venerable tomes of poetry, dictionaries of a dozen kinds, atlases and scrolls of ancient maps, all the works that are lately preying on the popular imagination, adventure novels by Fernández y González, Alexandre Dumas, Pérez Escrich and Jules Verne. And, of course, who can forget the catechisms and Lives of the Saints that are pored over endlessly by the Meridanos during the *sobremesa*, that hour after the Sunday meal has been consumed when the tablecloth is lifted, an oil lamp is solemnly lit, and the family congregates around the table to listen to the elder sons read.

It is late February and although the heat is building it has not yet reached its peak. The scorching winds have begun to blow from the south, bringing with them the scent of freshly burnt forest scrub. The air inside the *librería* is being cut by the blades of a fan— *swoosh, swoosh, swoosh*. The sound is comforting, it silences the doubts, the many worries that are plaguing Sofia's mind. Well, in truth, one worry looms large among the crowd. One worry is growing bigger and bigger with no end in sight.

It has to do with the dance of the eyes.

Carlos Blanco Torres, the dandy who had once restricted himself to merely gazing at her during the Sunday evening promenades, is growing bolder with the passing of time. Of late, he has even begun to appear at her father's store, where he asks for books he is unlikely ever to read. François Coppée's *A Romance of Youth* the first day. Rudyard Kipling's *The Seven Seas* the next. *El Gran Galeoto* by José Echegaray y Eizaguirre the following day; a copy of Fowler's *The King's English*, the revised edition, for his library the day after that.

Whenever the young man appears, Sofia makes herself as invisible as she can at the back of the store, burying her nose in whatever book happens to be near lest assumptions should be made and she is forced to listen to yet another lecture on decorum from her aunt, or worse, from her grandmother, who has suddenly taken to staring at her intently as if attempting to extract Sofia's very thoughts from her head.

Seated at the back, her face buried inside the pages of the most ample tome she can find, Sofia can still feel the weight of the dandy's eyes as they travel down her face and her side. Good God, can it be true? Can this man be arriving at the *librería* with more than a book in mind? She hesitates to think it so—not out of any false humility, mind you—but because she refuses to believe she could be cursed with such ill luck.

She lifts her eyes every so often, turns her face to gaze at the front where Carlos speaks to her father about this title or that, and then, just as quickly, returns her eyes to the book that shelters her, trying with all her might to concentrate on the blurry words.

Finally, after weeks of this routine, after weeks of doubting her instincts and then confirming them with the occasional furtive glance at the front, she admits to herself what she will from that moment on attempt to conceal from everyone else. Carlos Blanco Torres has most definitely fixed his eyes on her, has begun the dance of the eyebrow *la tía* once so aptly described.

Horrors! she thinks, aghast. Calamity! she writes inside the journal she has kept since she was old enough to write. And then she brings her pen to her lips, thinks hard, dips pen into inkwell and adds: Something Must Be Done. She underlines it once, stops, and then underlines it again, anxiety pouring freely from her hand.

Above all, above all, she thinks, heart beating rapidly, nerves aflame, this is a disaster best kept to oneself. If the three mad-women of Mérida should learn of the news, things will surely go from bad to worse. The pressure to join in the dance will be tremendous, unbearable, she will be made to tango whether she likes it or not, for she has been put on this earth, it seems, to fulfill the schemes of those three women no matter how distasteful, how insane those schemes may be. Because despite Carlos Blanco's position, despite the fact that he is the son of one of the region's most important henequen magnates, despite the lure of the box in the theatre, the diamonds, the access to the European *modistes,* Sofia is sure she does not want to engage Carlos's eye in a dance, does not want to begin the lengthy flirtation that will lead to the altar even at the advanced age of twenty-two.

No, Sofia has been planning an alternative future for some time. She is determined, against all odds, to travel down a much differ-ent path.

Yes, the dandy must be stopped, she thinks. This silly dance must be brought to an end, she writes. But how, Sofia? Think.

There is Mr. Nelson, yes, the most wonderful man in the world, a trusted friend of her father, who welcomed the American natu-ralist into his house when he first arrived in the Yucatán almost fifteen years before. She has thought often of approaching Mr. Nelson, of asking this man who has watched her grow from a young girl into the woman she is now, a woman who has a special place in his heart—she knows this, she can see it in his smile—she has often considered asking for his help. He had, after all, on her insistence, taught her how to classify mammals and birds, what to look for, what to record, what to omit. And he is an American, never forget. Women in America can do many things, are allowed moments of liberty that their Mexican sisters cannot even aspire to in their dreams. *Las locas*, is the way the Mexicans refer to the women who dare to stray too far from the nest—the crazy ones, despised, ridiculed, exiled to back parlours and madhouses so they may not be seen or heard. Yes, what Sofia needs is to make her way north, find a way to be allowed to forge her own path, make her own decisions, live the life she wishes for herself. *But how?* she asks herself. *How?*

She thinks resentfully of Diego Clemente, Mr. Nelson's Spanish assistant, who disappeared into the backroads of the region to begin work on Mr. Nelson's bird guide. She has thought many times of the Spaniard, the usurper who has taken her rightful place by Mr. Nelson's side. Yes, he may well be talented with the brush, but she too has been much praised for her abilities, can beautifully depict a trogon, a jay or a hawk. Mr. Nelson himself has told her so. What is more, she has been trained in the finer points of species identification, has watched and learned from the American since she was old enough to be entranced by his work.

A passing fancy, her father had called it, when she had first asked Mr. Nelson to teach her all the things he knew about animals, plants and birds. She is just ten years old, her tastes will change as she grows. Teach her, teach her, it will amuse her, but be careful around the other women of the house eh, Edward? her father had added, a chuckle in his words. He loved to indulge his daughter, but he was wary of the territory, knew better than to throw himself unarmed to the dogs. His daughter's interests were fine now but later, later, well, later, he reasoned, she herself would surely abandon them to the things that entranced those of the fairer sex—embroidery, the piano, all manner of dances and balls.

Who would have thought he could have been so wrong? Sofia thinks, smiling to herself. Like her father, and his father before him, Sofia is in love with the feel and the smell of paper, in love with the possibilities waiting inside the pages of obscure volumes where she learns the secrets of apothecaries, the size and look of the heavens; where she can roam the streets of Victorian England or the plains of sixteenth-century Spain. She is thankful her father has no such misgivings about her, a daughter, taking an interest in what has clearly been written for the eyes of men, that he has stood firm in the face of her grandmother's strident objections about bringing the girl to a place of possible ruin. "Nonsense," he had told his mother, "Sofia is never there alone. What could possibly happen to the girl inside the confines of a bookstore?" *Harrumph,* his mother had replied, "That store will addle her brain, *mi hijo,*" she warned him. "That store will corrupt her weak feminine heart." But he had held his ground—poor Papá, only this once maybe; he was not usually able to withstand his mother's violent assaults— but here she was, in her own private sanctuary, away, in the mornings at least, from the old woman's grasping claws.

And why in heavens not? She is, after all, a *señorita hecha y derecha,* a woman down to the tips of her toes, and she loves to be useful, loves to spend the mornings here helping to catalogue the books that arrive from the United States, England and Spain. Never mind that there are few customers to pore over the volumes that arrive here in crates. Never mind her grandmother's loud objections, her complaints about young women wandering into men's areas of concern, wandering into a world which does not belong to them, venturing too far from the realm of needle and thread.

She thinks again of Diego Clemente and envy once again darkens her face. Another emotion weaves its way upwards as well, curiosity perhaps? Interest? No matter, all other thoughts are quickly suppressed—after all, more than two months have passed since their eyes locked in the cathedral. She cannot even recall his face with any clarity anymore, does not even remember why her eyes had been drawn his way at all.

And, just as if the usurper had heard each of her thoughts, a few minutes later it is Diego Clemente himself who enters through the door, with Mr. Nelson and Very Useful following closely behind.

Sofia looks up as she hears the door open; her mouth prepares to form a greeting, but, finding it is the Spaniard who is before her, the words quickly dissolve. For his part, Diego, who has until that moment been listening pensively to a story being told by Mr. Nelson, is suddenly frozen to the spot looking not—as you would imagine—at the young woman, but the book she holds in her hands.

It is, as it turns out, one of the most important books in her father's collection, one that will never be offered up for sale. It had been acquired with the aid of a New York bookseller by the name of Richard Smith who, wandering through Mérida once on his way to explore the by now famous Mayan ruins, would declare himself forever indebted to Don Roberto for his kind assistance, his enthusiasms, his intimate knowledge of the beloved terrain.

What is it, you ask?

Ah, in a million years you will never guess. For it is none other than one of the volumes of the famed octavo edition of Audubon's *Birds of America,* published in 1842, hand-coloured and magnificent with all of the plates intact so that she can admire the Brewer's Black-bird or the Crimson-Throated Purple Finch if she likes. And there are so many other treasures to be had in between. There, in all their glory, are the Cape May Wood Warbler, the Burrowing Day Owl, the Louisiana Tanager, the homely but comforting Brown Finch.

"Careful with that, *hija,*" her father never fails to warn her when the beloved book is in her hands, for he cannot help himself, cannot suppress the fear that surfaces around this book, an anxiety he rarely feels even when contemplating the dangers that could afflict his own children or the state of his deplorable finances as he sinks further and further into debt.

Sofia is careful. A book like this is a treasure, she thinks, and although she cannot keep herself from wanting to touch it, she is careful to ensure no harm comes to it—it is, after all, in such a pristine state.

For Diego Clemente, who is standing there with a stupefied look on his face, the book is bringing to mind memories he had thought permanently erased. He is thinking of a ten-year-old boy who had once sat in another bookstore an ocean away, hiding behind that same book, trying with those beautiful birds to drown out the unhappiness that trickled down from the floors above.

"May I see that book?" Diego asks now, voice tight, stepping forward abruptly and leaving Mr. Nelson with the remnants of a half-finished thought on his breath.

The young girl cocks her head, moves her eyes quickly from the usurper to the two men who stand next to him. She ignores the Spaniard's request and stands up instead, runs to Mr. Nelson and offers him her hands, which he covers immediately with his. "How nice to see you, *chata,*" he says, using the affectionate name he has called her since she was a child. Pug-nose—the name no longer fits well now that Sofia is a woman—*hecha y derecha*—to the tips of her toes. But it sounds appropriate somehow on this one man's special lips.

"And Very Useful too, you rascal," she says now, tugging playfully at the assistant's ear until he grimaces and begs her to stop.

"And what, may I ask, brings you this way?"

Sofia has her back to Diego, is pointedly ignoring him as she showers attention on the other two men. It is bad enough that the usurper has taken her rightful position by Mr. Nelson's side, that he, a stranger, has been allowed to accompany the naturalist on his explorations through her very own Yucatán, but it is worse, so much worse, that he had chosen to ignore her completely just moments before, that he had rudely asked for a book without having had the decency to wait for the proper introductions to be secured. There are no limits to his infamy, she will later tell her friend Patricia in the privacy of her room, nothing that this *malcriado,* this miscreant, will not stoop to do.

In truth, Diego Clemente is shame-faced and uncomfortable by now, has realized too late the extent of his indecorous behaviour and is desperate to offer up an apology if only the lady will allow.

"Señorita," he says, finally spotting a space in the clearing and jumping in before she ploughs forward with another topic and leaves him looking like an errant child, "I am so sorry to have barged in like that earlier. You must forgive me for my inexcusable abruptness. I did not mean to offend." He wants to tell her about the importance of the book, of what it once meant to him, but she interrupts him before he has a chance to proceed.

"And you are Mr. Nelson's assistant I assume," she asks, poison in her eyes, "recently arrived from Spain?" *And a lout like all of your countrymen,* she adds to herself, *the odious* gapuchines *we kicked out a century ago and had hoped would never return.*

"This is Diego Clemente," Mr. Nelson says, "Diego, this is la Señorita Sofia Duarte, the delightful daughter of a good friend. And you are right, Sofia, Diego is my new assistant but he is not so new to the area anymore. He has been in the Yucatán for over two months now, in fact."

"Oh? And how does the *señor* like our region?"

"I like it immensely, Señorita Sofia, thank you. It is beautiful in every way," Diego rushes to say, trying still to make amends for the abruptness of his first words, trying too to come to terms with the fact that it is this girl, the very girl whom he had searched for in vain in Mérida's Plaza Mayor, who is now standing before him, who just moments before had been holding Audubon's sacred book in her hands.

But if Sofia has been placated Diego cannot tell, because her father, Don Roberto, has suddenly appeared and a new round of introductions takes place followed by the usual commotion that ensues from the reunion of good friends. Everyone sits to drink *agua de lima* and iced tea and update each other on their news since last they met.

"Tell me, Very Useful," Don Roberto asks, "are you able to keep up with our two scientists as they traipse through fields looking for birds to classify and paint?"

"Keep up? Keep up, you say? Well, I do not know if I am keeping up exactly. Certainly my head is mostly down, burdened by the weight of the equipment I am, as the assistant, expected to carry about—pots, cups, plates, rope, knives and instruments of all kinds, a camera, field glasses, paints, paper and even a bottle of arsenic to prepare the skins. And have I mentioned the skins? Ah, yes, dozens of skins of birds with unpronounceable names and all the other assorted bits and ends—scissors, bags, cotton, and boxes to hold the fancy bird eggs. But I am grateful, Don Roberto, grateful indeed, to have been made an 'assistant' at least, for I cannot even imagine the weight on my back had I been made a servant instead. Yes, as a servant I would surely be traipsing along with my nose on the floor, inhaling the scrub from the forest, the weight of the pack pushing me down every step more."

"*Bueno, bueno,*" Don Roberto says, laughing and patting Very Useful on the back. "Be thankful I introduced you to Mr. Nelson all those years ago or what would a man like you be doing with his time? You were, after all, named Very Useful for a reason, as your own old father once said."

"Yes, yes, my old father, may he rest in peace, he was such an old father indeed." Very Useful turns now to Diego, who is seated there quietly sipping his glass of *agua de lima*, trying to keep from irritating the *señorita* further, trying his best to disappear into his shell. "My poor old Papá having fathered twenty children and finding me, the twenty-first, newly arrived and lying next to him one day on his bed, declared himself *agotado*, finished, no longer able to come up with any names. For it is reasonable for a man to think of twenty, he told my mother, but it will surely drive the mind to the brink of madness having to come up with the twenty-first. So Very Useful it was and Very Useful I have proved. And, *ojo, eh?* For I do not hold the old man accountable with having burdened me with such an undistinguished fate. There is, after all, more to a man than his looks, his accomplishments, his wealth. My own father, may he rest in peace, owned only the trinkets he sold on the streets and my great-grandmother's book of dreams which had been passed on from generation to generation, and which was full of symbols and scribbles that presaged all manner of important things but that, regretfully, no one could understand in the least.

"Yes, my poor father, may he rest in peace, father of more children than he could name, drunk on every day but Tuesdays because every man should dedicate a day to rest; the finest man on earth for getting nothing accomplished from sunrise to sunset; never needed on committees of importance nor councils nor departments of any note; an indefatigable apostle of a life lived from the spoils of others' sweat; a gem, in short, *señores*, a glorious, indestructible gem."

The men laugh, more *agua de lima* is offered, a cigar is lit.

"Tell me, Mr. Nelson, is your new assistant all that you had hoped for?" the *señorita* asks, thrilled to be allowed in the company of men and eager to learn more about the usurper who is sitting there, eyes lowered, lips tightly shut.

"Yes he is! He is a wonderful artist, wonderful indeed," Mr. Nelson replies. "And entirely self-taught! He is a quick study too, has shown an impressive aptitude in distinguishing among various species of birds. Yes, I am very grateful to Mr. Raleigh for having sent him my way."

Diego smiles slightly, nods his head in gratitude, utters a humble "thank you" and then says nothing more.

"How lucky he is!" Sofia says, trying to keep the bitterness from creeping into her tone. "If only women were allowed to wander out into the fields to collect birds—I too would dedicate myself to drawing the beautiful creatures. After all, it is well recognized that women have a better eye for colour, for detail, for the nuances that separate one thing from the next. Just think of our ball gowns, for example. Any woman can point out with perfect precision what another woman was wearing at the previous night's ball, the colour, the texture, the designer's origins, where every button and every pearl was placed, the nature and colour of all the accessories from the shoes to the headdress. And this they can do even if there were a hundred women to account for in one single event."

Mr. Nelson laughs. "Ah, that is indeed true, *chata*. But why would a woman want to be tramping across the countryside with her boots filled with mud? Why, there is only one woman ornithologist I've ever even heard of—a Martha Maxwell of Colorado, and from what I hear, a more eccentric woman could not be found anywhere in the world. Besides, *chata*, bird collecting, unfortunately, requires the proficient use of a gun. It requires climbing trees and scaling cliffs at times. Many a man has perished doing this arduous work—even a well-known and experienced collector like John Cahoon fell to his death trying to make his way up a two-hundred-foot cliff. No, Sofia, bird collecting is not really women's work." And he pats her head like he once used to in the days when she was a girl of ten, not noticing the anger, the disappointment that have travelled the length of her body and turned her face a bright red.

Another man has noticed the anger, her barely suppressed bitterness, the desire that underlies her words. Well after the conversation has turned to other things and Sofia has withdrawn into her own shell, long after the thirst has been sated and plans to meet again have been made, until the time for goodbye arrives and everybody begins to disperse for their afternoon meal, Diego's attention remains fixed on the girl. And then he looks boldly again into the *señorita's* eyes, acknowledging the enormous weight of the dreams that lie trapped in her heart. He looks at her with compassion mixed with some other emotion—appreciation, respect?—Sofia cannot tell for sure, but she does know she feels drawn to this young man, that there is a fatedness about their coming together that is impossible to deny. Like the heroes and heroines of her favourite stories, she thinks, the adventures, the romances, the plays. She offers up her hand to him as the men take their leave, and their eyes lock for a moment until the *señorita* lowers her head first and shyly looks away.

In the flurry and activity as goodbyes are being said, only one other person is aware of the young people's exchange. It is Mr. Nelson, lifelong bachelor, renowned naturalist, responsible for the identification of so many Mexican mammals, plants and birds—in love with the young woman whom he has known since she was a girl, the woman he calls *chata,* knowing full well that he is too old to contemplate anything beyond an affectionate name, but age does not always relieve a man of being saddled with his own impossible dreams.

Some things are best left in one's head, he thinks, his words bittersweet. But this thought does not offer any comfort, does not ease the pain nor make the dream any less burdensome, any less likely to dissipate.

*

Centre stage stands an enormous *ceiba*—the sacred tree of the Maya—tall, majestic, so strong that no hurricane can hope to topple it, dignified in its perennial cloak of brilliant green. At its feet Very Useful and Diego sit on a blanket of *estribilla* surrounded by odds and ends—ropes, hooks, field glasses, notebooks and paints.

They are feasting happily on tropical fruits: tamarinds, mangoes, mameys, sour oranges, *gingo* leaves.

"*Hombre,*" Very Useful is saying to Diego, "could you have been more of a *bruto* earlier on with Sofía? Are men in your country not familiar with the rules of courtship? How one is to approach a young girl? One does not storm the castle like a bull inside a church, trampling over altar, chalice and cross. What on earth am I to do with you, my boy?" Very Useful rolls his eyes, slaps his forehead once, twice with his fist.

Diego would like to respond, would like to say he made amends to Sofía for his shoddy behaviour in the end, but he thinks better of it and says nothing at all. Some things, he knows, are best kept to oneself and besides, he cannot be sure his assessment is correct. Only eyes met, after all, no actual words had been exchanged.

In the two months since Diego's arrival in the Yucatán, Very Useful has made it his business to take the young Spaniard under his wing. "*El patrón* can show you all there is to know about birds, mammals and things of the like but Very Useful, *mi'jo,* Very Useful is here to show you how to extract the marrow from the very bones of life."

He said this to Diego on that very first day in Mérida, after they had watched the promenading of the young people around the Plaza Mayor and after Very Useful had declared that enough was enough, this was a thing for dandies. They were not flowers but men, virile, strong, as *feos y fuertes* as the best of them and it was time to move on, to the barrio del Maine where women of a certain reputation were waiting to be bought. Once there, Very Useful had purchased a whore's time for Diego's edification and for his own sanity as well. "Listen," he told him, "I have served one monk well for the last decade but I am not prepared to dedicate myself to another one of your kind. Yes, *mi amigo,* serving another one will surely drive me writhing and screaming into the bowels of the monastery myself."

And so it was that Diego had gone inside the ill-lit house with a young girl with large eyes and skin the colour of weak tea, skin that glistened with a fine powder made from ground eggshells that, up close, smelled of roses, cinnamon and the sea. Inside a small hot room with a rusty fan, the two had fumbled and groped and grunted for as long as it took, neither deriving any great pleasure from the exercise, both grateful when the thing had been consummated.

How could I have refused? Diego had asked himself later. How could he have confessed to his own self-imposed monastic past? How could he have admitted that he was a true innocent in the things of the world? That he had lived only for his books, his maps, that his youth had been squandered, lost, devoted to caring for a frail and disappointed mother and the great-uncle who tormented her from the attic above?

"An opportunity is about to present itself, my boy," Very Useful tells him now, excitement coursing through his words. He is referring to the invitation that has just been extended by Roberto Duarte for the men to spend a week at his hacienda, which lies just over one hundred kilometres southwest of Mérida, near the beautiful Mayan ruins of Uxmal. Nelson and Very Useful know it well, have been frequent visitors in the past; it is a delightful place, they assure Diego; the air is sweet, the birds are divine.

Diego knows it is useless to deny that he is smitten with the *señorita*, to deny that the girl has caught his eye. "I am all-knowing, Diego," Very Useful has warned him more than once, "God may have cursed me with the body of a misshapen child but He has compensated me by giving me powers beyond the range of most men."

Yes, it would prove impossible to keep things from him, especially something as obvious as an infatuation with a girl Very Useful knows so well. And in any case, what was there to be gained from such subterfuge? Diego asks himself, when Very Useful could prove to be of assistance in the matter, could play the confidant or a go-between.

Once they finish eating, the two men place their heads inside their hats and lean back against the tree for a moment of rest. Soon their *patrón* will return and their work will commence again. But for now, the sun overhead is strong and the air is still and the *wook wook* of a Blue-Crowned Motmot that hovers nearby serenades them as each falls into a blissful sleep.

A hacienda on the outskirts of bliss itself

Don Roberto's hacienda Arroyo Negro had been a sugar cane plantation until the advent of the henequen boom in the 1890s, when it had been converted, like many of its kind, to the cultivation of the astounding plant with the grey-and-blue spikes. It is a medium-sized one by regional standards though it does sit on a particularly lush piece of land. The main house at the hacienda, the *casona*, is modest but still large enough to accommodate the extended family and up to a dozen guests at a time. It has a large dining room that can sit thirty for a meal, a parlour for entertaining both family and guests, a study where Don Roberto writes his voluminous correspondence to booksellers around the world, and half a dozen bedrooms that can sleep up to four people side by side on hammocks made from the region's highly prized plant.

Just five years before, a washroom had finally been built at the back of the house, replacing the isolated outhouse situated so deep in the fields that those who used it were forced to arm themselves with a shotgun in case they were to encounter a wild animal and were made to pay dearly for their walk. Attached to the side of the house is a small kitchen where the servants prepare the meals for the family and for the workers who live in a long, rectangular building at the back. The hacienda also includes a company store, a *cenote* in which to immerse the body during the hottest hours of the day, and a small chapel complete with its own patron saint, Saint Tomás—whose effigy sits, with a handlebar moustache and a beaded *sombrero* on his head, near the altar.

"It is not one of the most splendid haciendas of the area," Don Roberto tells Diego when he extends an invitation to the three men, "but neither is it the most humble of its kind."

Like many of the *hacendados* of the time, Don Roberto leaves the running of the hacienda to an overseer, a certain Arnoldo Lamas from the town of Valladolid, who manages the workers with a strict hand and, when needed, the use of a whip. Don Roberto has never liked the man, but he knows that he is loyal— Arnoldo's own father had been the overseer before him and had served old Miguel well and, in truth, Don Roberto has little interest in the business of the henequen, wants only to dedicate himself entirely to his hobbies and his books.

The family travels to the hacienda four or five times a year to celebrate the children's birthdays and, on the day of San Tomás, to honour the saint with a sumptuous patronal feast. On that day, after the celebration of the Mass, workers and family gather behind the saint with the handlebar moustache for a procession around the perimeter of the hacienda followed by a splendid meal of four courses followed by dancing and fireworks after dark.

Compared to the castle that is Don Victor Blanco's hacienda, Don Roberto's is a most humble home indeed—no Austrian chairs here, no Persian rugs, no prized oil paintings of deceased ancestors, no fine crystal of any kind. Instead, all through the house are the mismatched furnishings that have been inherited from the dead. Over here a Louis XV chair that had belonged to a great-grandfather and had been the fashion in that age, over there an armoire that had belonged to a forgotten great-aunt and had been made for her to house the better part of, as it turned out, a never-used marriage trousseau. Some rooms seem to have been forgotten and have no furniture in them at all while others are overflowing with crudely made odds and ends—tables veneered with rosewood, walnut and oak, shoddily upholstered chairs that are as uncomfortable to sit on as they are hideous to look upon and piles of assorted discarded bits—an empty birdcage, various hat boxes, a cardboard toy horse, a number of oddly-sized books. In the parlour, the piano has long ago warped in the heat; the music sounds distended, as if the instrument is suffering from exhaustion, and no efforts to tune it can get it to sound as it should.

In the days when her husband still lived, Doña Laura had loved spending time at the hacienda, often staying behind whenever old Miguel returned to Mérida to attend to his world of books. Back then, there had been upwards of one hundred workers tending to the estate, a number that had been reduced by more than half in the intervening years as their son took over and the hacienda was converted to the cultivation of the blue-and-grey cactus.

Henequen. The very word weighs on Doña Laura's tongue. Fortunes have been made with this plant, it is true, but the fortunes have not been spread so far and wide. Doña Laura has heard the rumours that course through Mérida like a bout of the plague and she knows well the extent to which her only son is in debt. She rues the day sugar became rope, longs for a time that now lies in a distant and more glorious past.

What Doña Laura misses above all are her regular visits with the dead. Doña Laura is a woman obsessed with death, has been fascinated with it since she was a child when she had witnessed sparks emanating from the grave of a recently interred aunt. "There she goes," her mother had said, as they stood there watching over the grave in the dark. "Your dear aunt's soul has begun its journey towards heaven and towards God."

These days, alas, there are fewer workers on the hacienda, fewer bodies to bury when their time is up, fewer souls to observe making their astounding journey from earth to sky above.

During one of his previous visits to the hacienda, Doña Laura had even summoned the insufferable American scientist, Mr. Nelson, outside to be a witness to the spectacle of mist and spark that was taking place over the tomb of a recently departed worker buried in the hacienda's graveyard near the chapel of San Tomás.

"And what does your science make of this phenomenon, Mr. Nelson?" the old lady had asked, pointing with great excitement to the sparks as she challenged him with her eyes. "I'll wager not everything can be explained with tables and formulas and things of the like."

Doña Laura had never liked this thing called science; she had been suspicious of it from the start, could remember clearly that day in 1865 when the first telegram had been sent between the towns of Mérida and Sisal, how they had all stood outside looking up at the sky, hoping to see the message make its way overhead like a bird in flight. The telegram had been received in due time to enthusiastic applause and the victorious playing of a marching band, but what disillusionment the people had felt! Such anticipation, such fanfare, such celebration for something that could not be seen or heard. No, Doña Laura, for one, would not be easily tricked again.

Mr. Nelson had stood in front of the grave with her on that day and had smiled his infuriating smile—the smile of a hawk, Doña

Laura thought, for she had never taken a liking to this man, had never understood why her son had welcomed him so warmly into their lives.

"Our science would say, Doña Laura, and with all due respect, that what you are watching is none other than the sparks formed by the phosphorous that emanates from the bones of the dead. Sparks occur in these hot climates when the dead are buried in too shallow a grave."

He had gone on to explain how it was a phenomenon that could be seen in marshes as well, since the more decay there was, the more likely gases would be released into the air, gases that glowed and burned, making it appear as if the ground itself were on fire. "So you see, Doña Laura," he had concluded in his soft Spanish with the weak *r*'s, "there is no magic involved at all. Merely nature behaving in her astounding way which is, I grant you, magical enough."

"Harrumph," she had replied, bitterness filling her mouth. "You scientists always have a way of adding up what should be left alone, Mr. Nelson. It is as if you want to deprive the world of the beauty that everywhere abounds. But there are too many ghosts for your science to explain." And then she had told him the story of a certain Pánfilo García, a *hacendado* from the state of Hidalgo, who had been so evil in life, so vile, that the earth had not allowed his body to remain interred in her arms.

"No matter how deeply they buried this Pánfilo, Mr. Nelson, no matter how many times they tried, as soon as he had been completely covered, the earth herself would spew him out of the ground. In the end his family was forced to throw the corpse into a ditch, where the wild animals eventually disposed of his flesh. And what about María Juliana, who wandered the halls of her house for years after her death, leaving sophisticated French recipes behind for the cook? What, Mr. Nelson, does your science say about that?"

The scientist had raised his arms as if conceding defeat. "There is much we know very little about, Doña Laura, much we have yet to learn. And it is true, as Heraclitus once said, that much is lost to disbelief." And then he had smiled his gentle smile—the smile of a weasel, Doña Laura thought—and, bidding her a warm goodnight, had retired politely to his room.

And now Doña Laura is expected to withstand yet another visit from this egregious man who will be arriving, her son had informed her, with no fewer than two others of his kind. Doña Laura curses again her son's strange interests in things that have no merit at all, the friendships he makes with eccentrics like Mr. Nelson, but she stops well short of criticizing her prized son himself. No, if anything is wrong in this house it is due to his chatterbox of a wife, Gabriela, or her fool of a sister, Marta—both of them useless, capable of nothing but talk, and look what they have done to Sofia, turned her into a vituperative, waspish girl, a girl who, with every day that passes, is evermore in danger of living her life out as an old maid.

It is a growing concern for Doña Laura, her granddaughter's advancing age. Seven years have passed since the girl's introduction into society and no suitor has materialized, no offer has been made for her hand.

"It is all Gabriela's fault," Doña Laura complains to her septuagenarian friends. "She has managed to raise a daughter without any feminine graces whatsoever. Already twenty-two and incapable of attracting a look her way, incapable of using that fine face of hers to secure a future with a man of substance, one of those *hacendados*, for example, who regularly travel around the world."

At this very moment, the failure of a girl is watching her grand-mother from across the courtyard of the hacienda, observing the old woman as she sits in her high-back chair, arms crossed, a perpetual scowl stamped on her face, inspecting the work of the servants as they sweep and polish and scrub.

At times, during the long nights in Mérida where there is no bookstore to escape to, no promenade to offer her a breath of fresh air, Sofia longs for her childhood days at the hacienda, the way the time used to crawl there, the sounds that serenaded her at night, the humming that cradled her in the hammock, the same humming that often kept her grandmother awake, fretting, on the other side of the house. She longs for those days when she had accompanied her father on his daily nature walks, learning, over time, to distinguish among the various species of birds. She thinks with pride of her contribution to her father's obsessions, of her considerable talent with the quill. It is her drawings her father uses to distinguish between birds of a similar hue. "How else," he asks her, patting her head, "could I possibly hope to remember the difference between a Violaceous Trogon and the Black-Headed variety of the same bird?"

When Sofia remembers her childhood days on the hacienda, she thinks of Rosita, above all.

She was only eight years old when she befriended the little girl, the daughter of a servant who worked in the kitchen at the side of the house, cooking for the workers who tended to the henequen, work that kept mother and child in that hot room from morning until night.

Rosita had a wide face and a soft smile. She had the disposition of a saint, spoke with a hushed voice, had the charming habit of hiding her smiles behind a small, perfect hand.

She spent the day by her mother's side, helping to make the *tortillas*, helping to make the stew out of the meagre ingredients meant to feed fifty workers, but which would be more appropriate for twenty men at most. She ran food and water to the fields, where she was referred to as an angel of mercy by many an ailing worker trying to meet his quota despite the fact that his head was heavy with fever and his body shook violently in the heat.

It was during one of these jaunts that Rosita ran into Sofia, playing with a stick at the back of the house, singing a song taught to her by her mother, though she could remember only bits and pieces, was forced to hum the parts when the words would not come out.

Sapito, sapito
Anduvo,
Anduvo bajo del cubo

Sofia invited the girl to join her. "Sit," she told Rosita, delighted to find someone of the same age with whom to pass the time. Sofia's brothers Juan and Bernardo were too young to play eight-year-old games. Sofia explained this to the young girl whose eyes remained fixed on the ground, who wanted desperately to play with Sofia but who knew she would be punished for daring to desire such a thing. After some coaxing, Rosita did sit down. "Just for a little while," she told Sofia and Sofia smiled, promised her she would teach her this song so that they could sing it together, a song accompanied by the beating of two sticks upon the ground.

They agreed to meet there the next day although Rosita explained that she did not know when she would be sent on an errand—sometimes it was in the morning, sometimes not until late in the afternoon. "Don't worry," Sofia told her, "I will look for you, Rosita. I will watch the kitchen and wait until they send you out."

Over time they grew closer and found a way to meet each other three or four times a week. Sofia taught Rosita the names of birds, told her about the stories her father read to her before bedtime, tales of *conquistadores* and mermaids, knights upon white horses and princesses with long blonde hair.

One night, the workers rose from their hammocks and spilled into the darkness. They began to knock furiously on the trunks of the trees and upon cedar boxes. The noise woke everyone in the house, who ran to the windows, ran to the doors. "The *indios* are rising up against us," Doña Laura had screamed, fear in her eyes.

In the sky above, the moon seemed on fire.

"It is a lunar eclipse," Don Roberto told his mother, trying to calm her fears, trying to focus her attention on the beauty of the sky above. "Perhaps the *indios* are celebrating this miracle of nature." But his mother's fears were not so easily laid to rest. She fed on her suspicions of these dark people, impenetrable, dangerous, she thought, beneath their golden skins.

And then the moon turned white again and the drumming stopped. The *indios* rejoiced briefly in celebration and then retreated quickly to their rooms. The family returned to their hammocks as well, though Doña Laura did not sleep another wink, held tightly on to her crucifix throughout the long, dark night reciting prayers until the arrival of the morning light.

The next day, Sofia asked Rosita about the drumming, about what had brought the workers outside the previous night. "Evil spirits were eating the moon," Rosita told Sofia, "but the men scared them off with their drums." And then Rosita told her friend other things Sofia did not know. About the Chiquinic, the wind that blew from the west bringing the black butterflies that presaged all manner of difficult times ahead. About the power of Rosita's aunt to interpret people's dreams, knowledge that had been handed down from woman to woman since the beginning of time.

Over the next days, Rosita shared other stories with Sofia as well. She told her friend of the beatings that the overseer, Arnoldo Lamas, inflicted upon the workers, young boys at times, no more than ten years old. Rosita hoped that Sofia could help them, could help Rosita's brother, Jorge. He was an unruly child, had not learned to bow his head properly, was beaten often with a whip. Rosita thought that Sofia, with her white face, her kind face, had the power to make things right, that with a few words Sofia could wrench that whip from the overseer's hands.

Sofia had nightmares at night after their talk; she tossed and turned in her sleep. She woke with deep circles under her eyes. Her father heard her in the night and rushed to her side whenever she screamed for help. "What is it, *hija?*" He asked her, concern in his voice. It was not like Sofia to be screaming this way. She was usually so sunny, usually so content.

"The overseer is beating the children," Sofia sobbed. "Please, Papá, make the man stop."

Don Roberto tried to comfort her. "*Hala, hala,*" he told her, "it is a dream, Sofia, a bad dream that will disappear in the morning light."

But, no, Sofia insisted on it, insisted she had heard it from the children themselves. She told her father she could not sleep with this man so close to their house. What if he wished to punish her? Or worse, what if he hit little Bernardo, who was too lame to walk or run, who crawled around the house dragging a heavy leg behind, trying with all his might to keep up with his brother and sister as they ran freely around the grounds?

The next day Don Roberto took the overseer, Arnoldo Lamas, aside. "You are not to beat any of the children, Arnoldo. This is a strict order from now on."

Don Roberto knew Arnoldo Lamas considered him a weakling, knew that the overseer despised his eccentricities, the fact that he could not bring himself to reprimand a worker properly, the fact that he had never tended to the operation of the hacienda, the fact that Don Roberto was ignorant of the daily grind that kept Arnoldo busy from dawn until dusk.

"The Indians listen only with their backsides," the overseer told his *patrón* without emotion, repeating a maxim used often by the planters to justify their need to use the whip and the cane.

"I am ordering you, Arnoldo, to desist from beating the children on these grounds. This is a command, I repeat. Not open to question at this or any other time."

"As you wish, Patrón," Arnoldo replied, a half-smirk spread on his face. It was too bad he needed him so, Don Roberto thought, not for the first time. It was too bad indeed.

One day, Sofia and Rosita hid in the chapel. They brought the saint with the handlebar moustache down from the altar where he was perched and took turns playing mother to him—they patted his face and rubbed the sombrero that sat on his head and they called him their little Tomás. Their laughs and giggles filled the chapel so that they did not hear the door open, did not hear the rustling of Doña Laura's gown as she made her way inside.

It was Rosita who had the saint in her hands, who was humming that song taught to her by Sofia the first time they met. Doña Laura approached her quietly, ripped the saint from her arms and slapped the girl hard across the face.

"What do you think you are doing in here?" Doña Laura spat out. "How dare you touch the saint with your unwashed hands! How dare you leave the kitchen! Run. Now! Go quickly back before I let the overseer know where you are." Rosita's mouth was open in shock; her face had turned red. She ran out of the chapel quickly, eager to avoid more serious punishment at the overseer's hands.

Doña Laura turned then to Sofia, whose mouth was half opened as well, who was shaking perceptibly as if it were her own face her grandmother had slapped, as if she felt the imprint of Doña Laura's hand on her own cheek.

"You silly girl, do you not know that you are forbidden to play with *los indios*? Has your father not instilled any sense in that hard head of yours?" Her grandmother grabbed Sofia's cheeks and squeezed them hard. "Your father will hear of this, Sofia. Mark my words. We will teach you to distinguish between wrong and right. If it takes all eternity, we will teach you. I, personally, will make sure of that."

Sofia longed for the *abuelas* that appeared in fairy tales. The kind who told their grandchildren stories and showered them with sweets and toys. She knew it was wrong to despise her grandmother, but she could not help it. She could not remember hearing a kind word from this woman, could not remember a time when anything other than bitterness had emanated from her grandmother's bones.

Later, her father would tell her gently that she was not to play with the girl, that Rosita must help her mother in the kitchen, had few moments to spare to entertain Sofia. "And you have your brothers to play with, *hija*. And your books too, all the books you so adore."

Sofia would never play with Rosita again. The girl ran to and from the fields now with her eyes fixed on the ground. Sofia wished she could touch Rosita, talk to her, tell her she was sorry that it was Rosita's face that had been slapped and not her own.

One day, a year later, passing by the kitchen where Rosita and her mother prepared the worker's meals, Sofia noticed that her friend was not about. She returned the next day and the day after that, but still there was no sign of her. Sofia enquired after Rosita, was told by the girl's mother that her daughter was very sick. Some sort of fever had been spreading among the children of the workers at the hacienda. Sofia and her brothers had so far been mercifully spared.

That afternoon, after she was sure everyone in the house had settled for their afternoon *siesta*, Sofia ran to the worker's compound that lay to the south of their house. She looked through the bars of the windows, ran from room to room until she found Rosita lying inside one of them, alone on the floor.

"Rosita," she whispered, "it is me, Sofia." When the girl did not respond, Sofia entered the room, ran to where the girl was lying and picked up her hand.

Rosita looked up at her with swollen eyes, tried hard to smile but could not muster the energy to get the smile right. Sofia lay her friend's head on her lap, stroked her face as if she were her own child, sang her the song they once used to sing together, until Rosita drifted into sleep.

The next day she returned and again the day after that. Rosita seemed worse with each passing day, no longer even recognized Sofia. She could not smile, no matter how hard her friend tried to make her laugh.

On the third day Sofia entered the chapel and took Santo Tomás from his perch. She ran to the room where Rosita was lying and placed their make-believe son into her friend's arms. "Look," Sofia whispered, "our little baby Tomás. Let's sing him that song he so likes." Rosita's body was still; she did not even open her eyes. Sofia kissed their baby on the top of his head, kissed Rosita as well, told her she would be back later for Tomás once they had both rested some more.

She returned a scant hour later to find her friend in her mother's arms. The cook was crying softly as she gently stroked Rosita's face. Sofia told her she could go to the kitchen now, assured her friend's mother that she would take care of Rosita and their son, Tomás, the saint who stood nearby, staring at them with his expressionless eyes.

"God bless you, *mi niña,* but Rosita is already at rest," Rosita's mother told her and some time elapsed before Sofia realized that her friend had passed away.

Sofia walked then to the chapel, with the saint underneath her arm, tears rolling down her face. She thought of those hurried but precious moments spent with her friend, the songs, the stories, the laughter they had shared. She seethed when she thought of her Abuela, the woman who had deprived her of the girl's friendship, who dared even to mark the girl's face with her rage.

She looked up then to find her grandmother rushing towards her, pointing at Santo Tomás and raising her fist into the air. They stopped in front of each other, grandmother and granddaughter, like a pair of flamenco dancers, engaged in a duel where the only weapon was the rage that shone from each set of eyes. Although Sofia knew that she was to respect her elders, to love them despite their many faults, their tarnished hearts, she could not forgive her grandmother for this, not when the memory of Rosita's still body was so fresh in her mind.

Eventually, it was Doña Laura who took a step back. Sofia walked by her to the chapel, where she placed the saint on his perch, from which she would never again take him down. Grandmother and granddaughter would lock eyes many times in the years ahead. They were destined to engage in battle, destined to forever disagree.

Oh, yes, at times Sofia longs for her childhood days at the hacienda, longs for Rosita's smile, Rosita's touch. But she is all grown up now, knows that she is to leave the memory buried in Arroyo Negro along with the rag dolls with the porcelain faces and the fables of Jean de la Fontaine.

This trip will be different, she thinks, indulging in a moment of hope. This time they will be receiving a visit from Mr. Nelson and his two assistants; there will be much to do, much to learn, many opportunities to escape the oppression that lingers in the corners, many chances to avoid unpleasant encounters with the women of the house.

And there they are now, the three women, huddled together in the courtyard like three bees on a flower, dreaming up, no doubt, yet another one of their improbable plans. Yes, there is her mother seated on the far left, buzzing away as usual, with that vacant look in her eyes. And seated next to her, Our Lady of Bitterness herself, Sofia's grandmother, her lips pursed as tight as a miser's fist. Finally, as always, seated next to *fu* and *fa*, is her Aunt Marta, a pair of crochet hooks in her hands.

It was Aunt Marta who usually defended Sofia against Doña Laura's tirades, who tried to offer up excuses for the girl's refusal to consider any men the older women suggest. "*Bueno*, Doña Laura," she would say, "the girl has not descended into the lower registers yet. She is still young, still vibrant, can and does attract the eye of many a man in town. But just look at the men who are wandering about! It is not her fault that they are a collection of ostriches, strutting and preening, seeking to find only their own reflections in a young girl's eye."

"What nonsense you speak, Marta, what *bobadas* indeed!" Doña Laura would reply, "There are men of all kinds in Mérida, as there are everywhere else in the world. The fault lies not with the men but with Sofia herself." And then the old lady would embark upon a litany of Sofia's faults—disrespectful, proud, combative, picky to a fault—a litany interrupted more often than not by Gabriela, who had not been listening to a single word of their exchange and who would launch, incomprehensibly, into a detailed account of all the happenings in the house of Doña this or Doña that, what their children were up to and what their servants had been saying around town—and "Have I told you of the purchase they made just yesterday? A ham the size of a boulder—a boulder, sister, I do not exaggerate at all" and on and on she would go, chit-chat, chit-chat, chugging like a freight train, ignoring her mother-in-law's irritation, her sister's raised eyebrows, until she ran clean out of steam and came abruptly to a stop.

Yes, there they all are now, together in spite of how poorly they get along, complaining and sewing their way through another long hot afternoon. Thankfully, Mr. Nelson and his two assistants arrive just then, stopping to pay their respects to the women as the servants attend to their baggage and then guide the men to the office where Don Roberto is waiting for them.

Ah, freedom has arrived, Sofia thinks. Freedom and something else—excitement perhaps? No, she erases this thought quickly from her mind. Of course I am happy to see Mr. Nelson, she tells herself, he is a most prized teacher, and Very Useful is a most entertaining man. As for Diego Clemente—she will be watching the usurper carefully this time, gauging what kind of man has been lucky enough to assume the position she so wants for herself. For now, she is content to dwell on the opportunities that will present themselves during the visit from these men—opportunities to learn, to discuss, to wander into nature with field glasses and paints, opportunities to escape the boredom of the long afternoons with the three older women of the house, of being forced to play the warped piano as all good Mexican young ladies do, with decorum, with restraint, ever mindful that the mastery of music and embroidery are a vital route to a young man's heart.

*

Inside the hacienda's study, two old friends are taking turns discussing the afflictions that are accosting them with each passing year. Edward William Nelson, distinguished naturalist, noted ethnologist, known to the Bering Sea Eskimo as "the man who buys good-for-nothing things" because he had purchased from them as many of the bits and pieces of their lives as he could—boat hooks, ceremonial masks, ptarmigan snare sticks, fish traps, grass socks—over ten thousand pieces in all, each lovingly packaged and sent back to the Smithsonian Institution to be conserved there for all time. Edward Nelson, once vigour-filled, imbued with an almost superhuman strength, is of late feeling as if bits of himself are slowly drifting away. He thinks back wistfully to his days in the Arctic, the energy he had back then, the little thought he had given to making his way by dogsled and *bidarka* across the barren ice shelves into the Yukon Delta and the interior of Alaska, camping in often inhospitable territory in order to study any number of things—fish, butterflies, the breeding habits of the magnificent emperor goose. But those had been very different days indeed. Yes, back then Nelson had basked in the luxury of youth, could still boast good health, had been armed with the certainty that what he was doing would prove of lasting value to the world.

These days nothing is imbued with certainty anymore. Time has changed all things and now he feels battered, weathered, exhausted beyond his years. Right and wrong have blurred into one, the shadows he had once easily ignored have been illuminated, there are no clear lines of demarcation to be found anymore. The earth has melded into the ocean; all the lines on the map have blurred. What a curse to be burdened with memories; how difficult it was to feel so weighed down with uncertainty when he could still so easily remember his younger more buoyant days.

"Imagine," Nelson says to his friend, "it feels as if it was only yesterday that I was approaching the coast of western Alaska for the first time, glimpsing a bit of heaven in the gorgeous colours of the night-sea sky. Along the northern horizon, as the sun crept just out of sight, lay a bank of broken clouds tinged fiery red and edged with golden and purple light. In all my subsequent years in the Arctic I would never see such a beautiful sky again, and now I ask myself—was it really that beautiful or did I perceive it as such because I had come upon it innocently for the very first time?"

Duarte smiles. "Is that not the question we all ask ourselves, my dear friend? Is this not what makes each passing year a torture, the realization that we are trapped inside an aging vessel but think ourselves young boys still, no matter the evidence to the contrary, no matter the silly figures we cut? Yes, old age is a curse, my friend, a curse as wicked as those uttered by a witch's mouth."

"I have begun of late to wonder, Roberto," Nelson confesses after a pause, "whether I will be able to complete the work on the bird guide. It seemed a worthy idea at the time but I am now sinking in a sea of doubt. There is much to do back in my own country, so much research to catalogue, so many worthy projects to embark upon. And my revisiting Mexico four years after my work for the Biological Survey was completed seems foolish to me now. An attempt to relive experiences from another time." He drifts into silence then, lowers his eyes, inhales deeply as if he were trying with that breath to erase each of his doubts.

"A man cannot be blamed for wishing to relive his youth in some shape or form, Edward," Duarte hurries to assure him, "after all, we are older, yes, but still not hovering over the precipice of death itself. *Ánimo, mi amigo, ánimo!* Perhaps what you are experiencing is nothing more than a momentary slump."

"I fear it is not, Roberto. I fear this is something quite different indeed. A bend in the road. My own dark night of the soul."

The men fall silent for a moment. Outside, they can hear the voices of Don Roberto's two youngest sons, arguing over a game of cards.

"And then there is the issue of those two birds," Nelson says.

"Two birds? What two birds do you mean?"

"A pair of Passenger Pigeons, Roberto, a pair held captive right here in the Yucatán."

"Surely you jest, Edward! Who could possibly have those birds on their hands?"

"A man by the name of Victor Blanco."

"Victor Blanco?" Duarte repeats, surprise in his voice. Later, alone in the privacy of his bedroom, he will chastise himself for having expressed even a hint of surprise. Of course it was Victor Blanco, who else could it be? A man who has everything, who lives in a state of constant restlessness, forever in search of a way to quell his acquisitive thirst—art, land, jewels and now, it seems, even a pair of endangered birds.

He thinks then of what his friend Edward Nelson does not know about his life, the things that pertain to the hacienda, for example, to all matters relating to the cultivation and sale of the henequen. The two men share a love of nature, have travelled through the region together on many occasions in search of a trogon, a manakin, a weasel or a bat. They have compared notes, gloried in scenes of spectacular beauty, but they have never, during the eighteen years they have known each other, discussed any details of Roberto Duarte's life.

Would it surprise Nelson to learn then that there is a rope that binds Roberto to this Victor Blanco? Would he be surprised to hear the extent to which Roberto is so penuriously in Don Victor's debt? Edward has arrived in the Yucatán to document the wildlife of the region, to produce a written testament to the natural riches of this blessedly beautiful area. He knows much about animals, about plants, can recite the scientific properties of the *Agave fourcroydes* in his sleep, but he knows little of how this plant makes its way from the Yucatán to the plains of the American South.

He does not know, for example, that a few men control all aspects of the henequen trade in the region, Don Victor Blanco being one of them. He does not know that it is these men who own the export houses, it is these men who make the deals with the buyers, it is these men who channel the capital loaned to them by the Americans to the small *hacendados*, such as Roberto Duarte, but only on their terms and always at usurious rates.

Five years later, these larger landowners will be referred to derisively by the Revolution's General Alvarado as the "divine caste," ever intent on consolidating their landholdings, consolidating their wealth. And how easy the lesser landowners make their task for them, assuming increasingly greater debt just so they can own the trappings of power exhibited by the members of this almost superior race—the jewellery, the houses designed by European architects, the automobiles and the yachts. One by one, the smaller landowners collapse under the weight of their debts, are left with no option but to surrender their henequen haciendas to the likes of Don Victor Blanco, who show no mercy in calling in their loans.

Every fourth Saturday, Roberto Duarte appears at the company of this Don Victor Blanco and sells his henequen for a half or even a quarter of the going rate. It was Don Victor who had advanced him the funds to convert his hacienda to the cultivation of hene-quen back in 1891 and Don Victor who advanced him capital to keep his Mérida bookstore afloat as well. So it is that as the henequen magnates in the Yucatán reap the extraordinary benefits of the furious demand for rope, as they bask in the profits of a plant growing dearer with each passing day, Roberto Duarte sinks evermore into a morass of his own making, humiliating himself at the doorsteps of Don Victor's company, trying to unload his fibre in an effort to pay his own accumulating debts.

"Sorry, my friends, we already have more than we can use," Don Victor's men tell those who line up there on Saturdays, those who, like Roberto, find themselves indebted up to their very ears and who can find no way out of their predicament except to come here to peddle their wares.

Ah, but he is a generous man, this Don Victor, and after much shaking of heads, and many jovial apologies, "No, really, we cannot buy any more. Sorry, really sorry we are," inevitably, there is a change of heart. "Because how can I not help you, my friends, my *compadres,* each and every one of you, and friends are here for each other, no?" Don Victor himself will say, appearing before them now in his white linen suit, a cigar hanging from his lips. "Perhaps we can unload the fibre in the next shipment. Yes, yes, I will see that it is done. But it will prove impossible to unload it at your prices, eh? No, *señores,* you too have to give a little back. To unload this much fibre we need you to cooperate as well," he says and then proceeds to offer to take their henequen off their hands for a fraction of what it is worth. Many families have already lost their haciendas, have been unable to hang on after a bad harvest, have succumbed to their own indebtedness, their own inability to live within their means.

Roberto Duarte has miraculously found a way to hang on. In some ways, Roberto's fortunes parallel those of Mexico herself. Consider the nation's capital, Mexico City, for a moment and you will see what we mean. In 1803 no less a man than Alexander von Humboldt could already declare it the most beautiful city founded by the Europeans in any hemisphere, but beauty does not feed mouths or cure the sick. Consider the city's location, over two thousand metres above the sea, caged in by mountains and volcanoes, prone to earthquakes, sinking evermore into the moist subsoil on which it sits. This city is not a city, it is a catastrophe waiting to unleash.

And yet.

Two hundred years after von Humboldt inhaled the air, untarnished as of yet by pollution and waste, the city stands grander than ever, the beauty still there, the disasters kept mostly at bay.

Consider then the Yucatán itself, a limestone ledge with its poor soil, its few forests, no hills and little rain. Consider its location, miles and miles from the centre of things. Consider the difficulties encountered in even the simple act of growing beans and maize.

And yet.

It is this limestone rock that the Maya used to build their spectacular jungle cities, a source of awe still to those who travel from all corners of the globe to admire these miracles of stone. And it is on this arid piece of the earth too that a plant worth its weight in gold not only thrived, it transformed a region into a haven for some of the most spectacular fortunes in the world.

Yes, so far Roberto Duarte has managed to avoid losing his hacienda, has managed to hang on by a tenuous thread. But times are changing, his luck is fading, things will soon be coming to a head.

It is true, he thinks to himself, as Edward Nelson, with anguish in his heart, speaks of those two birds, there is a lot my friend does not know about my life. Roberto Duarte considers the possibility that perhaps his friend prefers to remain in the dark. After all, there are many who abhor the system of slavery that allows the region to reap the extraordinary profits from the henequen. Roberto himself does not venture to think much about the issue. Things are as they are, he thinks, they are as they have been for centuries now. Since time immemorial there have been masters and those who live under their protection and command. Thinking too deeply about such things will not prove useful in the least, not when the world is full of much more interesting things—his birds, his books, the many interests he has in all manner of things—bells, metallurgy, French literature and, lately, a new interest—the Eskimo of the Bering Sea.

Yes, he thinks, looking at his friend's crumbling gait, the exhaustion that is stamped across his face, it would be better to keep his own relationship to Victor Blanco to himself. There is much in life to speak of, to share—why sully it with a moment of darkness, a reminder of all the rot that lies beneath the surface, always threatening to rise up.

*

On the other side of the house, inside the parlour with the distended piano, a dead great-aunt's armoire, mismatched tables and chairs and dozens of potted plants—reed palms, jasmine, scented geraniums, red ivy, lilac, narcissus and hyacinths, all tended to by the voluble Gabriela, with a tenderness her children have rarely been privy to—in this parlour of shabby furniture and luxuriant plants, seated upon badly upholstered chairs, are Very Useful, Diego, Sofia and Aunt Marta. Crochet hooks as always in hand, she is there as chaperone for the young man and woman who are engaged at this moment in a most curious exchange of words.

"A congregation of plovers," Sofia is saying, a spark in her eye.

"A cover of coots," the young man replies.

"A dole of doves!"

"A fall of woodcocks."

"A murder of crows!"

"*Bueno, bueno,*" Aunt Marta jumps in, putting crochet needles aside, mouth twisted, perplexed eyes opened wide. "What is this nonsense you two are speaking about?"

"A peep of chickens!" Sofia says, laughing heartily, ignoring her aunt.

"A siege of pigeons," Diego replies, smiling wide.

"A parliament of owls!"

"A muster of storks."

"Stop, *niños*, stop!" Aunt Marta cries out. "I am asking you again to tell me what in God's earth all this talk is about."

"Allow me to explain, Doña Marta," Very Useful jumps in, wiping some juice from the mango he has been feasting on from his chin. "The young people are engaging in one of Mr. Nelson's favourite pastimes. My *patrón*, you see, has a genuine fondness for language and likes nothing more than to unearth improbable words used for a particular group of birds."

"Aaaahhh," Aunt Marta replies, head cocked, curiosity now sufficiently quenched. Then, not knowing what else to say, she returns to her crocheting, dismissing the affair entirely with a quick shake of the head.

"A wedge of swans!" Sofia continues.

"An unkindness of ravens," Diego retorts.

"A wisp of snipe!"

"A murmuration of jays."

"Aha!" Sofia screams out. "It is not, Señor Diego, a murmuration of jays as you say but rather a murmuration of starlings instead."

Diego brings his hand up to his forehead, slaps it loudly, shakes his head back and forth. "Of course. A murmuration of starlings, of course! You win, Señorita Sofia, but you must admit that you have had an enormous head start. I have been learning these terms for only three months while you have been learning them all your life."

"I will grant you that, Señor Diego, though only grudgingly. I hope you understand."

A silence follows as the young people lower their eyes and Very Useful fixes his own on the basket of tropical fruit that rests nearby. "Tamarinds, plums, guavas, mameys," he exclaims, "what a wonderful assortment of our region's riches we have here today." He offers the basket to the others, each of whom declines in turn.

"Mr. Nelson tells me you are a very talented artist, Señorita Sofia," Diego says.

"He does?" Sofia answers eagerly, too eagerly she immediately thinks, as a blush creeps up her face. She quickly adds, "Mr. Nelson is very kind," in a tone that indicates she does not for a moment believe the older man's words.

"Would you permit me to see some of your work, Señorita Sofia?" Diego asks.

"They are trifles, Señor Diego, amateurish attempts of little use to anyone with a serious scientific bent."

"Nevertheless, I would so like to see them. I am, after all, an amateur myself."

"Very well," Sofia says. "But I would also like to see your own drawings, Señor Diego. Mr. Nelson speaks very highly of your own talent as well."

The young people agree to go and retrieve their respective work and meet back in the parlour, where Aunt Marta has by now abandoned her crochet hooks and placed a sleepy face in her hands.

As they walk out, Sofia nudges Diego with her elbow, pointing to her aunt, whose eyes are closing at that moment, her hand finding it increasingly difficult to prop up her head.

"Just you watch, she will be in a deep sleep by the time we return," Sofia whispers to Diego, smiling at the sight of her aunt's head bobbing up and down. And indeed by the time they return, drawings in hand, her aunt is fast asleep, her head resting now on the side of her chair, her mouth opened wide. His stomach full, Very Useful has also lowered his head into the side of the chair and is snoring loudly, his hands clasped across his chest.

Sofia and Diego sit at a large table by the window and agree immediately to drop the Señorita and Señor from their names.

They place their work gingerly on the table, Sofia first, Diego next, each of them nervous, each eager to please the other with their respective drawings of the area's birds.

"Yours first, Sofia," Diego says and the young woman nods shyly, handing him the first drawing from her folder—a Yellow-Throated Euphonia, the colours vibrant and magnificent from the slate blue back to the yellow forecrown, underbelly and throat.

"This is beautiful," Diego says after a pause, examining the drawing up close as if he were trying to memorize each of the pieces that make up the whole. A Turquoise-Browed Motmot, a Cave Swallow, a Yucatan Wren and an Olive-Throated Parakeet follow next, each exquisitely rendered, the colours brilliant, painted from the stuffed specimens her father had himself pre-pared, the birds carefully suspended by wires among plants and fern to make them appear as if they were still in mid-air.

"All right then, it is your turn now," Sofia insists, eager to see an example of what Mr. Nelson called "an exquisite talent"—words, it is true, that had seemed torturous when she had first heard them and which manage to still feel heavy in her chest even now that the enmity between them has been erased.

Diego produces a watercolour of two Orange Orioles first, one depicted in mid-flight as the other perches on a tree branch below.

"I call these paintings 'feather maps.' I try to get the details of the birds first, aided by the photographs taken by Mr. Nelson, and then to convey an overall impression of the bird," Diego explains. He examines her reaction nervously as if trying to gauge her opin-ion of his work from the expression on her face.

"This is magnificent, Diego," she says, a strange vibrato distending her words, a look of awe emanating from her eyes. It seems to Diego that another emotion moves across her face—disappointment, perhaps? No, he dismisses this thought immediately—he is incapable of attributing any ill will to this young woman now.

And then Sofia says nothing more, sifts silently through each of those pictures, some of them sketches, mere skeletons awaiting flesh, and as she sifts she feels her heart sink deeper and deeper into her gut. She had so wanted to dismiss Diego's talent—even now, after their playful exchange of words, after admitting to herself that perhaps not all about this young man was unworthy, that he was not the villain she had imagined, nor the usurper in the classic sense of the word. Even now some part of her needs to believe her own talent has been ignored, that she has been passed up for a foreigner ignorant of the area's birds, but these beliefs simply cannot be sustained after seeing the young man's work. It is not only the exacting detail with which the birds are painted, the perfection of an eye, a crown or a leg—no, much worse, infinitely worse than the perfection of the detail is how real each bird seems, how intensely alive it appears.

It is at this point that Aunt Marta's eyes open and she brings herself up abruptly, returning to her needlework as if she had not missed a stitch to sleep. She looks around then, disoriented, and notices that Sofia and Diego are now seated at a table instead of on the chairs where they had been before she had surrendered to her impromptu afternoon nap.

"*Hija?*" she asks Sofia, confusion in her eyes.

"Ah, *tía,* you have resurfaced at last. Señor Diego and I were just sharing with each other some of our work on the area's birds."

Her aunt smiles, nods her head. In truth, nothing interests her less than the area's birds. She had once attempted to teach her niece needlepoint, embroidery and other useful things for young girls, hoping to discourage her from her eccentric interests, but had quickly given up in defeat. Her niece is unusual, of this there is no doubt. Birds, books, atlases and dictionaries are clearly more to her liking than playing fine music on the piano or embroidering a sheet. But then, it is true that colours have been invented to satisfy every taste. And her niece's interest in drawing birds has always seemed quaint to her aunt, an example of the talent that courses through their blood—what does it matter if that talent is best expressed with the needle or the brush?

"*Bueno, hijos,*" Aunt Marta says to Sofia and Diego, waving her hand as if implying that they are free to continue perusing each other's work.

But Sofia has seen all that she needs. She bundles her drawings back into her leather pack—orioles, terns, hawks—smiles a broken smile and excuses herself before Diego, who watches, confused, as the girl quickly exits the room, hurrying out as if something inside of her has been dispersed and she needs time alone to regroup.

*

Inside Roberto Duarte's study, Edward Nelson is finally revealing the cards that are close to his chest. "What would you think, Roberto, of you finishing the bird guide, with the help of Diego, if I am not able to do so myself?"

Roberto Duarte looks up, surprise in his gaze. He has not been taking his friend's complaints too seriously until now. We all have bad days, he thinks, days when our lives seem unbearable. But we move through them, we move on.

"Are you serious, Edward? Do you really think you will not be able to finish the work yourself?"

"One can never tell, Roberto, one can never tell. However, I would like it to be finished one way or another and I know you are the best-equipped person to do it in my stead. You would have Very Useful at your disposal and I would continue to pay Diego, of course." Here Nelson pauses briefly and clears his throat. "You could also have Sofia help, Roberto. She is extremely skilled, knows those birds as well as we do, can draw splendidly herself."

"Sofia?" Roberto Duarte seems surprised by this suggestion, because he would have never considered it himself. True, his daughter is a talented artist and experienced with the area's birds, but she is a young woman, not meant to be traipsing through field and forest in search of rare specimens in bushes or in trees.

"I doubt very much that my mother would allow Sofia to be involved in such a thing. She is of late pestering me with the worry that she is still unmarried, and you know our culture, Edward. Her age could prove to be a liability soon."

"She is only twenty-two, Roberto."

"That is old enough, Edward. Some would even say she is almost too old."

"Still, she is not married yet and before she is packaged off to some local dandy she could prove immensely helpful to Diego and yourself."

Roberto Duarte looks up sharply, startled by the bitterness in his friend's words.

Nelson draws back, lowers his voice and adopts a more honeyed tone. "I'm sorry, old friend. If I sound abrupt it is merely a reflection of how tired I feel, the exhaustion that has lodged itself deep inside my bones."

Would it surprise Roberto Duarte to learn of the loneliness Nelson feels, a loneliness that had never assailed him so thoroughly before, not even in the Arctic when the days seemed as long as weeks and he was alone for torturous dark periods? Would it have surprised his friend to learn of the regrets Nelson now feels, how he longs for the first time in his life for the warmth of a family, for the company of a woman upon whose lap he could lay his doubts to rest? There are many things Roberto Duarte does not know about him, the small secrets that are barricaded inside a starched breast, the turbulence that hides behind gold-rimmed spectacles, the longing that is barely suppressed inside an aging heart.

It would certainly surprise, upset and unhinge his dear friend, he is sure, to learn of Nelson's feelings for Sofia—his subversive thoughts, thoughts more appropriate to a man half his age—to Diego, for example, than to him in his weathered, fifty-four-year-old shell.

He realizes now that returning to the Yucatán a full four years after he had finished his work for the Biological Survey was a serious mistake, no matter how useful a bird guide to the region would prove to the cause of conservation he so believes in, no matter how much he tries to rationalize it to himself. Shoot the birds with a camera and not a gun, he had said in his speeches to the ornithological societies in the United States. Learn to care for them; list them in your private diary as if you were the first to lay eyes on that particular species of bird. We will help you, provide the guides that will make identification easy, complete with range maps and accurate drawings of the birds.

He thinks now of the two birds in Victor Blanco's possession and feels himself sinking further in despair. In his mind, his feelings for Sofia and the fate of those birds are inextricably bound, two sides of the same coin—their fates futile, impossible, leaving behind a hole in the heart too cavernous to fill.

The men leave the study to wash up before the midday meal. From across the courtyard they watch as Sofia leaves the parlour, drawings in hand, anxiety in her stride. They watch as Diego runs after her, watch as she turns back.

"Sofia, have I done something to offend you?" the young man asks.

"No, of course not, Diego. I am merely offended at myself. Angry for having thought myself an artist when I see now that my drawings are nothing but depressing, static attempts."

"Sofia, that is not true at all," Diego says, placing a comforting hand on her arm.

From across the courtyard, a duet becomes a trio as Don Roberto shouts out, "Are you all right, my child?"

"Of course, Papá, of course. Just the ravings of women, as you always like to say!" Sofia replies.

The four voices come together now at centre stage.

Nelson speaks and a trio becomes a quartet. "I am sorry for overhearing what you said, Sofia, but I must tell you that you are very mistaken in your belief. Your drawings are not static at all; they are, in fact, very fine indeed."

"Yes, of course they are, *hijita*," her father jumps in. "Why, Edward was just asking me to lend your services to the completion of his bird guide. That says it all, does it not, my child?"

Sofia issues the barest of smiles. "Of course, Papá, of course it does."

Diego smiles reassuringly, "I told you, Sofia, did I not?"

Nelson's smile is bittersweet. "You are an artist just like the best of them, *chata*. Never, even for a moment, allow yourself to doubt it at all."

It is Roberto Duarte who now brings the matter to a close, "Dear friends, it is time to retire to the dining room for a well-deserved meal."

Offstage, far from the glare of the lights, underground movements are afoot. It is 1910, a venerable year in Mexican history. The centenary celebrations of the nation's independence are being prepared in Mexico City, where the dictator of thirty-three years resides, never doubting that he will be presiding over the bicentennial celebrations a hundred years from now. Dictators like him have been known to live for thousands of years in different guises and names.

But beneath the firmament, in hidden coves and alleyways, a revolutionary movement is brewing, a chorus of dissent rumbles, growing evermore intense. The voices are building, one on top of the other—contralto, soprano, tenor, baritone, bass. Listen, listen, for they will soon reach a crescendo, a zenith, a holy peak, signalling to all that life as they know it is about to come to an end.

But for now the voices recede, the tidal wave is held at bay as an intermission is granted, one last invitation for those in the cheap seats to arise and stretch their legs.

ACT THREE

Inside the oldest cathedral of the New World

From stage left a shot now rings out in the dark.

It is a cool evening in December 1910 and the Mexican dictator of more than thirty-three years, General Porfirio Díaz, is seated behind a solid walnut credenza table contemplating his uncertain fate. In just five months he will be forced into the arms of exile inside la belle France, but for now the old man with the generous white moustache and the inscrutable gaze is still trying to change the progress of history, still trying to forestall his inevitable fall from grace. In the half-light of the early evening, he stares listlessly at a map of the land under his now tenuous command. Mexico—the horn of plenty, the North American tail, the nation that has been completely his for so long and that is now slowly but surely escaping from his grasp. Just a month ago a wealthy landowner by the name of Francisco Madero had called for a day of insurrection. The insurrection failed, but the thirst for change remained. In the South, a peasant's son by the name of Emiliano Zapata is at this moment organizing a guerilla force to attempt to do away with the hacienda system for all time. In the North, an ex-bandit by the name of Pancho Villa is bringing Mexico's cowboys together in an army of freedom fighters. There, too, another army is being formed by a peasant named

Pascual Orozoco, who is sick of the inequality, of the abject poverty that the majority of the people have lived with for centuries now.

With the tip of a fat finger, Díaz traces the areas on the map where insurrection is rife—east, west, north, south. *Surrounded,* he thinks. And then, more ominously, he adds, *all of the portents were right.* Porfirio Díaz, the strongman of the Americas, the colossus, the general with a thousand lives may have spent the last three decades steeped in every imaginable luxury—gold, diamonds, yachts, telephones, cars—but he has a peasant's cunning, a peasant's heart. That very year, they had all seen the comet that had appeared in the heavens, had watched in awe this spectacle of light, this harbinger of the disasters that would surely be coming to pass. Across the nation, nervous people began speaking of the unthinkable—plague, famine, war.

General Díaz's scientists had scoffed at the people's ignorance, had dismissed all the talk of disaster that this spectacle in the heavens supposedly presaged. "We have been waiting for this comet to arrive, *Su Excelencia.*" They told their president, incredulity in their eyes, "It portends nothing other than how accurate our scientific calculations are."

Porfirio Díaz had nodded, but felt fear in his heart. Mexico is a land of prophecies, a land where the future is forever being revealed. Had not comets appeared in the heavens in the year 1519, when the Spaniards had arrived? Had not the Mayan *Chilam Balam* warned the people to prepare themselves, that the white twins of heaven would come to castrate the sun, bringing night and sadness and the weight of an incalculable pain? And is it not true that Francisco Madero, the very man who had called for the day of insurrection that began this revolution, had Madero not been assured that he would be president of Mexico by a ouija board? No, the general's fears are not so easily laid to rest. He remains anxious about the future, afraid of what is coming, unsure any longer of his role in this New World. Above all, he feels exhausted. Eighty-four years old. Too old, surely, to be fighting any unreasonable wars. He moves his finger over the map, across an ocean, stops abruptly in France. There could be worse fates, he thinks, worse places to spend the rest of one's life. But for now, the general will stay put. Watch as things unravel. Perhaps this revolution is nothing but a hiccup, a minor disruption that will peter out with the morning light.

Yes, yes, he thinks as he sits back in his chair, I will have the patience to wait it out. As he leans back, the stage slowly grows dark and we find ourselves transported from inside a palatial study to the city of Mérida once again.

A year has passed since Diego Clemente's arrival in the region and already bits and pieces have been added to his map. On all four corners birds have suddenly appeared—an Aztec Parakeet in the west, a Turquoise-Browed Motmot in the north, a Ferruginous Pygmy Owl in the east, a Violaceous Trogon to the south.

And there is more. Shading has been added to the rivers, colours have become more intense, the earth has acquired texture and the oceans depth. The country that had so awed him when he first arrived has grown more impressive yet. Is it the beauty of the region that has added shading to his map—the sheen of the white city of Mérida, the majestic *ceibas*, the windmills, the city's spectacular main square? No, surely it must be the birds, the miracles of colour that roam the skies—robins, jays, kingfishers, orioles, woodpeckers, hawks. Or perhaps it is the days that stretch out languorously until they come to a close, or the quality of the light, unmatched, unequalled in any region of the world? Yes, all of these things have contributed, some more, some less, but they are not the main reasons for Diego's tumble into ecstasy, into a heady state of grace.

There is only one real possibility for this marvellous explosion of colour, this added depth. Can it be that our Spanish lead has fallen madly and irremediably in love? Yes, what else but love can intensify the blues and the reds, add texture to surfaces that once were flat? What else but love lies at the heart of any opera, *buffa*, *seria* or any other kind? And so it is with our own tenor, who has plunged headfirst into this amorous abyss with pencil, paper and field glasses in hand. There is no turning back for this young man; his voice has soared in the last few months, he no longer feels in command of his own emotions, he has grown wings and learned to fly.

And there he is now—inside the great Mérida cathedral attending a Mass in the name of the Virgen of Guadalupe, the great heroine of the people, carried from Spain by Cortés himself, and adopted by the Mexicans, who promptly gave her dark skin and cast her in a central role as the nation's very own patron saint. Inside the cathedral on this December twelfth of 1910, while in a distant capital city a dictator lives out the last days of his regime, the people have come together for this most sacred affair—a celebration unlike any other. Dozens of priests are in attendance, a bishop, two governors and all the illustrious families of the region dressed in the sumptuous finery recently ordered from the couturiers of Paris. There, too, scattered throughout the less hallowed places of the cavernous cathedral nave, are all the players in the story that has brought us here on this day.

On the left stands a bespectacled Mr. Nelson. He is flanked on one side by a jovial Very Useful, dressed in his usual attire of bright oranges and greens, and on the other by Diego Clemente, groomed to perfection on this day though his hair remains unfashionably long and he has not yet adopted the moustache that is all the rage with the dandies of the town. As a chorus sings its heavenly music in the background, Diego furiously scans the crowd.

Who is he looking for? Surely you need not ask! It is of course Sofía, that rare bird who at this moment lies hidden from sight, lost amidst the throngs that have packed this cathedral today, from the splendid altar to the imposing doors.

Well ahead, in the pews reserved for the most glorious of the glorious, sit some of the members of the more illustrious families—Don Victor Blanco for one, boredom in his eyes, and next to him his long-nosed, phlegmatic wife, Doña Alicia, sitting stiffly, bedecked from head to toes in diamonds and silk. Next to her, their son Carlos, dressed in one of his impeccable English suits, his bowler hat placed respectfully beside him, his eyes closed as he listens enchanted to the chorus singing from above. Scattered all around them are the other members of Mérida's upper crust—the Medinas, Villarreales, Peniches, Molinas, and de la Cruzes.

On the other side of the cathedral, seated well back from the dignitaries, are Roberto Duarte and his wife, Gabriela, sons Bernardo and Juan, who are seated between them, and in the pew behind the four are Aunt Marta, Doña Laura and Sofía. She is dressed in an elegant pale blue dress, a dress that will be abandoned later as she dons a more spectacular gown, a gown that has caused a furor in the Duarte household of a kind usually reserved for more serious affairs. Doña Laura is at this moment poking at her granddaughter, trying to iron her dress with the back of her palm, ignoring the frowns that greet her every pull and tug, defiant in the face of Sofía's obvious distress.

Every so often the young woman looks about the cathedral, tries to spot Mr. Nelson and his assistants, only to be repeatedly thwarted in her quest. The people are packed chin to chin on this day, they are like leaves on a laurel tree, thick, crowded, obscuring all manner of treasures from view.

Defeated in her attempts, Sofia thinks now of how things have changed over the past year. *From boredom to triumph.* Where once she had nothing to look forward to but the morning hours spent at a bookstore, dreaming of all the possibilities that were denied to her, now she can look forward to outings in the field, as a valued contributor to Mr. Nelson's last project in the Yucatán.

There has been much arguing in the household about Sofia's participation in the venture since it had been suggested during the first visit Diego Clemente had made to their hacienda. It had been Doña Laura who, predictably, opposed it with the most vehemence, challenging her son as she had never done before, convinced that an already suspect reputation would now be ruined for good.

"What are the people of Mérida to think about a decent girl traipsing about the mud with a group of badly dressed lunatics in tow?" she had asked, despair in her words. Her son tried to reason with her, but there would be no convincing her, no way to make her see the importance of their work.

To Doña Laura's dismay, her son had held his ground. He had made a promise to a friend and was determined to keep it, no matter how vehemently it was opposed by the others in his house. It is true, his wife had expressed her own doubts about Sofia's participation in the project, had voiced opinions similar to those of his mother but she had at least acquiesced once assurances were given that the girl would never be left alone. Eventually, a compromise had been struck. Sofia would participate only if accompanied by her Aunt Marta, who thought privately that nothing was less appealing than the prospect of spending the early evenings wandering about in the wilds full of crocodiles and bloodthirsty insects, just so she could keep an eye on her niece's virtue. And would not the girl's father be there with her in any case? But, no, Doña Laura argued, no man, not even her son, could be trusted to notice the truly important things. And so Aunt Marta had consented in the end, reasoning that it would be a small price to ensure that peace reigned in the house.

Sofia's contributions are indeed proving fruitful to the creation of the bird guide. Not only does she spend the time in the field with the group, she also often works well into the night sketching the specimens they observe and photograph during their excursions into the field.

Las Aves del Yucatán, she whispers to herself, sounding out the title of the proposed guide much as if it were the words to the Our Father itself, reverentially, with awe. In all of her life she has not felt such contentment, such peace. It is as if someone has opened the doors to heaven and, for once, has let her wander in.

Seated at the cathedral next to her grandmother and her aunt, she thinks now of Diego Clemente, the man who has so thoroughly insinuated his way into her heart. It is true, no words of love have been exchanged between them—they have merely shared tips, stories, ideas on how to approach a particular drawing of a bird. But there is a current that courses between them, an electrical charge. She thinks of their equal devotion to the bird guide, to Mr. Nelson himself, to his ideas on conservation that are slowly but surely making them both see the world through a very different lens. A bird guide is one way to ensure the safety of the birds of the area, Mr. Nelson often says to them, passion in his words, determination in his stride. We are here to defend them, to make people admire them, to make them come alive in their minds. A camera and not a shotgun, he proclaims. A photograph and not a mounted bird.

Sofia feels her grandmother pulling at her skirt now, watches, irritated, as the old woman reaches over and irons the folds with her hands. Ah, but there are storm clouds hovering, Sofia thinks, feeling the anxiety suddenly surging in her chest. Not all has unfolded perfectly in the last six months. Some things have grown more complicated, more difficult to manage than her participation in the creation of the bird guide.

The bookstore, for one. Carlos Blanco has not, as she had hoped, exited from her life. She no longer promenades with her friends on Sundays—too much to do, too much to think of, she tells them—uninterested as she now is in participating in the ritual of walk and talk. She had hoped Carlos Blanco would understand that a message was being conveyed. That she was not interested in his attentions, did not want his notes filled with the titles of arias, the names of operas, allusions to the leading artists of the day that she is supposed to decipher, as if embedded in these names and titles is the very meaning of life itself.

Instead of being dissuaded, the fool seems more determined than ever to pursue the dance. He has begun appearing at the bookstore almost daily, asking for increasingly obscure titles, staying for up to an hour at a time as she hides in the back, hoping that he will take his leave quickly so that she can emerge into the light.

Sofia is determined to keep her grandmother from learning of the young man's interest in her. Sofia does not doubt for one moment what the old lady's reaction would be to even the tiniest possibility of a marriage between her granddaughter and the son of one of the wealthiest *hacendados* in the land. She is obsessed with marrying her off, the sooner the better; the minutes are ticking, the days and months are passing by. Soon, she tells the women during their afternoon sewing circle in the courtyard, Sofia will be of little interest to even the most desperate of men.

"And a woman is meant for marriage," Doña Laura has declared to Sofia's mother more than once. "Whatever else is she to do with her life? Look at Marta—lost in her world of foolish remedies with nothing to live for but her needlework and her deck of cards."

And then, suddenly, disaster struck Sofia hard. One afternoon in early November, arriving home from the bookstore, Sofia found the women of the house in an uproar, her mother and aunt screaming at each other in delight, words spilling furiously from their mouths, their sewing momentarily put aside. Even her grandmother had abandoned her usually sour demeanour and was sporting a wide, almost maniacal grin.

Good God, Sofia thought, whatever has happened must be astounding indeed if my grandmother has actually allowed a smile to creep in.

"What, what?" Sofia asked impatiently, excited already by whatever it was that had the women beside themselves on this day.

Aunt Marta rushed in, determined to be the first to deliver the magnificent news. "We have been invited to a ball, *mi niña*."

"And not just any ball, *hijita*," her mother jumped in, elbowing her sister to one side, "but a ball given by none other than the Blanco Torres family. Can you imagine anything more splendid than the Blanco Torres family including us in one of their affairs? No, I can hardly believe it. I can hardly take it all in."

Before Sofia had time to respond, her mother planted in her hand the invitation, a thick envelope with their family name printed in gold where inside, Doña Alicia Torres de Blanco requested the pleasure of their company at the family's annual Virgin de Guadalupe Ball.

And then Gabriela was off—reminding herself aloud of all the French terms that belonged to the dance—those terms that had once rolled so easily off her tongue, once, so long ago it seemed to her now, when as a young girl she had been invited to almost all of the city's grandest affairs.

Balancez, glissade, traversez, vis-à-vis, quatre en ligne, chaine des dames, le moulinet.

The commotion in the house had not subsided for the next three weeks. Among the women, it was silently agreed that this was more than a ball, it was an *opportunity*, a chance to secure a husband of substance for Sofia, and opportunities like these, they told each other, were meant to be seized by the neck.

"The girl seems to be growing less interested in the business of marriage with each passing day," Gabriela said to her sister.

"Growing stranger too," added Doña Laura, who could not forgive Sofia for being prey to such ridiculous interests, for desiring to partake in things as unfeminine as a walk in the fields. Oh yes, a ball was just what the girl needed, a glimpse into a more feminine world. It might knock some sense into her, pry her away from inside the covers of a book, wipe that smile of victory from her face, the one she had been sporting since being allowed to join the men in their trivial bird-loving pursuits.

"*Por favor!* She is not strange, Doña Laura. She just has her own particular style, her own way of doing things, if you like." Gabriela hurried to her daughter's defence, because although tensions in the house had diminished of late, not even this great event, this *opportunity*, could possibly erase all the damage from the war that had been going on between them for so long. Indeed, her mother-in-law's opinions continued to irritate Gabriela right to the tip of her toes.

"What she means, *hermana*," Aunt Marta said, in that special tone of hers, a tone she usually reserved for people she considered simpletons at best, "is that Sofia is *different* from the rest of the girls her age. *Mira*, all of her friends are interested in dances and such things. But Sofia, *bueno*, there can be no denying that there is a touch of the eccentric in our dear girl . . ."

"Can we just concentrate on having the most divine dress made for her, please?" Gabriela interrupted, irked by her sister's siding with the old woman and even more annoyed that, deep down, she agreed with them both. If they were to achieve their aims, however, if they were to make use of this *opportunity*, it was best to put aside their differences for now. The time, she knew, was not right for internecine wars.

Sofia herself could not be less excited. Trepidation accompanied her through the long days and all the talk of the ball merely made her retreat further into her work, where she at least found consolation cataloguing and sketching her beloved birds.

It was in this spirit that she tried on the dress—a golden gown, shimmering and loose, embroidered with sequins of faceted crystals that caught the light whenever she moved. "An exact copy of a design by no less than Callot Soeurs," her mother hurried to tell her, congratulating herself on her luck in having found a picture of it in an issue of *Harper's Bazaar* that had arrived at the store and having found a dressmaker talented enough to copy it stitch by stitch.

It was beautiful indeed—even if the colour was all wrong, or at least according to Doña Laura, who, having been left out of the decision, eagerly pounced on the deficiencies of the gown, who complained about it unendingly as if it meant the *opportunity* itself had been frittered away. "Anyone with taste," she told whoever would listen, "anyone would have known that a girl like Sofia, with her dark hair and her white skin, would be favoured not by yellows but reds."

And now the grand day had finally arrived and despite all the commotion, the mad scramble to get everyone properly attired for the event, Sofia's dejection had not been lost on her grand-mother, who had a sharp eye for detecting all that did not accord with her own worldview.

"What is the matter with the girl?" Dõna Laura had asked Aunt Marta that morning as they all hurried to dress for the morning Mass. "Because I can assure you that with that attitude Sofia is unlikely to attract the eye of any of the fine young men who will be in attendance this evening, fine young men wishing to dance with gay young ladies and not a sour-faced fish. And they espe-cially won't look at one dressed in yellow, a colour that lights up a face inappropriately, which manages only to enhance that sullen, bitter look."

"*Bueno,* Doña Laura," Aunt Marta hurried to assure her, "the girl is nervous, that is all. And who can blame her? She may have been invited to other affairs but nothing on the scale of a Blanco Torres ball. She will be fine once we have arrived and she has had time to adjust to it all."

Seated in the cathedral now in her simple morning dress, stiff as a board and bored stiff by the incessant droning of the priests, Sofia is already feeling much better about things. She has overheard a conversation that took place between her father and Mr. Nelson outside the cathedral doors, has learned that the scientist has somehow secured an invitation for himself and his assistants to attend the Virgen de Guadalupe Ball. To what end, she does not know. Sofia is quite certain that Mr. Nelson has no interest in society affairs, knows that if he has accepted an invitation it is for more important reasons than dancing until dawn. She is certain something else is afoot. For days now she has watched as Diego and Very Useful exchanged pointed looks, has noticed how they often grow quiet when she appears before them unannounced, has caught them red-faced and nervous as they were interrupted discussing God-only-knows-what. She has affected ignorance, has played the innocent while keeping her ears primed, her senses sharp. She has stood behind doors, strained to listen to whispered conversations, has even resorted to sifting through Diego's notes, but she has uncovered nothing that reveals a secret plot. She was beginning to think that she had been imagining things until this—Mr. Nelson's revelation that he and his assistants would be in attendance that night at the ball.

On the other side of the cathedral, far from his beloved's eyes, Diego Clemente is occupying his time not with prayer but with trying to get the rhythm of a waltz right. One, two, three; one, two, three. Forward, side, close; back, side, close. He stops. Is it not forward, side, close; back, forward, close? No, no, he thinks. Back to first principles! Count, Diego, count. One, two, three; one, two, three; one, two, three.

Such madness this is, he thinks, exhausted by all the counting, the trying to remember the differences between a polka, a mazurka and a waltz. To what end? He feels foolish now for having allowed himself to be convinced by Very Useful that the Blanco Torres ball would be his one chance to declare himself to his one true love.

That he was attending in the first place seemed impossible to believe. Just two weeks earlier Mr. Nelson had broached the subject while the three men were busy cleaning the lenses of their reflecting cameras, putting the equipment away after an early-morning shoot.

"Señores," he had said, his voice expressionless, "prepare yourselves. We have been invited to a ball that will be held at the home of Don Victor Blanco."

"A ball?" Very Useful had asked, his eyes opened wide. "We are invited to a ball? Inside the home of Don Victor Blanco?" He glanced over at Diego, who had stopped cleaning and was looking up at Mr. Nelson in stunned surprise.

"And what are we supposed to do at a ball, Mr. Nelson?" Diego asked.

"Why, dance, Diego, what else but dance?" Mr. Nelson had replied and he had turned around then, putting the equipment in his pack, making it clear nothing more would be discussed.

That evening, after much conjecture, much mulling over the reasons for the invitation, the reason their *patrón* had for including them in such an affair, Very Useful had abruptly changed course and had declared the reasons to be irrelevant, that the important thing was that Sofia would be there as well.

"An opportunity has presented itself, my boy! A door has opened, a tunnel has appeared through which to crawl. Don't you see? You must seize the moment, grab the iguana by the nose."

"You mean the bull by the horns, do you not?" Diego replied, amused, lying on the ground and cradling his head in his hands.

"Iguana, bull, flounder, who cares? Think, *amigo*, think!" Very Useful slapped Diego gently on the forehead, pulled at his arms until Diego sat up.

"And how, tell me, genius in a bottle, am I to declare myself? I certainly cannot dance, I know nothing of how high society works. I will be a fish out of water, flapping about like a fool."

"Ah, man of little imagination! Of little faith. Am I not here to serve you, to teach you all the ins and outs, the thises and thats? Have I not shown you the ups and the downs, the *turulus* and the *taralas?*"

"Be serious for a moment, Very Useful, please! Is this Victor Blanco not one of the richest men in the land? Does his hacienda not extend to the Caribbean Sea and back? What, pray tell, do you know about a man like him, about the way he conducts his life?"

"You offend me, Diego. For although you are indeed green around the eyes, I myself am a native of this land, have served in houses grander than Victor Blanco's pitiful shack. More important, *mi amigo*, much more important than that, is the fact that Very Useful can teach you to dance!" And with this, the little man jumped into the air and twirled about a few times.

"I have no intention of learning how to dance, Very Useful. I have come here to paint birds, not to squander my time with high society balls. There is, I insist, a reason for Mr. Nelson's strange invitation, and although we may not know it yet, it certainly has nothing to do with a waltz."

But Very Useful had stopped listening, was twirling around the perimeter of a *ramón* tree, hands outstretched, *one, two, three; one, two, three*, nodding to an imaginary partner, madness in his hair, wild enthusiasm in his eyes.

One, two, three; one, two, three.

"Very Useful, please!" Diego cried out, laughing at the sight of the little man dancing about in his bright orange breeches, arms extended wide, lost in his secret music, sporting that wide, toothless smile.

"Get up, *gapuchino*, get up," he demanded of Diego, pulling at his arm until Diego had no choice but to stand up, though he continued to laugh, continued to insist that Very Useful was thoroughly and irremediably mad.

"*One, two, three; one, two, three, venga,* come on, Diego, join me in the dance."

Diego rolled his eyes, placed his hands in Very Useful's own, twirled with him now around a bush of violet *Bugambilia*, fell into the rhythm that was being set by Very Useful's words; *one, two, three; forward, side, close; back, side, close.*

"Jesus and Maria!" Very Useful screamed out suddenly, holding on to his foot. "What in God's name are you doing, stepping on my delicate toes with your big elephant hoof?"

"Elephants do not have hooves, Very Useful," Diego replied, arms on his hips, watching amused as the other man hopped back and forth.

"*Hombre,* what makes you think you can lead when you have only begun to learn how to dance?"

"Is the man not supposed to lead, Very Useful? I know little about such things, but that I do know for sure."

"And what is this then, you barbarian?" Very Useful asked, holding on to his groin, "A bowl of *frijoles,* perhaps? Some decorative marbles? Why can I not be the man?"

"Because I am taller and more *feo y fuerte* than you by far."

"Bah! First you learn, then you lead, *mocoso.* Now stop wasting my time."

Very Useful grabbed Diego's arms once again. "*Venga!* Do you not want the girl? Or do you want to leave her to the machinations of that operatic fop, Señorito Carlos, with his English shirts and his French cravats? Come on, Diego, concentrate, learn!"

"Wait, Very Useful, wait. What Señorito Carlos are you talking about?" Diego asked pushing his friend away, all traces of a smile now entirely erased from his face.

"Ah, do not worry, Diego, do not worry. He is, just as I said, a complete and utter fop, walks about the town with a gold-tipped cane and a pince-nez on his nose. Has a good voice, that I must admit, likes to bellow out Italian songs at the top of his lungs. But do not worry, my friend, do not worry at all. I have on many occasions observed our dear Sofia hiding inside a bookcase at the store just so she doesn't have to exchange words with this tedious popinjay."

"He is not like us then, Very Useful, not *feo y fuerte* at all?"

"Ugly and strong? Ha!" Very Useful screamed out. "Of course not, not at all! Dainty and weak, I would say. Buffed and perfumed. Laced and rouged. Almost a woman, in fact. Now dance, Diego, dance."

They twirled around the tree once again, humming the one, two, three; one, two, three in one voice.

"Oh, one more thing, Diego."

"What?"

"This Señorito Carlos? He is also the son of Don Victor Blanco."

"What?" Diego asked, alarm in his voice but before he could ask any more questions, another voice interrupted from afar.

"What in God's name are you two doing?"

It was Mr. Nelson. The words were curt but his expression was not. He was smirking widely, watching as Diego's face turned a most unbecoming shade of red.

"Why we are dancing, *patrón*," Very Useful replied, dignity in his voice. "Practising for the Blanco Torres ball." He sniffed loudly then and brought his chin up high.

"Very well, gentlemen, very well," Mr. Nelson replied. "But before your enthusiasm transports you to more distant realms, come over here and listen to what your real task will be at this event."

The two men exchanged looks and then walked solemnly over to their *patrón,* who had sat down by a rock and closed his eyes, seeming in danger of losing himself already inside the rollicking whistles of a Spot-Breasted Wren that hovered nearby.

*

Is it ever really possible to leave the past behind, to cross an ocean and put the memories of what has been abandoned to one side— the taste of a fine sherry, the scent of distant olive groves, the feel of stone-cobbled ancient streets beneath one's feet?

Once upon a time an Arab caliph, Abd al-Rahman, forced out of his ancestral home in Damascus, made his way north to begin life anew in Spain. There he founded one of the greatest cities of the day—Córdoba, the heart of the new kingdom of Al-Andalus, a city of fountains, running water, glorious libraries, paved streets— all this at a time when the rest of Europe was mired in medieval warfare and disease. Still, as old age approached, Abd al-Rahman remained haunted by the smells and the sounds of Damascus and longed to return to the land of his childhood, now banished forever from his sight. Drenched in an overwhelming nostalgia, he sat in his courtyard and stared at the palm trees he had brought from the East and he thought, I am like those palms, exiled from their rightful home, empty, mournful, surrounded by voices and yet always alone.

Hundreds of years later the Spanish would carry the riches of their ancestral home across the ocean with them in their ships— horses, pigs, honeybees, bananas, lilacs, wheat. Once on New World shores they honoured their memories by baptizing the cities they found there with the names of the places they had left behind—Guadalajara, Mérida, Valladolid. What had been aban-doned had not been forgotten; it had been replanted, renamed, transformed. Granite became limestone; wheat gave way to corn; chilies grew bolder; rattles, drums and clay flutes mixed with harps, guitars and violins and altered the rhythm of familiar child-hood songs.

On Diego Clemente's map we can see that as the strokes of his brush grew bolder and brighter on New World shores; what had been left behind seems to stand out even more. From the hidden recesses of memory, scents, words, songs had begun to emerge unbidden, leaving him with a feeling of vertigo, unsure of where he was standing or where he was heading, confused, at times even forlorn.

"Nostalgia!" Very Useful had declared when Diego confessed his uneasy feelings to him one day. "Don't worry, *compadre,* I have seen this before. It is an affliction of all those who leave their land, no matter how much improved their lot may be in their new homes. But it too will pass, Diego, these feelings may not disap-pear, but they will surely diminish in intensity over time."

But was it nostalgia or was it something more? At night Emilio appeared to Diego in his dreams. Other times it was his mother who materialized, dressed in her habitual grey, shoulders slumped in defeat, a fleeting figure, the fire of reproach still in her gaze. And at other times yet it was Uncle Alfonso who made his presence known, dancing improbably in a brightly lit Mérida square. *Sobrino,* he would ask him then, waving his arms wildly in the air, have you forgotten the figs, the olives, the scent of jasmine, the taste of bitter orange, all that is waiting for you back here?

And yet he was happy. In all of his life he had never been happier. For once he was responsible for himself only, had only to worry about pleasing one master, a master he adored. He thought of his youth then, of all those years after Emilio's death, toiling to keep his mother alive, assuming responsibilities more suited to a much older man, and the memories made him feel suffocated, as if the ghosts of his past had their arms still wrapped tightly around his neck. At times his mind would wander briefly to that moment at Don Ricardo's house, to the weight of his mother's disappointment, but just as soon as the memory surfaced he would violently block it out. No, he would think, eyes closed, lips tight, no memory shall so easily pollute my mind.

Whenever a spare moment presented itself and he found himself alone, he would resume work on his ever-evolving map. A Pygmy Kingfisher, a Collared Aracari, a deep bay, an imposing mountain and the ocean, always the ocean to delineate. What lay inside that ocean he did not know for sure, but he added layer upon layer of indigo blue and brilliant violet as if attempting to tame whatever lurked beneath the waters, trying with all its might to surface and be heard.

His thoughts would return then to that day's events, to the blissful moments spent by Sofia's side, to the companionship provided by Very Useful, to the admiration he felt for his *patrón*. Strangely enough, it was Mr. Nelson's manner, his curiosity, his unending drive to explore the hidden alleyways that lead to new and greater truths, it was these aspects of Mr. Nelson's personality that made Diego pine for the days of his early youth, though it would take him some time to understand his feelings for the man for whom he worked. It is not until one day, after many hours spent learning the finer points of photography by Mr. Nelson's side, that Diego suddenly realized how much his *patrón* reminded him of his beloved father. From that moment on, his devotion to Mr. Nelson would grow to resemble that of an acolyte to his God. There was nothing he would not do for him, no request he would hesitate to fulfill.

As he sat next to Mr. Nelson, waiting for him to reveal what he had planned for them at the Blanco Torres ball, Diego was ready to embark on any assignment his *patrón* might propose. And it was a good thing too because his *patrón* was about to make a most unusual request. He was hoping his assistants would not question his judgment, would not balk at their assigned task, especially as he himself felt so uneasy about the whole affair, knew that he was crossing a threshold from where there would be no turning back.

"Gentlemen," Mr. Nelson told them, pointing down to the ground, "come over here so that you can see what I am to draw." In the earth at their feet, Mr. Nelson now began to fashion a map with the end of a stick.

"Don Victor's hacienda—parlour, study, kitchen, billiards room, dining hall."

He extended his stick north—drew a factory, workers' quarters, machine room, train tracks and then stopped to make a large **X** on a spot just behind the house.

"And what is that, *patrón?*" Very Useful asked.

"That is an aviary, my man. The reason we will be in attendance on the night of the ball."

Nelson's assistants looked at each other expectantly and then waited in silence to listen to what their *patrón* would reveal next.

It is about two birds, he began.

*

On that same day, less than a kilometre away on the vast Blanco Torres henequen estate, some of the most powerful men in the region were leaning over a very different map. They were contem-

plating the dots that had once been minor henequen haciendas
—the dots that these men had swallowed into their own estates
during the last decade as the former proprietors, one after the
other, sank under the weight of their debt. Here the Carrerra
estate, over there the ancient lands of the Beltráns. Near Progreso,
the hacienda of Tomás Diaz, at one time as proud a man as could
be found anywhere in the Yucatán.

"And here, near Mérida, Señores," Don Victor Blanco now
boasted to the other men, "is my latest acquisition, the lands of
Pascual Seguro, the deed to which I now hold in my hands." The
men laughed, raised their glasses in the air and showered Don
Victor with applause. Little by little, they were inching their way
towards their goal of consolidation. Little by little, their lands
were becoming fiefdoms, towns in their own right.

"There is one small problem," Don Victor told them, the laughter now disappearing from his eyes, "a minor thorn in my side.
One Roberto Duarte, to be exact." Don Victor brought the men's
attention back to the map. Arroyo Negro. A hacienda surrounded
by acres and acres of Blanco Torres land.

"Our goal, Señores," Don Victor told the others, "is to get this
man to assume a greater burden of debt so that we can push him
off his land."

"Duarte is a lunatic, Victor. A bird lover, a freak of nature, an
eccentric interested only in obscure subjects and encyclopedic
books, a man who even looks the part of the fool in his ill-fitting
suits." A certain Don Máximo was speaking now, a corpulent man
with the unfortunate look of a turkey vulture. A *Cathartes aura*,
Nelson would say, to be precise: large body, a red, unfeathered,
bald head, given to preying on dead animal carcasses and occasion-
ally even attacking young animals as well.

"Why don't you just offer to buy his land outright?" Máximo Cuevas asked his friend. "He is out of his league on his hacienda anyway. You would not believe the stories Duarte's own overseer tells about the man."

But Don Victor did not like the thought of being bested by such a fool, did not wish to pay for what he had taken so easily from other more capable hands—hands, it was true, that unlike Roberto Duarte's own, had borrowed and borrowed until the only way out of their debt was to pay with their land. No, Don Victor would wait. He had waited long for other things before and had always managed to win out in the end.

In the meantime, the henequen magnates of the Yucatán had greater things on their minds. The conversation turned to the talk of revolution that had been sweeping through Mexico City during the last month. The men shook their heads, lamented how things were on the verge of falling apart in other parts of the realm. They dismissed the notion that any such revolution would ever arrive in the Yucatán, reassured each other with their sarcastic laughs. But make no mistake about it, these men were nervous. You could see it in their eyes.

*

Having heard the Mass and confessed to their sins, the people now stream out of the cathedral, congregating in the main square to assess each other's festive clothes in the bright midday light—from the elaborate hats that adorn many a head to the dainty shoes that squeeze many a woman's toes. The air is electrifying and gossip is rife. What a fine day it has turned out to be, they all exclaim in delight, with the air so still, the temperature so pleasant, the sun so bright in the sky. They promenade this way and that as the band of men dressed in starched white *guayaberas* and matching breeches plays *fiesta* music on a red platform, as children shout and dogs bark and the orange-sellers entice them with glasses of freshly squeezed juice.

By a bench, Nelson and his assistants encounter the Duarte family in full—Mamá and Papá and the two sons, Aunt Marta and the irritable Grandmother not far behind, and standing far away enough that it is difficult to tell if she is with them at all, is Sofia herself. A wide scowl is still on her face for she has not yet rid herself of the rage she has felt at being pinched and poked by her grandmother throughout the long and tiring Mass. She smiles now that the men are before her, asks Mr. Nelson to confirm that they will indeed be attending the ball. "Why yes," Mr. Nelson, replies. "And I would so very much like it if you would save a dance for me, *chata*," he adds, taking her hands into his own.

"Of course, Mr. Nelson, of course," she replies and her smile grows wider until it erases the last traces of an ill mood from her eyes. In the meantime, Doña Laura's own smile has disappeared from her now stark face. Storm clouds darken her brow. Just my luck to have these *ignorantes* ruin the day, she thinks bitterly. Just my luck they will be following us straight to the season's most important event.

The group breaks up then; Aunt Marta chases after the boys, who have wandered off in search of a sweet; Very Useful and Mr. Nelson take a seat on a bench next to Don Roberto to share news about various species of birds; Gabriela walks away in search of a spot of gossip to tide her over for the afternoon.

Off to one side, Diego and Sofia exchange pleasantries while looking down at their feet. "And do you know how to dance, Señor Diego?" the young lady asks, assuming this formal address knowing her grandmother is hovering nearby, listening intently to each word.

"No, Señorita Sofia, in truth I do not. Very Useful has tried to teach me during these last few weeks but the exercise has proved nothing short of disastrous, I must admit." Diego laughs now and Sofia joins in, imagining Very Useful waltzing around a room in his bright orange breeches and his wide, lopsided grin.

"Well, all is not dance at a ball in any respects. There will be plenty to eat, I suppose, and much in the way of other entertainment to keep us amused." Sofia now raises her gaze and meets Diego's own. Eyes lock for a moment, no more than a beat, four sacred seconds that seem to last much more than this—enough time for young hearts to skip, for the music to soar, enough time, also, for a spark to suddenly ignite in Doña Laura's suspicious head. *Good God, but can what I see be true?* she asks herself. *No, no,* she tries to erase the thought immediately—after all, had she not herself ensured the two were always accompanied by a chaperone? Ah, but what a chaperone! That fool Marta with her crochet hooks and her cards, always falling asleep at the most inopportune times. She will have a word with her later, yes indeed, she will accuse her of being blind to even the clearest of signs.

But for now, the old lady has already seen more than enough. She grabs her granddaughter roughly by the arm, pulls her away from Diego, announcing curtly that it is time for them to make their way home. "You will excuse us, of course, young man," she says to Diego, and before he or Sofia can utter another word, Doña Laura has already steered her granddaughter north, away from her beloved and towards the safety of a closed door.

At the Virgen de Guadalupe Ball

It is true that we can be torn apart by competing emotions, attempting to balance what nature simply will not. Sofia is wary, yes, fearful of what lies ahead, yet she cannot, once at the ball, be but swept away by the sheer excess—the jewellery, the carriages, the dresses embroidered with diamonds and gold, the men in perfectly pressed black suits, the servants in impeccable uniforms. Stunning Venetian lanterns are given to the ladies as party favours by gondoliers *to light your loved one's heart* they are told; silver hearts trimmed with roses are given to the men so the women can comply.

Outside, yes, there is hunger, there is despair among the masses who subsist on meagre rations of beans and maize. But inside it is all warmth and succulent smells, chicken in bougainvillea sauce, beef filet in tequila sauce, salmon in *chaya* sauce and, to tempt a man's soul, the more exotic fare—walnut-mayonnaise sandwiches, lobster à la Newburg, oyster à la poulette, sweet fruit and sherry compote.

Just outside, the slaves on the Blanco Torres estate toil from dawn until dusk, thousands of them—no one can hope to know their numbers anymore, not when they die so fast and so young; but take no heed, they will be replaced *inmediatamente.* After all, the henequen must be processed, the henequen must be sold.

We close our eyes; we cover our ears. Eyes that do not see do not suffer. Ears that do not hear do not despair. Besides, without excess there is no chance for a revolution, and the winds of a revolution are blowing in Mexico City already. It will not take long for them to arrive here, where they will coalesce into a storm.

Inside the ballroom, after hair has been carefully arranged, dresses brushed and the appropriate look stamped upon the face—the women of the Duarte house appear, eyes enlarged by the spectacle and the utter grandness of the affair. "Have you ever seen such a thing?" Aunt Marta asks Doña Laura, who has to concede she has never been a witness to grandeur such as this: the marble stairs, the Persian carpets, the fine art on the walls, gold and silver everywhere, the fine crystal clinking from every corner of the room.

The women head towards the receiving line, a still despondent Don Roberto trailing behind, burdened not only by the thought of his debt but a fish out of water in an event of this kind. Don Roberto is meant to be scanning the sky for birds or browsing a book on more esoteric affairs, is meant to be discussing things of cosmic significance and not standing here in a ballroom cursing the shiny black boots that torture his feet. Ah, but the torture will be momentary at least—dinner at eight, dancing to begin at ten, the affair officially done by three.

In the receiving line, standing in her privileged place as hostess and matriarch of the Blanco Torres clan (and one who rules her family with an implacable hand, it is rumoured, Gabriela quickly and discreetly informs Aunt Marta) is Doña Alicia Torres de Blanco herself, resplendent in silk and diamonds, with what looks like a tiara sitting atop the tight curls that frame her face.

"So kind of you to come," she says to one person and then the next. "So good to see you," she utters perfunctorily just to vary the theme, the phrases escaping languorously from her throat as if she is attempting to avoid exerting herself unduly with her own words.

Then the Duarte women are before her, Don Roberto still lingering at the back, and the good lady—who seemed until now not to be paying attention to those she has been greeting—suddenly stops in her tracks. She does not know these people, looks at her husband and her sons who are standing behind her, raises her eyebrows to indicate that she is in need of their help.

Carlos Blanco Torres steps forward. He introduces his mother and then his father to Don Roberto Duarte and waits for Don Roberto to present the ladies in his group to them. Sofia, who has been demurely eyeing the floor until then, looks up and encounters the eyes of the young man she has been avoiding for so long now, the young man who has invited them to the affair. There is no longer any use in hiding from him; her hands are tied. She has finally run out of luck.

"Enchanted," Carlos says, lifting up her hand and bringing it to his lips.

"Señor," she hears herself say, smiling briefly and then moving along as fast as decorum will permit.

"I hope you will save me a dance, Señorita Sofia," Carlos calls after her, but the girl has already walked quickly ahead and is spared having to respond by the pressure of the receiving line which is moving everyone inexorably forth.

Gabriela, in the meantime, is all effusiveness. She has focused on only one thing. The eldest Blanco Torres son has fixed an eye on Sofia, has asked her daughter to dance. "It is the dress," she tells the other women her face bulging with joy. "I knew it would be the perfect dress." Aunt Marta nods, equally enthused. She too has gleaned some promise from the momentary exchange. Only Doña Laura is unwilling to concede the appropriate choice of attire had been made. While it is true the young Blanco Torres has been kind to Sofia, it is just as easy to thank the stars as a golden and, in her view, badly stitched dress.

The dancing is to begin shortly after ten o'clock. No sooner has dinner ended and the orchestra begun when Carlos Blanco Torres is standing before Sofia requesting the pleasure of dancing the very first quadrille with her.

The older women are beside themselves now. A Blanco Torres asking Sofia for the very first dance! Oh, they can hardly believe it. Fans are produced and waved vigorously as the happiness suffuses their faces with heat—even Doña Laura is prepared now to concede that the *opportunity* has not been squelched with an inappropriate dress.

But then . . . no, it cannot be. Have they heard Sofia demur, have they heard her say she cannot dance, that she does not know the steps? Doña Laura is instantly at the helm. "Now, now," she says to Sofia, turgid words emerging from tight lips, "anyone can walk gracefully and easily through a quadrille, Sofia. Follow el Señor Carlos, he will guide you through the moves."

And before she knows it, Sofia is out on the floor, Carlos Blanco Torres confirming with the way he looks at her now what she has feared from the start, that inside the store those eyes had indeed been dancing for her while she hid behind a book at the back.

The young man tries to make conversation. He speaks of the things he thinks will warm her heart: questions about Schiller, Pérez Galdós and Lord Byron, and when his words elicit no more than a nod from Sofia (who, it is true, has plenty of opinions about all of these things but suppresses the desire to speak for fear of encouraging further talk), Carlos turns desperately to the subject of her beloved birds.

But then, thankfully, the dance is over without as much as two words being strung together by the girl who now walks quickly to join the older women, unaware that they have watched every move she has made, have witnessed, with each step, the young man's enthusiasm wane, have stared in horror as Sofia kept her eyes glued steadfastly to the floor. She arrives to three scowls. It is her grandmother who, predictably, begins to chastise her, reproaching her for the disgrace she has brought upon them all, only to be interrupted by the arrival of Mr. Nelson and his two assistants—Diego handsome in his formal dark suit, Very Useful attired more soberly than usual in muted yellows and browns.

"Ah, Mr. Nelson," Sofia breathes in relief. She offers her hand to the older man and then greets Diego and Very Useful.

"I did not see you during dinner," she tells the men. "I was beginning to despair you would not arrive at all."

"Not arrive? Why, of course we would arrive, my girl. Come now, you owe me a dance, as I recall." Mr. Nelson offers her his arm and they step out onto the dance floor, where the young lady giggles and talks her way through a waltz.

"Harrumph!" Doña Laura snorts to the other women who stand beside her, watching wide-eyed as Sofia comes alive in Mr. Nelson's arms.

"Notice how the girl is all giggles now. All coquetry. All talk. Could she have spared a smile or two for the Blanco Torres boy? Ah, that of course she could not."

"*Bueno*, Doña Laura," Aunt Marta responds. "Mr. Nelson is like a father to Sofia; it is only natural she should feel so comfortable in his arms. Carlos Blanco Torres, on the other hand, is no more than a stranger to the girl. It is no wonder she felt so shy and tongue-tied."

"Tongue-tied? My granddaughter? You are a fool, Marta, an innocent of the worst kind." And she is about to launch into a full-fledged attack, is about to reveal the suspicions she has nurtured all afternoon, that Diego and Sofia share more than an interest in birds, but the waltz has ended and her granddaughter and the American are standing before them once again.

No matter, the old lady thinks, biting her lip; there will be time later for her fury to be properly unleashed.

In the meantime, off to one side, Very Useful and Diego are having a whispered conversation that is growing more heated with every beat.

"Ask her now!" Very Useful urges Diego. "This is your one and only opportunity, *compadre*. Take it, come on!" He is pushing Diego forwards but the young man has dug in his heels, will not take the formidable step of moving forward to the spot where Sofia is standing with their *patrón*.

"Stop it!" Diego whispers hotly. "You know I am here for a much more important matter than a dance. I simply cannot let Mr. Nelson down. Now take your hands off my back, you crazed man."

"All matters of importance can wait for one dance, Diego. *Venga*, do not hide your cowardice behind a pledge of duty. You forget who I am, a mind reader, a seer of great truths, the one person on this earth who can see your weaknesses right through to that unbecoming hole in your sock. One dance, Diego, just one dance, my boy. An opportunity to reveal your feelings to your one and true love."

But Diego will not budge. He is all nerves and adrenaline, feels torn between a desire to act and a frantic desire to flee. Amid the exchange of words with Very Useful, his mind is alternating between two very different concerns. Parlour, study, kitchen, billiards room, dining hall; forward, side, close; back, side, close. *Concentrate, Diego,* he tells himself, *think!*

Things have gone smoothly so far. The men have missed the dinner and skipped the receiving line. The most important thing now is to avoid being noticed, to avoid being caught. Even one moment on the dance floor might make Diego conspicuous and he knows that will make his task more difficult, impossible perhaps.

"I am going, Very Useful," he says, his voice hardened, his determination incorruptible now. And before Very Useful can argue, he has turned on his heels, is moving slowly through the room, trying to make himself as invisible as possible in the throng.

Out of the corner of her eye, Sofia has observed the argument that was taking place between the two men, has watched Diego look around nervously and quickly take his leave. *Where is he going?* she asks herself, nodding vacantly now at Mr. Nelson's words.

She excuses herself abruptly and starts to follow Diego, anxious not to lose him in the crowd. Thankfully, he is quite tall and can be seen moving about easily even in this unruly horde.

She walks well behind him as he makes his way through servant-filled corridors—men in starched shirts pass by him carrying crystal flutes of French champagne on silver trays; women in white dresses follow, carrying freshly cut tropical fruit artfully arranged on gold-rimmed plates. He walks through a courtyard lit by hundreds of candles, where groups of people mill in the shadows, talking, laughing, whispering things to each other in the privacy of a half-lit night. He walks at a leisurely pace, bows to a group here and there, smiles as if he is merely in search of a spot of fresh air, walks and walks until casually, without drawing suspicion, he reaches the back of the house. He conjures up the map Mr. Nelson had made for him in the dirt and heads east, thinks fleetingly of Isidore of Seville and the path he had once travelled to a house in the city of his birth, the humiliation he had felt, the slap that still lingers on his face.

Along the path a figure now appears before him in the dark, golden, shimmering, more spirit than flesh.

"Who is there?" Diego cries out, fear rising sharply and then dissipating as the ghostlike figure comes into the light.

"Sofia!" Diego exclaims.

The girl runs up to him, takes his hand into hers. "Take me with you, Diego," she says and in the confusion of the dark, in the sudden surge of feeling that has coursed through his body like the electrical current that once lit up a ball in Mérida's Plaza de Armas—with that beloved hand in his and time on the clock beating on, Diego pushes forward, quickly blocks any misgivings that arise from his mind. Perhaps, he tells himself hopefully, his *patrón* has informed Sofia of his monumental task. It seems improbable, he knows, but now is not the time to consider the reasons for her being here, now is the time to move forward towards his goal.

Nearby they hear the rustling of wings. Toucans, manikins, hummingbirds, owls and two rare pigeons await in a cage. The aviary is poorly lit. Only a waning gibbous moon outside helps to reveal the birds' splendid colours to the sight.

And what a sight! Sofia cannot believe her eyes, has never seen such a splendid collection together in the wild. She tries to identify the birds she knows, only to be distracted by those she has never seen before.

"Come here," Diego whispers to her, moving ahead. "The best part of all is inside this cage."

Sofia joins Diego, stares at the two pigeons with the scarlet eyes, the slate-blue heads and rumps, the grey backs and the wine-red breasts.

"A bird that once passed overhead like a thought," Diego says quietly, quoting the incomparable Audubon. "A bird that is now on the verge of disappearing from the earth."

"No!" Sofia exclaims, crouching down to look at the pigeons up close. "But what is the bird's name?"

Another voice now answers in the dark.

"Those, Señorita Sofia, are a pair of *Ectopistes migratorius*."

Diego and Sofia turn around in shocked surprise. Standing before them is Carlos Blanco Torres, a thin cigar in his hand, a cane in the other, observing them intently from across the dimly lit room.

In the face of their silence, the young man speaks again. "Well, in fact, that is their scientific name, what men such as your father, Señorita Sofia, would call them, at any rate. To us more simple folk, they are merely pigeons, Passenger Pigeons to be exact."

Sofia is the first to recover, the first to stammer out a response.

"Señor Carlos, I do hope you are not displeased with our being here. We simply could not resist. Señor Diego and I are helping Mr. Nelson with his guide and we could not leave without taking a look at your beautiful birds."

Young Carlos merely nods, mumbles a dismissive *Of course not*. He looks over at Diego now, "I do not believe that you and I have been introduced."

"No, no, indeed we have not. I am Diego Clemente, assistant to Mr. Edward Nelson of the Biological Survey. I too apologize for our indiscretion, Don Carlos. I am an obsessed bird artist and that is the only way I can possibly explain myself."

The young man merely waves the apology away with the back of a hand. "Do not concern yourself, Don Diego, the grounds are open to all of our guests on this night. Though I would have been quite happy to have shown you the birds myself."

He calls for a servant now, has him light up the area so that they can better admire what is inside. Diego and Sofia follow Carlos through the aviary in silence, hearts beating in equal time, unable to enjoy the birds in the face of this sudden turn of events.

Diego is mulling over just one thought. *I have failed Mr. Nelson, I have failed my* patrón, for it will be impossible for him to leave now with those precious birds in his hand. He has been spotted, has been registered by none other than the son of Don Victor Blanco himself. He chastises himself for not having been more careful, chastises himself for having been foolish enough to be followed by not one but two people outside. His face falls, his heart sinks. No bird, no matter how rare, can now possibly hope to light up his eyes.

By Diego's side, Sofia is cursing Carlos Blanco with every step that she takes. *Of course he would follow me here,* she thinks. Of course the dandy had arrived just in time to ruin a budding duet. She is careful to keep smiling, is careful to give nothing more away to this young man, but inside she is seething, her mood worsened by the fact that she has noticed the distance that has opened suddenly between Diego and her. A chasm, she thinks, a wound that may not be so easily healed.

Once the tour is done, the three walk together back along the same path Diego had travelled before. In a well-lit corner of the courtyard, they come upon Don Victor, standing there surrounded by a group of his friends. He spots his son, *and what is he doing here?* he asks himself, unnerved to see him with these two unknowns, while inside his mother has assembled a collection of the most distinguished young ladies in the land. Will he never learn? What a disappointment! How difficult it is to be burdened with such a son.

Don Victor calls the three to his side and asks to be introduced to his son's companions in a voice that is tighter than tree bark.

"Over here, Papá, la Señorita Sofía Duarte, daughter of Don Roberto Duarte."

"Ah, yes," old man Blanco says, issuing the barest of nods.

"And next to me, Señor Diego Clemente, assistant to Mr. Nelson of the United States Biological Survey."

"Of course," Don Victor says, waving a cigar Diego's way.

Nonentities, Don Victor thinks, *just exactly as I had thought.*

"Now, son, perhaps you should make your way back to the hall. There are many young ladies searching for you inside so that they may dance a quadrille or a waltz."

Ah, my loving, devoted Papá, Carlos thinks, scorn in his eyes. *Always trying to bend those around him to his will. Always looking to reshape the world to fulfill his infinite needs.* Ah, but the boy has his own arms with which to fight.

"You are so right, Papá," the young man says with a triumphant smile. "But I cannot think of a woman I would rather be dancing with than the *señorita* who is standing next to me now."

He turns to Sofía, whose face is now a bright pink, who can feel the tension that is coursing between father and son and who dares not look at Diego for fear of his reaction to Carlos's words.

But Diego is unaffected by what he hears, is much more concerned by what he can see. *Is it really ever possible to leave the past behind?* he asks himself, as he stares at Don Victor Blanco, whose appearance and demeanour catapult him back into a distant time. *Don Ricardo Medina,* he thinks, resuscitated in a new country and in different dress. The voice is similar, the way he holds his head exact and those sea-bream eyes—it is the eyes, above all, that remind Diego of the Andalusian aristocrat he had seen but once.

"Forgive me," Diego hears Sofia say. "But I have been nursing a most violent headache and would prefer to be sitting down."

Carlos blinks hard, offers to show Sofia to a quiet space inside.

Don Victor's smile grows tighter until it seems etched upon his stone face.

Rejected by a nonentity, he thinks. *The clown! And right here in front of my friends.* He will have a word later with the boy's mother, threaten to cut his son off entirely if he continues with these pubescent charades.

The young people leave now, Sofia walking quickly ahead, the two young men behind her, strolling silently in the half-lit night.

Inside the ballroom, Sofia is greeted by her mother, her grandmother and her aunt with a mixture of anger and relief.

"Where have you been?" they ask. "We have been worried sick," they accuse.

Sofia pleads for understanding. "I am not feeling well," she says, one hand cradling a hot cheek. "It is better that we leave."

Leave? Surely not now! No, the women will not have it, are not prepared to sacrifice this opportunity to one of Sofia's ill moods.

"And just what were you doing with those two young men?" Doña Laura whispers to the girl, taking her aside. "In my day, girls were decent, knew what was expected of them. Ah, but how we have fallen. How one girl can ruin a family reputation that has been pure for centuries now."

But Sofia is not prepared to appease anyone at this point in time—has had enough of the evening, will not respond to threats issued by her enraged grandmother, the urgent pleas from Gabriela to stay, or even Aunt Marta's gentle admonitions that they must not appear rude by leaving precipitously.

Only Don Roberto seems unconcerned by his daughter's wish to leave the hallowed Blanco Torres ball and will remain unconcerned even after his wife has complained bitterly and unendingly to him once they have left, to the point of accusing him of having allowed Sofia to wander down dangerous paths, of not having been careful to inculcate the good breeding expected of a girl of her kind. He will sleep soundly all through the night, knowing that the rest will be much needed to face his mother's wrath the following day. But for now, contentment! A soft bed, his feet liberated finally from the boots that have tortured him all night. He thinks he will throw them out when he awakens, remembers to thank God that the affair has ended with no one bringing up the issue of his debt.

"Come on woman, sleep!" he implores his wife, who has moved on from Sofia to the horrendous ball gowns that had been everywhere in evidence that night.

"The dress on that Ballesteros woman!" she prattles on. "Does she not have a mirror to tell her the truth? And what about Doña Magdalena, with those cherries in her hair as if she were a piece of unripe fruit! A disaster, Roberto, from the top of her fruit basket of a head right to the tips of her oddly shaped feet.

"Roberto!" Gabriela exclaims now, turning to her husband, who has begun snoring audibly by her side. But it is no use, no amount of poking will awaken him from his sleep and so Gabriela takes her place next to him on the bed, cursing, not for the first time, her husband's lack of interest in anything that does not have wings.

Ah! je vais l'aimer
— Béatrice et Bénédict

Forget about it.

It is Nelson speaking, trying to lay Diego's guilt to rest. It is the morning after the ball and all across the now quiet city, the chickens are coming home to roost.

For Diego, it is his bare hands that weigh the most—hands, he thinks, that should have been capable enough to honour a simple request. For weeks he had rehearsed over and over in his mind the path he would take. Parlour, dining room, hall, across a courtyard and then east towards home. No, not home, he corrects himself, the anger rising in his chest. Towards the aviary, towards the birds, two Passenger Pigeons trapped in a cage.

"It was an insane idea, Diego," Nelson adds. "I was obviously not thinking clearly when I asked for such a thing to be carried out."

The two men are sitting on the edge of a forest just five kilometres outside town, trying to erase the bitterness of defeat with the consolation provided by nature's bounty in the spectacular early-morning light. Nelson begins to whistle a tune, trills that rise in pitch from beginning to end, attempting with his song to lure a Long-Billed Gnatwren to his side. Diego burrows deeper and deeper into his shell, watches listlessly as the bird darts quickly through the low forest brush, weaving in and out of sight.

"There is an undertone in the bird's song, do you hear it, Diego?"

"Yes, Mr. Nelson. It seems sad, dark and alone."

The intricacies of birdsong, which had provided the weightiest challenges to Diego's understanding of bird life at the beginning, now seem more interesting to him than the look of the bird itself. *Eyes, ears and mouth,* Mr. Nelson had repeated over and over during their first jaunt into the field. Eyes to see with, ears to listen with, mouth to whistle a song in return. For the past year, Diego has immersed himself in the language of the birds. Tempo, pitch, pattern and quality have become his measuring sticks. Over time he has come to know if a song is buzzy or clear, liquid or fluting, loud or soft. He has learned to distinguish between the various types of songs, knows how to interpret the pauses between the calls. A year after his arrival, a year spent learning at the master's feet, Diego has become obsessed with the songs of the various species of birds.

"Yes, Diego. The bird is indeed singing in a minor key."

The Gnatwren embarks on a series of long trills now, a much happier tune. Diego strains to listen, but his efforts to reproduce the tune are all for naught today—his mind is distracted; his worries will not let him focus on the subtleties in the bird's song.

"I am sorry, Mr. Nelson," he says, shaking his head. *Another failure,* he thinks, still mulling over the disastrous events of the previous night.

"Don't worry, Diego. These things take their time." Nelson whistles out another song, in a different pitch and a greater length. "I was thinking about the moon," he says, once the song is done.

"The moon?"

"Yes, the moon. I was thinking back to my days in the Yukon—of a morning when an entire village had come together to make sense of the lunar eclipse that had occurred the previous night. Various interpretations were bandied about, the most popular of which seemed to be that the eclipse presaged an epidemic or a war. Some people were even more specific though. They thought it meant they would be raided by the Tinné who lived up the river, as revenge on the Eskimo for having killed some of their moose the year before."

Here Nelson stops. He picks up his field glasses and investigates the other birds hovering up above.

"The ancient Maya thought that an eclipse was caused by a giant jaguar devouring the moon. They feared that this jaguar would descend to the earth afterwards and eat people until it was full.

"Is it not astounding, Diego, this need that compels peoples all over the world to interpret nature, to see messages inscribed in every natural event?"

A silence follows and then Nelson embarks on another series of trills.

These are the stories Diego usually loves the most, the moments when out of the blue, his *patrón* recounts an experience he had had in the Arctic or in northern Mexico or in the American southwest, moments when he shares a theory, a thought. Today, though, Diego is in no mood to listen with the careful attentiveness he usually lends to Mr. Nelson's words. Diego is carrying a hot coal in the pit of his stomach, a smoldering, painful reminder of his failure to get the task done. Try as he might, he cannot rid himself of the shame, rid himself of the rage at having failed to save a bird from the very precipice of extinction itself.

Two birds in hand, he thinks, two birds that would have been on their way to Cincinnati today had he been more careful from the start. He thinks then of Don Victor Blanco, of those sea-bream eyes, and his thoughts suddenly lead him to the one place he hoped never to return—the house of Don Ricardo Medina, his father, the man for whom his mother had pined all of her life. *Bastard!* he says to himself, thinking of Don Ricardo and then of Don Victor. *Bastards both.*

"Do you know what overtones are, Diego?"

"No, Mr. Nelson, I do not."

"In music, overtones are what make up a complex note. They give an instrument its timbre or tone colour. In life, I have observed that these overtones correspond to those elements in every experience that linger long after the experience itself has passed—memories, shock, emotional residues, reactions and things of the like.

"Overtones make for the finest poetry, Diego, the most sublime songs. But I have found they are not so useful when it comes to dealing with the vagaries of everyday life itself."

Diego feels as if his *patrón* can read each of his thoughts. He would like to appease him, to put the sorry episode behind. He knows Mr. Nelson feels no anger at his failure to secure the birds, is relieved even that things turned out as they did. But Diego cannot let the matter go. Until yesterday he had thought he had put an ocean between himself and his past. But oceans too are full of overtones, overtones to torture those who, like Diego, are blessed with a discerning ear and a sensitive heart.

"Forget about it, *muchacho*," Mr. Nelson says again, gently, and he places his arm around the young man's shoulder, delivers some reassuring pats to his back and then returns to the bounties of nature that, alone on earth, have the power to make things right.

*

Across town, Sofia slept fitfully all during that long, treacherous night. Guilty thoughts kept her awake. If only I had not followed Diego. If only I had been less impulsive, less curious. *But then what?* a little voice interjects. She knows something awful occurred the night before, knows that a train had derailed in Diego's head, but she is uncertain as to the destination of this train or who the passengers were. One question obsesses her, above all. What task had Diego been entrusted to carry out at the ball? All through the night she searched her brain for clues—snippets of conversation she overheard, the notes she had once rummaged through—but things seem as murky in the morning as they were in the thick of night.

It is all right, she tells herself. *Time will bring all things into the light. Right now I must find a way to see Diego, apologize for having ruined his plans, whatever they were.*

First, though, she must face the prospect of breakfast with three women who have still not overcome their shock at the missed *opportunity,* who will talk about this missed *opportunity* until they grow weary from their words, until they have hashed and rehashed the memory of the night and have thoroughly exhausted themselves with the sorry bits.

Luckily, her father appears, fresh from a dressing-down by his mother, fresh too from having stood up to her on his daughter's behalf. Backbones are emerging in Mérida on this glorious day. Let us just see if they will be used for greater things than holding meddling mothers back.

"Ah, there you are, Sofia," he says as she approaches the table, where three sets of eyes stare at her with muted rage. "Eat quickly so we can head out to the bookstore. A shipment is arriving from New York and I need to get it sorted out before we open at ten."

Sofia sits down and stares at her breakfast of sweet buns, tropical fruit and soft cheese. She is not hungry in the least and the prospect of eating with those three sets of eyes fixed upon her can only make the situation worse, but she chews on a piece of fruit in any case, careful to keep her mouth full, careful to avoid meeting any one set of furious eyes.

Mercifully, the two leave quickly, Sofia with head bowed down, Don Roberto sporting a satisfied smile. He is feeling well rested, well fed, content, almost, despite the burdens he guards so close to his chest.

"What are we to do with that girl?" Gabriela asks as they leave, shaking her head in defeat, and for once it is Doña Laura who offers a *there, there* in consolation, putting aside their historical enmity so that they may band together now against this much greater ill.

Thankfully, there is much to occupy Sofia at the store since Don Roberto's mind is occupied with other matters. Later, he will need to attend to business at the hacienda once again. Things are getting worse; indeed, they are spiralling right out of control. The harvest had been good, but there are fewer bodies to process the leaves once they have been cut. Don Roberto cannot afford to purchase one more worker to do the work, let alone the fifty he realistically needs. To purchase such help would mean going further into debt and the hand that once freely offered the money has of late turned into a clenched fist.

"*Hombre*," Don Victor Blanco had told him the last time Don Roberto approached him for help, "you understand that it is not the time to put out but to receive what is already owed."

Sofia spends the morning trying to quell the butterflies that flutter in her gut, jumping every time the door opens, expecting to see Diego walk in as if they had agreed to such a meeting the night before. Few customers of any kind arrive that day. They sell no more than a child's workbook and a copy of *La Hacienda* magazine. A henequen planter places an order for a technical manual published in France. The morning moves at a snail's pace. Finally, as they are ready to close the doors at midday, Very Useful makes an appearance, smiling from ear to ear, his hair tousled, his happiness a welcome respite for the father and daughter, who have spent the morning nursing their respective worries to themselves. Sofia is the first to jump up, welcomes Very Useful to the store with an effusiveness that seems out of place.

"Señorita!" Very Useful exclaims in surprise. "Really, it is just me, a lowly assistant and not a divine apparition who has fallen from the sky."

Sofia smiles, beckons him warmly to her side. A suspicious light suddenly turns on in Very Useful's mind. He is no fool, knows that the *señorita* is not seeking him personally but whatever information may be lying in his head. He starts to walk backwards, inching ever closer to the door, issues a hurried apology, insists he must take his leave at once, go in search of the other two men. But Sofia has already arrived at the door, has positioned herself in such a way as to make it impossible for him to leave.

"Señorita?" Very Useful asks, mouth twisted, eyebrows raised high. He is looking at the door, trying to find a way to escape quickly before he is made to speak.

"What was Diego doing in that aviary last night?" Sofia asks quietly, trying not to draw her father's attention their way but making it clear with her tone of voice that she is determined to extract the truth from Very Useful no matter the cost.

"Why, looking at birds!" Very Useful cries out. "What else does one do in an aviary, my girl?"

"Looking at birds in the dark?"

"Well, how was he supposed to know that the birds had been kept in the dark? The whole hacienda was lit up like a fireworks display last night. One could easily have supposed the birds had been granted a night of merriment, a night of frolic and dance."

"There had to have been something else, Very Useful," the young lady insists, but Very Useful will not budge, is not about to reveal anything that will incriminate even one single hair of Diego's unsuspecting head.

"Do you know, Señorita Sofia, how well that young man dances a waltz?" Very Useful now asks, trying to change the subject of the conversation before he accidentally reveals more than he should. "Yes, I taught him myself. He wanted nothing more than to try his new skills on you but alas, you took your leave so early and so suddenly last night. Really, Señorita Sofia, you could at least have had the decency to leave a glass slipper behind!"

But the *señorita* is in no mood to play games. She is about to threaten to pull him by the ear, but Very Useful has already clasped his hands dramatically in prayer.

Te rogamos, audi nos, he says in plainchant mode.

"What?" the Señorita asks, confused. *Hear us, we beg you.* Hear what? She opens her mouth to ask but is stopped by her father, who has now joined them at the door.

"Leaving, my good man?" he asks Mr. Nelson's assistant.

"Running," Very Useful responds, and with a quick bow to Don Roberto he is already out the door.

*

The bookstore closed for the afternoon, Sofia heads home with a heavy heart. Bad enough she has not received a visit from

Diego, bad enough she has not been able to figure out the mystery, but worse, infinitely worse, is the prospect that awaits her at home—facing the three sullen women still fretting over the thought of a wasted dress. *May God protect me,* she prays. The disappointments of the day will only make their anger seem harder to bear.

She arrives to a much different picture instead.

There in the parlour Sofia finds the women in a happy uproar, hands clasped in other hands, excitement spilling from all sides. *What can it be now?* Sofia asks herself in fear, for the little scene before her does not bode well.

It is Aunt Marta who rushes in first. "You have been invited to an afternoon gathering at the house of the Blanco Torres, *hijita,*" she tells her, pressing the invitation into her hand.

"See, I told them they liked you, that you made an impression, that the ball would not be the only gathering where you would have an opportunity to shine. Everybody is nervous the first time out, I told them. You cannot expect any better than that."

The "them" in question, her mother and grandmother, are not so ready to divest themselves of their earlier anger, not when it was so clearly merited, not when they have been stewing in it all day long, not, especially, when they sense that the defiance shown so freely on the dance floor last night is rising to the surface once more.

"I will not go," Sofia says, nervous words escaping from trembling lips.

"Oh, Sofia!" Aunt Marta exclaims. "Whatever has gotten into you, *hijita?* I simply do not understand." And then she sits down abruptly, clutching the invitation to her chest with dismayed hands.

"You will go," Doña Laura says in a tone that will allow no opposition, and then she goes on to call her a selfish girl, a spoiled child who thinks of no one but herself because what about the opportunities she is denying to the family as a whole? "You will go," she repeats once more, and Sofia, feeling the sharpness in her grandmother's tone, realizes that this battle has been lost—only momentarily of course. Sofia will not be prepared to concede defeat until the last skirmish has been fought.

The afternoon affair is to take place three days later—three days spent locked in the house on the orders of Doña Laura, who has tightened the noose around her granddaughter's neck. For now, she is confined to the bookstore and her room, where she works on bits of the bird guide that have been assigned to her while she waits for her next foray into the societal web. It is Aunt Marta who is to act as chaperone at the affair. "And spy," Sofia tells her friend Patricia, when they talk later that afternoon. "You can be sure Mamá and that *arpía* of a grandmother of mine have instructed her to watch me like a hawk—to make sure I do not commit some further unpardonable social sin. *Dios*, how those two plot and scheme like a pair of medieval kings!"

In the meantime, Sofia has been busy concocting her own plan. She is not a part of this social circle, but she knows something about their unspoken rules, about the way the women are expected to behave. Quiet as clams. Gentle as doves. *Fools*, she thinks. *Dead weights surrounded by the thick planks who call themselves men.*

She has other ideas in mind.

Sofia and Aunt Marta arrive at the afternoon gathering (chocolate for the women, scotch and tequila for the men, chit-chat for the young women, boisterous talk for the young men) after being escorted out of their own house by Gabriela and Doña Laura, both of whom continue to offer up advice even as Sofia and Aunt Marta disappear around a corner and the women can no longer be seen or heard.

"Try to smile a bit more, *hijita*," Gabriela calls out into the wind after her daughter, who has looked glum the entire morning. Qué barbaridad, *it is as if she were being sent to slaughter and not to a grand social event,* Gabriela complains to Don Roberto later that day, who isn't interested in the least in having his daughter attend such an affair but who is wise enough to keep this indifference to himself.

"There is nothing more dangerous to the health than the machinations of women," he will tell Very Useful later on and Mr. Nelson's assistant will nod, thinking—*and especially those women,* señor!

At the gathering Sofia and Aunt Marta are welcomed with such effusion by Carlos Blanco Torres that the whole room falls into a hush. There already are several of the good *señoritas* of the upper echelons, their hair and dresses carefully arranged, their minds blank slates, their displeasure at the sight of Sofia and her aunt on full display. They will not be indulging in chit-chat with this girl, have nothing to say to someone of her social position, someone who, judging by the dress, is in possession of so little taste as well. *El colmo,* they whisper to each other. The very worst. They bring their cups to their lips in unison, regale each other with knowing, secret looks, allow only the odd giggle to escape from their perfectly polished lips.

Sofia follows Carlos into the parlour, where she is seated next to none other than Diego Clemente himself. Sofia freezes; her eyes nervously scan the room. She spies Mr. Nelson standing off to one side and is overwhelmed by relief.

"Sofia! How good to see you, dear girl!" the scientist says, walking over to her and delivering an affectionate peck on her cheek.

"Mr. Nelson!" Sofia exclaims, delight in her eyes.

"And how pleased I am to have such eminent scientists with us today," Carlos Blanco announces to the small group he has assembled for the afternoon affair.

"Do you know," he asks, addressing everyone in the room, "that Mr. Nelson and his assistants are at this very moment working on the first bird guide to our lovely region? Mr. Nelson himself has spent more than fourteen years collecting specimens right across Mexico itself."

The young women tilt their heads at this announcement, roll their eyes, pick up their fans and begin to fan themselves, their blank looks growing blanker still.

From across the room, an old man speaks up.

"Science! We here in Mexico know plenty about science. Are not the *científicos* in power in Mexico City? Have they not been in power for decades now?"

"Ah, Don Máximo," the young man retorts, "those *científicos* you speak of are not scientists in the classical sense. They are economists, determined to sell the bits and pieces of Mexico to the highest bidders up North."

An awkward silence ensues. Doña Alicia de Blanco, Carlos's mother, looking every inch the aged queen with her abundant jewels in evidence and her neck stiffly held, silences her son with a searing look.

"Let us not engage in talk of politics, Carlos," she says, "this is not the time or the place."

"Is there ever a time and place then in this great nation of ours, Mamá?" her son retorts, clearly undeterred by the anger that is coursing through his mother's voice. "I was under the impression we were living in a country where certain things are never to be discussed."

Doña Alicia opens her mouth, is about to venture an opinion but is cut short by her son's pronouncement that they must all thank the American scientist for his extraordinary efforts in their region.

"Mr. Nelson, come here by my side, if you please."

Nelson walks forward tentatively, unsure of where the young man is heading with all of this talk.

"Is it not true that you are compiling a catalogue of all of our region's beautiful birds? Just think, Señores, soon we will have a complete listing of Yucatán's natural riches at our fingertips."

"If we should want to look at such things, I suppose," one man says, sniffing disdainfully.

"How interesting," Doña Alicia utters dryly, eyes downcast, thin lips growing thinner yet.

"I am rather intrigued by your interest in my work, Don Carlos," Nelson says. He thinks of Don Victor Blanco, of his evident disdain for soiling his boots. He assesses Carlos himself, makes note of the impeccable shirt, the gleaming spectacles, the expensive British suit.

"Ah, Mr. Nelson, I must confess that my real love is the opera. Nothing fascinates me more, in fact. But lately I have taken to listening to the songs of birds and have been enchanted by what I hear. Music in any form, you see, brings rapture to the ear."

("Birds," Doña Alicia will scream at her husband that very night, "they were boring the gathering with stories about birdsong and such things. What has gotten into my son, what illness has ravaged his brain, dear God?"

"He is a *payaso,* a clown," her husband will respond, cigar as always in hand, his face as expressionless as stone. "A *payaso.* Just as I have always suspected, just as I have always said.")

Sofia spies a clearing in the forest, knows that the moment to speak up is at hand.

"Have you heard, Don Carlos, the remarkable song of the Spot-Breasted Wren, the rollicking whistling phrases the bird makes?" she asks. "The call resembles the sound made by running a finger-nail down a comb."

And then, to the dismay of Aunt Marta and the scandalized gasp of Doña Alicia, Sofia begins to imitate the bird, *wheet-we-wi-we'yu-you*.

Carlos claps heartily at Sofia's birdcall. "Yes, I have heard the song of that particular bird and it is just as you say it is. Tell me, what other songs do you know?"

"How about the song of the Violaceous Trogon? I was mesmer-ized by one just the other day." And then Sofia begins to whistle a loud, high-pitched tune, her nose pointed straight up, wholly oblivious to the sudden hush that has descended over the room.

It is Mr. Nelson's turn to clap in delight. "*Brava*, my girl. Yes, that particular song resembles the call of the Ferruginous Pygmy Owl."

Another young man now walks to their side, whistling his own tune as he walks. "Yes, it is the song of the *Voluptuous Bolero*," he announces to all in a booming voice, "a stunning and forthright bird found all too rarely in the parlours of the best ilk." He stops. "Now Carlos," he says, wrapping an arm around his friend's shoul-der, "I must regretfully interrupt, but the young lady's wonderful birdsong is bringing all of Mérida's cats howling to the door. Per-haps she can explore some other animal. Or, here is an idea, perhaps you can even try engaging your most delightful friend in something different, like plain, simple talk."

Aunt Marta quickly steps in. "You must forgive my niece's enthu-siasms. She is so young" (not as young as you would like, the other ladies think) "and her father has a very great interest in birds . . ." Aunt Marta's words trail off. She brings a handkerchief up to her mouth in an effort to slow her breath.

How is she to explain this episode to her sister and, even worse, to Doña Laura, who has entrusted the girl into her hands? There is nothing, she thinks, nothing that can repair the damage, and Sofia, such a thoughtful young woman it seemed to her until now, a young woman who, moreover, she herself had been careful to instruct in the ways of courting, is laughing loudly again, speaking most inappropriately to el Señor Carlos, both of them seemingly unaware of the outrageous picture they are painting in the parlour with their talk.

Don Máximo brings the conversation back to the question of science once more.

"Did you know, Mr. Nelson, that Isaac Newton's theories only arrived here in Mexico a full century after they had been disseminated in Europe and other parts of the civilized world?"

"No, I was not aware of that, Señor," Nelson responds.

"Well, of course in those days we were ruled by the Spanish and the Church, who kept even works of literature from entering our borders, fearing their contents would incite us to revolt. That is why Díaz has been so good for Mexico. He has let science do its work. He has built railways, roads, hospitals, insane asylums for those who suffer from sickness of the brain. Why, look at you, Mr. Nelson, allowed to travel through every hill and valley of this nation collecting any specimen you like."

"Long live Porfirio Díaz," a man now shouts out from the corner of the room.

Damn him to hell, another whispers underneath his breath.

The talk turns, then, to more frivolous things—a lively discussion of who was dancing with whom at the ball, recent developments in the henequen trade.

Sofia turns to Diego, who has been sitting there immobile as stone, watching the scene unfold.

"Where have you been?" she whispers.

"Out in the field with my *patrón*," he responds.

"I need to speak to you. Alone," the girl says, still whispering, looking ahead as if she were not speaking to him at all.

"Where, when?" the young man replies.

"At the bookstore tomorrow."

"I will be there."

Across the room, Carlos Blanco Torres has been watching this whispered exchange unfold. He has noticed the intensity in the young woman's body, has noted the way Diego is stealing looks at her out of the corner of an eye. *Like two lovers engaged in a secret tryst,* he thinks, the disappointment slowly sinking in. He has invited Sofia and Diego to this afternoon affair precisely for this—to investigate what is transpiring between the two.

My suspicions have been most grievously confirmed, he now thinks. But no matter. Carlos Blanco Torres knows how deeply indebted Sofia's father is to his own, knows her family is tottering on the edge of financial ruin.

There are many ways to repair a debt, he says to himself, many ways to collect what is due.

What a fine day it turned out to be, Sofia will think later, once the whole affair is done with and she is in the safety of her home, much later, after she has tried everything in her means to console Aunt Marta, who blames herself for everything, the strident laughing, the inappropriate talk. She will stop, however, at the birdsong.

"After all, enough is enough, one should feel responsible only to a point and I for one," she later tells her niece, "know as little about birds as I do about the nature of the sky above." But still, only a cup of chamomile tea will help her, only the prospect of an early night and a warm towel over her head will allow her to erase the memory of the afternoon completely from her mind.

Gone with her tea and her towel, Aunt Marta leaves the other women to rage at Sofia, who has retired to the back of the house, unprepared to face the music on her own. And *qué música!* A *cante jondo,* a Cuban *son,* a hard and constant thumping on a metal drum—call it what you will, the women are in a mood to rumba. Gabriela cries at her daughter's betrayal; Doña Laura rails at her desire to ruin the family name for good. Both women have too much rage inside of them for just one villain—another one is exactly what they need. It is fortuitous for them then that it is just at this moment that Don Roberto enters the house, head lost, as usual, in his own private universe, ignorant of the events that have transpired while he was gone.

"It is your fault," they scream at him. "You with your birds and your store, your craziness. Look what you have done to your own daughter. Look at the disgrace she has brought upon us all."

He listens to their account of the afternoon fiasco, of the ravages that the debacle has wrought upon Aunt Marta's gentle and fragile heart, of the scandal that will result—*people speaking of us as if we were mentally unsound, Sofia's comportment the scandalous talk of the town.*

Don Roberto listens in silence at first, letting the accusations slide over him, secretly applauding Sofia's bravery, her gumption, her refusal to stand on ceremony when the ceremony was so clearly bankrupt. He listens until the women's accusations reach a deafening crescendo and then, "*Basta!*" he yells, "enough!"

"The only scandal, as far as I can tell, is the one you yourselves are unleashing right now," Don Roberto says, hands in the air, trying to block this frenetic duet before they run riot over the house.

"What? Why?" both women sputter in unison, unnerved by yet another demonstration of a burgeoning backbone. Really, they will ask each other later, what has gotten into our Roberto, no longer so meek, no longer so gentle, no longer a man who can be bent and plied at will.

"You," Don Roberto says to Gabriela, "are pushing our daughter into something much worse than social embarrassment. Because no matter how the young Blanco Torres boy may feel, the games he may play, he will never be allowed to marry our daughter or what do you think? That we have social standing, that we have something to offer to a family of such great wealth? Of course we do not. Leave Sofia to her own devices, for it seems to me she is the only one in this house with any inkling of how things work in this world."

He turns away from an open-mouthed Gabriela, directs his gaze his mother's way now.

"And you, Mamá, must not make Sofia pay for my lamentable errors in life. I am sorry to be such a disappointment, to have so bungled the hacienda's affairs. I am trying my best to salvage whatever I can." He takes her hands into his, looks sorrowfully into her eyes.

"What do you mean 'bungled'?" Gabriela screams out, forgetting all about Sofia now—for this woman, who knows every secret kept by the more prominent families in town, has managed somehow to remain completely ignorant of her own husband's business affairs, and is now shocked to hear words such as *bungle* and *salvage* come tumbling from his mouth. What has been bungled? What needs to be salvaged, dear God?

"Tell me, I must know," Gabriela is saying, hurrying after Don

Roberto, who will say no more, who is heading to his study, where he will try to forget all of this rot. He will focus instead on describing the Great-Tailed Grackle in all of her glory, attempt to dissolve his burdens with a moment of meditation and repose.

Only Doña Laura remains rooted in place, sits on a chair nearby, tries to settle her nerves, tries to cope with the fact that her suspicions regarding her son's finances have now been confirmed. Lose the hacienda? Be separated from all of the departed souls that lie there interred? No, she cannot stomach it, will not be able to withstand such a blow. She brings a hand to her mouth, attempts to press the fear away with her palm.

From across the courtyard, Sofia emerges from the shadows to see her Abuela sitting there, a pained expression on her face. She watches as the old lady's head drops into her hands, defeated, frail, resembling now only a fraction of her usual self, and she feels sympathy for her grandmother for the first time in her life.

What are we to do, dear God, the old woman is asking herself, knowing already there is only one possible way out.

Sofia.

Doña Laura's hands drop to her lap and she raises her eyes to the sky. A solution is making itself known to her; a light is beginning to shine in the dark. The old lady sits up. She lifts up her hands and then places them back on her lap. The tightness in her body has left; she is a woman defeated no more.

From afar, Sofia sighs. Her grandmother is back. She can see it in her posture, can see it in her eyes. But what could she be thinking? What plan would *la loca* be conjuring up now?

She will ponder it no more—has much better things to do with her time. She thinks of the upcoming meeting with Diego, sighs in the exaggerated way she used to mock in others until now.

Ah, *el amor!* Lovely, heady, a welcome respite from the tortures of the world. She walks to her room, forgetting about her grandmother, her aunt with the towel wrapped around her head, her mother who is still trying to get her husband to talk, still insisting that all secrets must be revealed. Only eighteen hours till morning arrives, she thinks. Eighteen hours that will seem as long as weeks to this young woman, experiencing the tortures of a real love for the first time in her life.

A song with wings

Over dinner two men have come together to discuss the events of that afternoon. Very Useful has tied a large napkin around his neck and is slurping loudly as he makes his way through a splendid *sopa de lima,* trying to tell Diego everything he knows, between spoonfuls of chicken- and lime-flavoured broth.

"Why would Carlos Blanco Torres have encouraged Sofia to behave in that way today?" Diego is asking, referring to her extraordinary venture into the world of birdcalls.

Very Useful shakes his head back and forth, spoons the soup eagerly into his mouth.

"The boy fancies himself a radical of sorts. Likes to create scenes to drive his parents stark raving mad. What better show could he have orchestrated than one with the girl of his dreams—the very unsuitable girl—at the centre of it?"

"And how do you know Sofia is the girl of his dreams?"

"How do I know? How do I know?" Very Useful drops the spoon, wipes his mouth with his napkin before answering him with a scowl. "What don't I know is a better question, you *petit* scoundrel—doubting me yet again when I am the only person capable of enlightening you about all matters of importance, from birds to dance to ghosts."

Diego raises his eyebrows, waits for Very Useful to go on.

"The *señorito's* interest in Sofia has been clear to me for some time, as clear as the interest in her shown by our very own . . ." Here Very Useful stops, brings the napkin to his mouth as if he is trying to plug himself up.

"As the interest shown by whom, Very Useful?" Diego asks, anxiety rising in his chest.

Very Useful changes the subject, tries to bring Diego's attention back to the afternoon affair.

"Why do you think you were invited to the event in the first place, Diego?"

"Because I am Mr. Nelson's assistant, I suppose."

"Mr. Nelson's assistant? The fop does not know Mr. Nelson. He has merely heard of his work from Sofia's father, whom he has been courting in an effort to get to the girl herself. No, no, Diego, your invitation had nothing to do with our *patrón*." Very Useful takes a sizeable bite from a *tortilla* and continues to talk as he chews. "It was the dandy's way of unearthing what lies between you and the girl."

Diego remains silent, thinks back to the afternoon affair.

"Why would Carlos be against the Díaz regime? Is it not odd for him to have such ideas, given the wealth under his father's command?" he now asks.

"Ah, his ideas," Very Useful replies, bitterness suffusing his tone. "Yes, it is quite common among the young of the fashionable set to indulge in such ideas—between their jaunts to the opera houses of Paris and New York, of course. First we hear the great voices sing in the opulent concert halls of the world and then we convene over cigars and scotch to devise the solutions to our problems back home. Do not be fooled by such radical ideas, *mi amigo,* they are merely one man's revenge on the father he despises and not anything felt deep in the gut."

"Very Useful, you surprise me. How much you know."

"Eyes, ears and mouth, Diego. Eyes to see with, ears to listen with, mouth to spew the dross back out that has been ingested during a long life of watching and listening to things unfold in this world."

Very Useful wipes his mouth now and puts the napkin on his plate.

"Let us not squander any more time on wastrels, Diego. The girl has invited you to meet her and we must devise a plan."

Diego looks at Very Useful and smiles. "I have a plan already, Very Useful, I have been thinking of it since the afternoon. Listen . . ."

Very Useful leans over and waits eagerly for Diego's words.

*

Morning!

Finally the sun has come up. Sofia gets up with a spring, hurries through the motions of washing and dressing. She has been counting the minutes to sunrise through a long night of fitful rest. She looks into the mirror, hopes her sleeplessness does not show on her face. Oh well, no matter, she thinks, the time is ripe for much more important things. She is sure Diego will be meeting her at the bookstore, is sure the moment of truth has arrived for them both. Inside a well-worn copy of Brewer's *Dictionary of Phrase and Fable* she has hidden the note she has tenderly written to Diego confirming the intensity of her love.

But first—a hurried breakfast after which she will take her brother Bernardo aside—the only one who has been privy to

Sofia's secrets, the only one who can help make sure that everything proceeds according to plan.

Outside her room she encounters her father on his way to breakfast too, storm clouds hovering over his tired eyes.

"Is everything all right, Papá?" Sofia asks, concern in her voice.

"Of course, Sofia, of course," he answers, thinking *Of course it is not*. In a scant two hours he will be meeting with Carlos Blanco Torres at the store. The young man had requested a meeting just yesterday and Don Roberto fears only one thing will be discussed: the debt he owes to the young man's father, the debt that has been mounting and mounting until Don Victor's admonition to him just last month that the time had arrived to pay up.

But how? he had asked himself all through the long and sleepless night, how to save the hacienda that has been passed on from generation to generation now that the time has run out?

At the breakfast table, a subdued Doña Laura is cooking up a plan of a different sort. She knows now that it is to Don Victor Blanco that her son is in debt, knows also that it is Sofia on whom Don Victor's son Carlos has his eyes set. What harm will it do to push her granddaughter a little his way? After all, marriage is the only means left for one to make one's way in the world and she does not agree with her son that a union between the two is impossible, given the differences in their families' position and wealth. Miracles can happen, can they not? It is true, this one could prove more daunting than turning blood into wine, she thinks now, looking over at Sofia, wondering if anything good could possibly be expected from the girl. But it will be worth a try. Doña Laura simply cannot think of parting with the hacienda that has been in her family for generations now. The loss would be the last nail in the coffin that has been waiting for her since her own husband's death so many years ago.

At the store, Sofia and Bernardo help their father take inventory of their stock. *Time to add up my worth, one book at a time,* Don Roberto thinks sadly, remembering the days when his father still lived and they had rejoiced over the bits of knowledge that arrived monthly in this blessed sanctuary, a time long gone when sugar cane had been the plant of choice and Mérida was still a quiet, backwater town. There is, of course, no way to turn the clock back now. The henequen boom had changed everything. His only hope is that he will not be forced to part with the most beloved items in his own collection—the books that have provided so much consolation during a long, exhausting life.

He leaves the store then, hoping to get help from the bank, hoping to be saved just as the last minutes tick on the clock. It will be a difficult proposition, he knows. No bank is of late prepared to take a chance on ailing landowners like himself, but Don Roberto feels compelled to make one more attempt. A man should give up only when he is dead, his father had often said. And miracles happen, do they not? He will give up hope only once all doors have been firmly closed.

Not long after he leaves, a customer arrives. Sofia turns around eagerly, expecting to welcome Diego into the store.

Before her, instead, stands none other than Carlos Blanco Torres, ivory-handled walking stick in one hand, a bowler hat on his head, all the confidence of an invading army stamped across his face. *And what is he doing here today?* she asks herself, crestfallen, fearful that her carefully conceived plan will now be ruined for good.

"Good morning, Señor Carlos," she manages to say.

"Good day, Señorita Sofia," he responds, smiling a confident smile, oblivious to the wariness that has come over the young girl who stands frozen before him now.

"What can we do for you today?"

"I have come in search of a book."

Sofia smiles her best shopkeeper's smile. "And what book would you be looking for?" she asks, hoping to be rid of him at once.

"In truth, not a book but a libretto," Carlos tells her and then, seeing her confusion, adds, "a book containing the words spoken or sung in an opera."

"I know what a libretto is, Señor Carlos," Sofia replies, her voice terse, trying to keep her impatience from creeping into her tone. "But I am afraid that we do not have any here. The Librería Maya specializes in other types of books—philosophy, poetry, scientific works. We do have Rousseau's *Dissertation sur la musique moderne*. I can get it if you like." She turns towards the back, calls for her brother's help.

"No, no, I am not interested in that book at all. Thank you, but I am very serious about collecting libretti, Señorita Sofia, have been doing so for many years now."

Carlos smiles at her confusion. "Your father is expecting me to discuss this matter. Is he not here?"

"No, he has just stepped out for a while. Can I get you some other book, Señor Carlos? Or would you like to return shortly, once my father is back?"

"I am waiting for two of my servants to meet me here, Señorita Sofia. Will you permit me to stay on?"

"Of course, Señor Carlos, of course," Sofia says, unsure of what more to add, trying with every breath to quell the anxiety that storms inside her gut.

Remarkably, two of Carlos's servants now enter the store carrying a large gramophone in their hands. On orders from their *patrón,* they place the machine gently on the counter and then disappear as quickly as they have come.

"Señor?" Sofia says. *And now what?* she asks herself.

Carlos points to the machine. "A Nipper gramophone made by the esteemed Victor Talking Machine Company, a magnificent specimen as you can see, straight off the boat from the United States, as a matter of fact. Imagine, you can actually store fifty-two discs in the space of eight cylinders. Would you like me to show you how it works?"

"No, I would not," the *señorita* answers, no longer able to keep the annoyance from creeping into her voice. "We are a bookstore, Señor Carlos, not a dance hall."

The *señor* ignores this comment as he begins to fiddle with the gramophone, bringing a hand up in the air to stop Sofia from expressing any further thoughts.

"*Shhh,* listen, Señorita, be still for just one moment."

Suddenly a song is filling the room, a song like no other she has ever heard before. It is the voice of the tenor Antonio Paoli singing from the stage of La Scala—Milan's venerable opera house:

Vesti la giubba e la faccia infarina.
La gente paga e rider vuole qua.

Sofia knows little about opera, has not been privileged enough to have attended one in Mexico City or indeed here in Mérida, where the occasional company arrives to entertain the distinguished men and women of the region, the *henequeros,* who attend the spectacle brimming with diamonds and pearls, eager not to see but to be seen. Sofia does not know anything about this art form, cannot understand a single word of the aria that is being sung, but her heart can respond to the anguish she hears in the man's voice. She can feel the man's pain deep in her bones.

E se Arlecchin t'invola Colombina,
ridi, Pagliaccio . . . e ognun applaudirà!
Tramuta in lazzi lo spasmo ed il pianto;
in una smorfia il singhiozzo e'l dolor . . .

Señor Carlos, who has been standing there completely still until now, listening to the music with eyes closed, can no longer contain himself. He bursts suddenly and dramatically into song:

Ridi, Pagliaccio, sul tuo amore in franto,
Ridi del duol t'avvelena il cor!

It is at this moment that Don Roberto walks through the door, just in time to watch as Carlos belts out the last phrases of that incomparable aria, hands on his chest, eyes fixed on the ceiling above. Her father spots Sofia nearby, standing rigidly, her eyes opened wide, clutching a book to her chest.

Jesús and María, he thinks, *what in heaven's name is going on here?* He cannot even imagine the possibility of his mother hearing of this. The consequences, he knows, would be too hard to conceive of, let alone borne by his weary shoulders, exhausted already from the troubles of the world.

"Señor?" he asks, looking at Carlos then at Sofia and finally at his son Bernardo, who is trying hard to say something but who is finding that despite his most earnest efforts, no coherent words will emerge.

Mercifully, it is el Señor Carlos himself who now speaks. "Ah, Don Roberto, just the man I came to see," he says, stopping to slap the older man heartily on the back, "I have some business I would like to propose."

Don Roberto nods and beckons the young man to the office at the back of the store. If he is going to be discussing his financial demise, he would at least prefer to do so far from his daughter's prying eyes.

The young man marches behind him but not before stopping to bestow Sofia with yet another of his infuriating, confident smiles. The *señorita* nods silently and returns quickly to the list of books she is compiling, hoping this business of his will be taken care of promptly so that she can be rid of him soon.

When the two men finally appear moments later, they are all smiles and good cheer. "We understand each other then?" Carlos is asking Don Roberto, who seems as if his burdens have been removed from his shoulders for good.

"*Sí*, Señor Carlos, I am sure we will be able to help you find what you want."

Carlos shakes Don Roberto's hand and then proceeds to the front, where Sofia and Bernardo sit engrossed in the business of the inventory, heads down, pens in hand.

"Good day, Señorita," Carlos says to her, bowing formally her way, whistling the last few bars of the aria once again before breaking out into song just as he opens the door.

Ridi, Pagliaccio, sul tuo amore in franto,
Ridi del duol t'avvelena il cor!

"An interesting young man," Don Roberto says, watching him leave and then turning his gaze towards the gramophone Carlos has left behind.

"What business does he want with us, Papá?" Sofia asks, doing her best to show only the slightest of interest in the matter, though her curiosity feels more like a barely contained tidal wave.

"The Señor is willing to pay us very generously to locate some libretti for him. I confess it is not my usual type of business, but he insists that you, Sofia, have expressed a great interest in the opera and have offered to help him."

Sofia would like to unmask Carlos as a liar, would like to insist to her father that she has never expressed such an interest, that the *señor* is taking liberties that do not belong to him, but she is aware of how much the business is needed at the store, feels humiliated by the thought that Carlos has found a way to purchase her agreement with this ruse.

"Yes," she says, to her father's open relief, "I would very much like to learn about opera." And there is some truth in her words—the music intrigues her, no matter the feelings she might have for the young man himself.

At the usual hour of one o'clock Sofia leaves the store in time to go home for the midday meal, devastated by the fact that Diego had not appeared for the meeting she had proposed. A battle now rages in her head—one side wishing to banish Diego permanently, the other unwilling to give up the fight before all hope has been completely quenched. She steps out to find Diego himself standing by the door.

"Will you come with me?" he asks.

"Go with you where?" she asks, annoyance and relief mingling in her chest.

"It is a secret," the young man replies, laughter in his eyes.

She pauses, trying to vanquish the last vestiges of irritation that still linger in her mind.

"Wait," she says. She runs back into the bookstore and instructs Bernardo on what he is to do and say back at the house.

Outside once again, Sofia finds Diego standing by a *calesa*, one of the horse-drawn buggies that transport the people of Mérida about. He helps her inside and she watches as the driver steers the buggy here and there without any clear direction until they are making their way out of town.

"Where are we going, Diego?" she asks, growing evermore confused about what he is planning, her anxiety quelled by the sheer joy she feels at being with him on this day, perfect, so perfect that when she remembers it later, she will be able to recall every moment, every sigh, every word.

They arrive at their destination in less than an hour's time—a field to which they have often travelled with the group led by Mr. Nelson during these recent months.

Sofia is now even more confused than before.

Diego helps her out of the buggy, leads her to a familiar clump of bushes and trees. Sofia remembers this spot well, remembers all the times she had come here as a child accompanying her father while he searched for his beloved birds.

"For the *señorita*," Diego says, handing Sofia a pair of opera glasses.

Diego lays out a cotton blanket and invites the *señorita* to sit, to wait for the performance to begin.

"Performance, Diego?" Sofia asks, eyebrows raised.

"Yes, Sofia, an opera of the most sublime kind," the young man responds as he takes a seat by her side.

Two Lineated Woodpeckers begin to hack at a tree, with a loud and insistent sound that resembles a series of drum rolls.

"Ah, the overture," Diego whispers, "to this private performance of *A Song with Wings*."

Diego and Sofia pick up their opera glasses and prepare to take it all in.

They sit there quietly, their eyes fixed on the sky and the trees. They watch the Cave Swallows dance their aerial ballet, admire the Rose-Throated Becard with its rosy-red throat and its blackish head. They listen to a duet sung by a pair of Green Jays, the birds' brilliant plumage resplendent in the afternoon light. The first one sings a tune and then waits as the second jay repeats the song in a higher pitch.

They admire the bearing of a Crane Hawk. "A bass, for sure," Diego says, pointing out the bird's long black tail, the narrow white band across the underwing, the assurance with which the bird stares at them from his perch.

More music follows—from the deafening *chaa* of a Brown Jay to the buzzy and clear whistled syllables of the Tropical Mockingbird. Aria after aria, bird after bird, so many performances to admire, so many birds to hear and see.

After some time, Diego puts down the field glasses and begins to speak, not of his feelings for her, not even of the birds that have serenaded them on this day, but of his past, his mother, Mónica, his father, Emilio, that fateful day when he had walked across Seville to be humiliated by the very man who had ruined his mother's life. He speaks about the futility of that time, of the memories that have been torturing him of late as if he had left pieces of himself behind, the feeling he has suddenly that the ocean that separates him from his own history is no longer vast enough. It is time to go north, he tells her, to follow the birds along their migratory path and find consolation, nourishment under skies of a different sort.

"Would you join me?" he asks. Mr. Nelson has offered him a position in Washington. They could travel there and begin working on other bird guides, embark on other projects, big and small.

There is little he could offer her but this. He is a man of little means, of no wealth at all.

"I have only my future to offer," he says, "the promise Mr. Nelson has seen in the work I have done."

He tries then to put his love into words but finds that his mind will not comply. He thinks back to the advice Very Useful has offered on how to court the girl—*praise her eyes, her smile, her fascinating mind*—but such talk seems impossible now that the moment has arrived. Diego is no poet, has no facility with words, his talent is in his hands and they seem useless now, hanging awkwardly by his side.

But there are, it turns out, no words needed, for Sofia is saying yes already, yes to the migration to the north, yes to him, Diego, yes to the life she has merely dreamed about until now. She takes his awkward hands into hers then and makes them come alive, all uncertainty, all fears banished for this one perfect moment in time.

*

Back in Mérida, as the duo trills and hums their love to each other outside of town, it does not take Doña Laura long to wrench the truth from little Bernardo, who is quickly made to confess to the fact that Sofia has left with Diego, their intended destination a mystery even to him.

Nelson and Very Useful are immediately summoned to the house by an agitated Doña Laura, who sees in Sofia's sudden absence all the portents of doom. In truth, it is not for Sofia that she fears but for the young woman's reputation, already tattered and frail, about to be delivered the last death stroke by this sudden disappearance with a Spanish *peón* of no known name or wealth.

"A wastrel!" Doña Laura raves. "A seducer of young girls!" she accuses, trying with the weight of her outrage to lay all of the blame at the young man's feet. Even now it seems impossible for her to believe that Sofia has been foolish enough to agree to such a thing. *Está loca, completamente loca. The girl has descended into madness,* the old lady thinks to herself.

Out loud, the old lady insists on an entirely different thing instead. "She is a decent girl who would never behave in such a way unless wickedly misled." She stares hard at Nelson, who is standing there stiffly holding his hat in his hands, his spectacles cloudy from the oppressive humidity of the day, watching silently as the old woman vents her considerable rage.

"Even if Sofia did consent to such a meeting—" (and deep in her heart, buried beneath her outrage, Doña Laura knows that Sofia did—after all, had she herself not witnessed a disquieting moment between the two? But she dismisses this thought immediately, no use revealing this to the others just yet.) "Even if the girl did consent," she says again, resuming her tirade, "I do not believe she could have known what that scoundrel had in mind."

"A walk in the forest, I believe," Very Useful now says, tired of this woman's vituperation, the exaggerated accusations that have silenced Don Roberto, that have reduced Aunt Marta to tears, that have Bernardo cowering in a corner and that have left even the usually voluble Gabriela bereft of words.

"A walk in the forest?" the old woman spits out, incredulity stamped across her face.

"Yes, Doña Laura, I believe they were going to be looking at some birds," Very Useful replies in his most respectful tone, his eyes expressionless, his mouth turgid and white.

"Birds? They were going to look at birds in a forest?" The old woman cannot believe her ears. She raises her hands to the sky, *harrumphs* loudly and brings her arms crashing back onto her lap.

"Edward," Don Roberto now says, ignoring his mother's theatrics as he attempts to make sense of the afternoon's events, "were you aware of the outing Diego had planned?"

"No, Roberto, I most certainly was not," a tired Nelson replies. All eyes now turn to Very Useful, who is still standing there rigidly, proudly, eyes staring straight ahead, chin held high.

Mercifully, Very Useful is spared, for it is just at this moment that the two lovers arrive, their joy instantly banished once they see the group that is waiting for them inside the courtyard of the house.

"Sofia!" Aunt Marta cries out, running to the girl as if she has just returned from the arms of death itself, enveloping her in a fierce embrace, worried more for what the girl is about to face than whatever ill she may have encountered until now.

Diego and Sofia walk up to the group, determination in their eyes. They have expected this scene, have anticipated the reactions during their long trip back. They are determined to announce their love, determined to declare their intention to be wed. Still, when Diego meets the eyes of his *patrón* he cannot but feel ashamed. He has failed him, he sees that now; there is a weariness in Mr. Nelson's gaze that Diego has never seen before.

"Scoundrel!" the old lady accuses as she gets up from the bench, hobbling over to them with her forefinger pointed in the air. *The finger of God,* Sofia thinks, her heart harder than stone, *attempting to push me into the* infierno *itself.*

But no, to that she will not consent. Twenty-two years have been purgatory enough. Sofia steps forward, lifts her own chin in the air, shields Diego from her grandmother, who is looking menacingly his way.

"No, not a scoundrel, Abuela. He is the man whom I have pledged to marry and will marry with your approval or not."

"Marry? Marry?" the old woman screeches out. "And what makes you think, Señorita, that this marriage will be allowed?"

"It will be allowed because I wish it to be so," the young girl replies, her voice firm, and now grandmother and grandchild are standing facing each other, in the same position they assumed the day Sofia's friend Rosita died.

The charged silence that follows is broken suddenly by the sound of the slap that strikes Sofia hard across the face.

"No!" Diego cries out. He has been transported in time, finds himself suddenly back inside Don Ricardo's house. The young man grabs Sofia, moves her gently to one side.

"And what is wrong with her marrying me, Señora?" he asks, his voice trembling, rage in his eyes.

"Sofia, marry you?" the old lady replies, mouth opened wide. "*Por favor!* A man with no name, no wealth to offer, nothing but a pair of dirty boots, not even a proper Castilian accent to speak his mother tongue with. A nobody from Andalucía, attempting to sully a decent girl's name."

"Señora, with all due respect," Diego answers, "do not speak to me about a name. My father was Don Ricardo Medina, a member of one of the most distinguished families in Seville, a *marqués*, in fact, and a distant relative of none other than the Duke of Medina Sidonia himself. Clemente was my mother's name."

It will take Diego a moment to acknowledge what has just escaped from his lips. Has he just admitted Don Ricardo as his father, dear God? Ah, but we are all sinners in the end, he hears his Uncle Alfonso say, all guilty of vanity and conceit, going straight to the Devil once our appointment with death comes up.

"Oh, and where is your father now?" the old lady asks, hope rising in her chest. Could it be, could it possibly be that her granddaughter has landed a much bigger catch?

"Dead," Diego responds flatly. "He died impoverished many years ago."

The hope that had swelled briefly in Doña Laura's chest now collapses like a house of cards. "A distinguished lineage will not feed my granddaughter, Señorito," she spits out. *Nor, more importantly, save this family from its ruinous debt,* she adds to herself.

It is now Don Roberto who steps forward, who takes Sofia by the hand. "Let us put this matter to rest for the moment. Take some time to collect ourselves. Can we agree to meet back here four days hence to allow us some time to think things through more carefully?" He looks to Sofia and then to Diego, waits for them to give their consent with nods of the head, silences his mother with a stare.

The group disperses then, Sofia walking with her father into his office, Diego, Very Useful and Nelson taking leave of the house after issuing a quick bow Gabriela's way.

The three men cross the street in silence, oblivious to the merriment that surrounds them as they walk. In the background on the edge of the Plaza Mayor a mariachi band is singing of lost love. Night is falling and Mérida looks especially beautiful now in the half-light of dusk, in that moment just before the electric lights are lit and everything has an otherworldly look.

They walk to the square, Nelson ahead, Diego and Very Useful following quietly two steps behind.

Once there, Nelson instructs his assistants to take a seat by his side. *There is much to discuss,* he says to them and his usual gentle manner has been replaced by an exhaustion, a weariness that has seeped into his face and that even in that beautiful half-light makes him appear much older than his years.

"My work here is done," he says flatly after a pause.

"Done, *patrón?*" Very Useful asks, alarm in his voice. "Surely not. There are more birds to study, infinite birds to draw."

"Birds that can be studied and easily drawn by Diego, Sofia and Don Roberto—with your help of course, Very Useful."

"No, no, *patrón*, forgive me but they cannot. Diego here is an amateur at most and besides, Doña Laura will string him up by the toes if he tries to get near the girl again."

"I will speak to Don Roberto myself. Make him see that Diego would make the perfect husband for the girl. His love of birds, his knowledge of books—I am sure my old friend will see it is for the best."

Nelson turns to Diego now, who is sitting next to him silently, looking down at his feet.

"And what do you think?"

"That I am sorry to have created a rift between you and an old friend, Mr. Nelson," the young man says, genuinely perturbed by what has occurred back at Sofia's house.

"Do not worry, my boy, do not worry one bit. The whole thing was worth it. How else would I have seen Doña Laura riled up to such a degree?"

"Ah, do not joke, *patrón*," Very Useful says, a shiver running down his spine. "That woman is the very Devil herself. A Medusa, a crazed witch. Why, I was certain for a moment that she was going to rip out my liver and chop my head into bits. No, no love in the world, *señores*, would persuade this man to marry into that viper's nest."

"Don Ricardo Medina was not my father," Diego says quietly

after a pause.

"Eh?" Very Useful cries out. "Not your father! What a quick thinker you are, Diego, inventing a *marqués* to provide you with some societal heft! Brilliant, utterly brilliant, my friend." Very Useful laughs, pats Diego heartily on the back.

But it is not brilliant, it is devastating, Diego thinks. He has spoken that despised name so as to quiet an old woman with pretensions to royalty herself. He has forsaken Emilio, the father who had raised him with all the love in the world, and he has managed, despite all of his *patrón's* assurances to the contrary, to fail Mr. Nelson once again.

He walks back to their house in silence, the splendid afternoon spent with Sofia forgotten momentarily as he castigates himself for his unguarded tongue, for the little loyalty he had demonstrated to the one person he had loved most in the world.

*

Back inside Don Roberto's house, father and daughter have retreated to his office to discuss the day's events far from Doña Laura's prying eyes.

"*Hija,*" an exhausted Don Roberto tells Sofia, disappointment in his voice, "this is not how things are done. You have made matters very difficult for me. I cannot see how I can now easily patch things up."

Sofia is aggrieved by her father's obvious displeasure, the exhaustion she hears flowing through his words. She notices for the first time the lines that have etched themselves on his face, the sudden droopiness in his gait. *How has this happened,* she asks herself, *when did my father suddenly succumb to the ravages of old age?* She would like to rise up and erase each of those lines with the tips of her fingers, but she sits there immobilized by her shame. Still, she has taken a decisive step, knows there can be no turning back. She has tasted the first breath of freedom; renouncing a future with Diego is simply not in the cards, even in the light of her father's disappointment, the futility that has come to mask his face.

"And what is wrong with Diego?" she asks him quietly after a pause. "Have you not always praised him, commended him for his talent, lauded his sense of responsibility, his quick mind?"

"*Hija,* this is not about the qualities the young man may or may not possess. This is about comportment, about how one is expected to behave."

Even to himself, his words sound hollow, barren of any of the truths he holds deep in his heart: for has the boy not indeed impressed him with his discerning eye, his knack for spotting the tiniest of birds that fly in and out of sight? Has he not often marvelled at Diego's abilities, how he can depict a bird so majestically that it seems to be caught in mid-flight? Has he not sworn those drawings could deceive him, make him believe, even, that he could hear the bird's call, the sound the wings made as they soar into the sky? And is he not hiding now behind convention, is he not cowering behind the very customs he has always claimed to despise? And what are the reasons for it, he asks himself, this disappointment that seems wedged in his bones—of course he believes his daughter's words, does not doubt her account of how things had unfolded earlier on, does not have reason to think that their venture into the field had not been prompted by the desire to rejoice in something he himself loves—the birds, as always, the birds.

Later he will suffer the indignity of having these very questions put to him by his dear friend Edward Nelson, who will arrive soaked to the bones from the torrential downpour that falls on Mérida all that evening, looking as if the weight of the world has fallen upon his shoulders too, as if he has cause to feel more exhaustion than Roberto. Not only does Roberto face the prospect of a looming battle with the women of the house but also the burden of his own uneasiness and why am I so uneasy? he asks himself again. He will be forced to listen as his friend expounds on the many virtues possessed by young Diego, the same virtues Roberto has enumerated silently to himself during the long afternoon, and he will have no choice but to agree that there is nothing deficient in the young man's character, that he is indeed as noble and as refined as they come.

And yet. There is no getting rid of that feeling, no way to fully unearth the objection that lingers just beneath his breath.

And now before him is his daughter, face tear-stained but an unshakeable conviction keeping her head erect, the conviction she has possessed since she was a child and which he has so admired, whether it applied to birds, to books, to the plight of the hacienda's labouring children or to the importance, now, of love—it is all the same, it is her strength he admires, that erect spine, that raised chin.

And yet, he tells himself again. And yet.

Sofia's eyes have been fixed on the ground all this time, though her head is indeed held high. After all, she has done nothing wrong except to defend her right to choose whom she loves, to carve a future for herself with a man who understands her need to express herself as he himself does, who will allow her the freedom to indulge in her heart's desires—field glasses and drawing pencil in hand, and the birds, yes, as always, the birds.

Later she will be forced to suffer a visit from her distraught grandmother, who will come to her room not with the battle axe raised high, but armed with a more potent weapon yet, her grief, her tears, the desperation that has been eating away at her flesh for years now, years of watching her son sink deeper and deeper into debt. What will become of us? she will ask her granddaughter. What will happen if you squander our one opportunity, our one chance at being saved from the claws of ruin?

And later still, it will be Diego himself who will knock on the window of her room, Diego who will stand there on the street, the rain dripping down his face, which seems luminous nonetheless, resplendent, for between the afternoon and the evening he has been building up strength, a strength he hadn't known was his, and he will reach across the iron bars of the window and take Sofia's hands confidently into his and he will kiss them over and over again, telling her not to worry, they will escape for the north, follow the path of the migrating birds, start life anew in Washington or even further north, Canada perhaps, but they will leave and soon.

But now, before her sits her father, a raging war building inside his chest, his eyes closed, his mouth a straight hard line. Although he does not say the words, Sofia can hear them nonetheless.

And yet. And yet.

It is then that Sofia raises her eyes, stands up slowly as the sad hard truth hits her squarely in the gut and she looks at her father as if seeing him clearly for the first time in her life. Silently she mouthes the words, Carlos Blanco Torres, incredulity tugging at her mouth, and before her father can utter a word, she has run out of the office to cope with the disappointment of that moment in the privacy of her room. Roberto has not heard her words, is still trying to calm the storm deep inside, and it is not until later, much later, after Edward Nelson has come and gone, after the women have shed the last of their tears and retired to their rooms, that the insidious thought that has been lingering just beyond reach finally rise to consciousness to torture him throughout the bitter night ahead.

Yes, Diego Clemente is a fine young man, an artist, a man subject to the same curious longings that he, Roberto, has always felt. The son of a *marqués* even, although impoverished, but it is probable that aristocratic blood courses through the young man's veins.

And yet. It cannot be forgotten; some thoughts are impossible to erase, though he wishes he could torch the idea, relieve himself of the burden of his need. But there, standing in the wings, is Carlos Blanco Torres, son of one of the most powerful men in the Yucatán, a man who at this moment holds Roberto's future in his grasp. Is it all that contemptible, all that unreasonable that he should desire a union for his daughter with the one man who can save him from ruin?

All night he remains awake at his desk, rueing the vicious hand of fate that can reduce a man like him to a rumbling, sea-tossed mess, at odds with the ones he loves most and, even worse, embroiled in a disheartening struggle with himself.

*

And now we see Diego Clemente, sitting in a chair at centre stage, head in his hands, plagued also by one devastating thought: I am a Judas, he is thinking, a traitor of the worst kind. How, he asks himself, how could the name of Ricardo Medina have come tumbling so easily from my lips?

"The dead have no ears to listen to the inanities we spew out into

the world, *amigo*," Very Useful assures him when Diego speaks to
him of how that name has scorched his tongue, made a mockery of
all that he believes. "Your real father would have forgiven you the
trespass because of the situation you found yourself in."

But no words will console his friend, no reasoning, no number
of earnest attempts to bring a note of levity to the affair. It is then
that Very Useful offers up the thought that will change the young
man's life.

"Diego, would you like to redeem yourself, my boy?" he asks his
friend, excitement suddenly coursing through his words.

"Redeem myself, Very Useful? But how?"

"Ah, watch and listen, my friend. Eyes, ears and mouth, as our
patrón always says. But the good man forgot the nose. And it is a
nose that I count on above all, Diego. A nose that helps me to sniff
out the most interesting bits of information to be had in this
world."

"What information, Very Useful? Speak!"

"First, Diego, we must go to a safer place . . ."

★

"An uprising?" Diego can hardly believe his ears.

"Shhhh . . . be careful, my friend, the trees and stones have ears
to listen with and mouths with which to speak."

It is later that night and Very Useful and Diego are sitting by the
enormous *ceiba* tree, where they often meet in the afternoons.

Diego lowers his voice, asks his friend to explain.

"Early Saturday, a group of insurgents will be leading an uprising at La pequeña Versailles, the splendid hacienda of none other
than our dear friend Don Victor Blanco."

"An uprising—but why?"

"Why?" Very Useful asks, outrage in his voice. He reaches over and cuffs Diego on the side of the head.

"Ow!" the young man screams out.

"How on earth can you ask such a thing?" Very Useful hisses. "Are your eyes, ears and mouth too full of birds, too full of a certain *señorita,* to notice what is occurring all around you, my misguided friend? Have you not noticed how the henequen workers toil on the estates, how much my people suffer under the weight of the *henequero's* fists? Bah! Sometimes you seem as empty-headed as a *lec!*"

"A *lec?*" Diego asks.

"Yes, a *lec*—that hollow gourd we store our warm *tortillas* in."

"It is not that I have not noticed, Very Useful. Of course I have," Diego says, rubbing the offended ear with the back of his hand. "It is just that I have learned to accept things as they are. Injustices are forever being committed. It seems to me to be the very nature of the world."

"Ah, *bonito!* And with that attitude, where would we be? Things would remain as miserable as they have been for all time. Mexico would never have become Mexico had we not fought tooth and nail to free ourselves from the grasping claws of Mother Spain."

"Are you going to be one of the insurgents yourself then, Very Useful?" Diego asks, alarmed now for the safety of his friend.

"Me? No, not this time, *compadre.* This time it is not my fight. There will be other opportunities for me to help set things to rights. But you, Diego, could be there if you like."

"And why would I be participating in an insurrection, Very Useful?"

"Why? Why indeed?" Very Useful says, his hands up in the air, his eyes fixed on the sky. "Think, Diego, think. What is lying inside that house? What does our *patrón* want more than anything in the world right now?"

"The birds!" Diego cries out.

"Yes, Señorito Diego. The birds. And do you think the insurgents are going to be concerning themselves with an aviary at the back of the house? No, they will set fire to the tapestries, to the fine furniture, to all the things Don Victor Blanco values most. In the middle of the mayhem, you can make your way to the aviary and bring back the goods. Who will notice later that a couple of birds have been lost? Nobody, Diego, I will assure you of that."

Diego thinks for a moment, his heart beating loudly in his chest.

"Yes, Very Useful, yes. I will do it. I will save those birds."

"Ah, *amigo,* I knew I could count on you. I know a *calesa* driver who will lend his horse and buggy to the cause. I will wait for you on the outskirts of the hacienda while you run in for the birds. And then, presto! The prize will be in our hands."

"When is this insurrection supposed to take place, Very Useful?"

"In less than forty-eight hours, my friend. Now listen up, we have precious little time to form a plan."

On the earth below their feet, Very Useful now begins to fashion a map with the end of a stick.

That very night, Diego will take out his own map and add two birds at the very top. He will draw them carefully, lovingly, from their long pointed tails to their graceful curved necks and heads to their brilliant scarlet eyes. The *Ectopistes migratorius*—how he longs to see the birds in mid-flight, their wings extended gracefully as they ascend swiftly into the sky.

No matter, he thinks. The moment for their liberation is finally at hand. He puts his paints away then and closes his eyes. In his mind, he can see the figure of Don Ricardo Medina, dressed in his dark suit made by Utrilla, the finest tailor in Madrid, smiling as he wades into a thick mud, walking, walking until he is immersed completely in that thick sludge and has finally disappeared for good.

Two birds in hand

The hour has arrived for those who have lingered in the wings to take their rightful place at centre stage—the men dressed in black with the look of emaciated intellectuals, centuries of oppression etched on each and every face. It will take twenty of them, carrying guns and sticks and canisters of oil, to lay Don Victor Blanco's vast henequen fields to waste. It is there that they begin first, setting the fields on fire as a warning that they will no longer be held hostage by the agave with the blue-and-grey spikes. But the insurgents do not stop there. They have not put skin and bone on the line to take a mere symbolic stance, not when they have so much anger coursing through their veins, not when they have come so far, have risked so much. The time for a revolution is ripe, they whisper to each other—the moment has arrived for a line to be drawn in the sand.

Diego and Very Useful arrive at the hacienda just as the first flames shoot out from the henequen fields at the back of the house. It is just past six in the morning and dawn is breaking all across the land. All around them, the birds have begun singing their spectacular morning songs. From somewhere above, they hear the eerie call of a Collared Forest-Falcon. Nearby, a Montezuma Oropendola is whining a single, heartfelt *euhh*.

Diego's own heart is beating wildly beneath his cotton shirt. He focuses again on remembering the details of the map Very Useful had just hours ago drawn in the dirt. This time, Diego will be bypassing the main house altogether and running straight to the aviary at the back. In his pocket he carries a handful of berries and seeds to help him coax the birds to his hands. It will be simple, he assures himself: grab the birds, run back to the horse and carriage where Very Useful will be waiting just outside the gates. In less than an hour they will be back in Mérida with the precious birds in their hands, a priceless farewell gift for the man they both love.

"*Bueno*, my friend," Very Useful says now, his voice grave. "The time has arrived. Do you remember what you are supposed to do? Keep your head low at all times. You do not want to be caught in the firestorm that is raging inside."

Diego nods, slaps Very Useful heartily on the back.

He runs then through the magnificent arch that has greeted visitors to the hacienda for over two centuries now, past the regal house, past the dozens of people who are emerging from all corners—workers, servants, overseers too, all united on this day by their single desire to flee from the inferno that rages in the fields.

Inside the aviary, the birds are on high alert. Smoke has begun seeping in through the open windows and underneath the door. The birds' frantic calls are raucous as they announce the encroaching danger to each other with squawks and squeals and the furious flaps of their wings.

In that half-light of early morning, his eyes stinging from the smoke, Diego is finding it difficult to make out anything. Even worse, the pigeons have been moved from the spot where they had been on the night of the ball. He looks around frantically but the light is too dim, the birds inside distinguishable only by the most obvious features—a large size, a pointed head, a prominent beak.

From somewhere in the aviary, a faint voice suddenly calls out in the dark, "Who is there? Answer me! Who is there walking about?"

*

It had been Don Victor's misfortune to be at the hacienda that day, having arrived the night before to tend to a group of American buyers who were coming the following day. His wife and son had stayed behind at their house in Mérida to indulge in the season of dances and celebration that were taking place as the month of December drew to a close. At the crack of dawn, Don Victor had been awakened by a commotion that seemed to emanate from somewhere at the back of the house.

Now what? he had asked himself, annoyed as he tumbled out of bed bleary-eyed, the beginnings of a headache announcing itself already at that early hour of the day. He shouted for his most trusted servant, Mariano, but no one responded in the shadows. *How unusual,* he had thought. There were dozens of servants in the house; why had none of them responded to his call?

He wandered out of the bedroom and made his way across the dimly lit courtyard to the other side of the house. He noticed that a faint light was shining inside his office. *A light there?* the old man asked himself, less irritated now than gravely concerned. The office was the one room in the house kept strictly under lock and key. Inside were the many papers and records of the henequen trade Don Victor considered too important for eyes that were not his. He hurried there, noticing that the door was slightly ajar. *Who is there?* he called out, anger in his voice, and it was just then that a shot rang out and then another one from somewhere deep inside.

One missed him, the other hit him in the thigh. He turned around quickly, desperately trying to make sense of what had just occurred, and, stumbling through the kitchen and the back of the house, made his way to the aviary, hoping to hide there until help arrived.

He had been lying there for some time when he spotted a dark figure making his way through the aviary in the dark. By then, Don Victor knew that he had lost a significant amount of blood. From outside he could hear the shouts of the people as they made their way frantically through to the front of the house, he could smell the smoke wafting in from the fields at the back. He knew with all the instincts of an injured animal that whoever was wandering about in the aviary presented his only hope—he prayed silently for a moment that it would turn out to be a friend and not a foe.

"Who is there? Answer me, I beg you!" he shouts out now.

Diego turns around sharply, spots a figure lying on the ground. He walks over to him and then slowly crouches down. *Don Victor Blanco*. Wounded, it seems—a hand is trying to stem the blood that is pouring from a twisted leg, his face is ash-grey, cadaverous already, Diego thinks, alarmed.

Two sets of eyes meet in the dark. A glint of recognition registers in Don Victor's gaze.

"Are you not the American's assistant?" the old man asks. And then, more sharply, he adds, "Does Nelson have anything to do with this?"

Diego shakes his head. "Nelson? No, of course not. I was in the area photographing birds—saw the commotion and thought of the Passenger Pigeons here inside."

"The pigeons?" Don Victor repeats, astonishment in his face. He pauses, tries to add up what he is hearing, but his mind is a jumble. There is no way, he realizes, to make sense of what is going on.

"Well, help me up then, my boy," the old man says in his hard, stentorian voice. "I am injured and cannot stand. If those bastards see me here they will shoot me again."

"Where are the birds?" Diego asks.

"The birds? The birds?" Don Victor's mouth opens wide; he stops as if to register the young man's question and then points to the other side, "Over there. But forget about the birds, *muchacho*, can't you see that I cannot walk? Do you have no pity in your heart?" The old man's anxiety is building, desperation is emanating from his sea-bream eyes.

Diego hesitates, knows the time is ticking by. The birds or this man's life? *It would be easy to leave him behind,* Diego thinks. After all, did men like Don Victor not bring this devastation upon themselves?

We are all free men, above all, he now hears Emilio say. *Free to be decent even in the absence of God.*

Diego pulls the old man up, puts his arms around his own shoulders, instructs him to hang on, as they begin to make their way outside, hurrying as much as they can along the cobblestone path to where Very Useful stands waiting just outside the gates.

"Thank you," the old man whispers, his head resting on Diego's shoulder, tears of relief streaming down his face.

From afar, Very Useful spots Diego making his way across the front of the house. The smoke is so thick by now that it is difficult to be sure why the young man is hobbling back. Surely those cannot be the birds he is dragging by his side?

Very Useful runs towards him and then stops abruptly once he sees that Diego is helping none other than Don Victor Blanco to the cart.

"Diego?" he asks, alarm in his voice.

"Quick, put him in the cart, find someone who can attend to his wounds. I am going back inside for the birds."

"The birds?" Don Victor spits out. "You fool, you will be burned alive if you go back in. Leave the birds there, I will purchase another pair if they mean so much to you"

But Diego has already run back into the grounds, past the arch, past the people who are still streaming out—coughing, crying, calling to the others who are following behind—back into the aviary to the spot that Don Victor had pointed out before.

*

In Mérida, just as Very Useful and Diego were setting out for Don Victor's hacienda, their *patrón* was awakening from a turbulent sleep. All night he had been accompanied in his dreams by old Don Pedro, a Maya curer from the town of Valladolid with whom he had once spent a week learning the healing properties of the local plants and trees. In his dream, Don Pedro was cleansing him with the freshly cut branches of a *sip che* as he invoked the help of the *balams*, the Jaguar Lords. Next he sang out the names of the plants and their properties in a hypnotic plainchant tone: resin from the *ch'ich'put* for skin eruptions; the bark of the *bacal che* for burns; leaves of the *x mex nuxib* for the evil eye and listen—here, Don Pedro had taken Nelson's face violently into his hands—to cure one of the tortures of memory, tea made from *boldo* leaves, which tastes like the Devil but which erases every sigh of lament from one's soul.

Nelson wakes up drenched in sweat. He laughs at himself, so old, he thinks, and yet still subject to the torments of a bad dream. Try as he does, though, he cannot easily shake the feeling of uneasiness that lingers in his chest. He busies himself with packing for the day's work: his long-focus, four-by-five Premo camera and a Kodak of the same size first, a dozen plates and films, ammonia, Persian insect powder, a bottle of formalin and his gun. It is just as he is closing his pack that he hears the tremendous commotion being made outside as the first servants from Don Victor Blanco's estate arrive on horseback, shouting for help. He runs out, listens to the story the men tell the group that has congregated outside and then runs quickly back into the house. He calls for Very Useful and Diego and, when there is no response, makes his way quickly to the house of Roberto Duarte, driven forward by a furious, relentless force.

Later he will ask himself, *how did I know, how did I sense what was happening, deep in the gut?* It is true, there is much science cannot account for, much science cannot easily explain. But for now he has only one thought: I must get to Don Victor's hacienda as quickly as I can.

Roberto Duarte emerges from his house, summoned by a servant. Tousle-haired and bleary-eyed, he is disoriented by the insistence with which Nelson has been pounding on his door.

"Edward?" he asks, eyebrows raised high.

"I am sorry for the commotion, dear friend, but it is of great importance that you allow me the use of your horse and carriage."

"Yes, of course, but why?"

Nelson provides him with the barest of explanations before insisting he must be on his way.

"But what would Very Useful and Diego be doing at Don Victor's estate?" Roberto calls after his friend, who has already started walking quickly towards the stables with one of Roberto's servants by his side.

"Pigeons," Nelson calls out.

"Pigeons?" Roberto repeats, tone incredulous, eyes perplexed, but before the good man can enquire further, Nelson has already disappeared from sight.

In the stables, a figure emerges from the shadows.

"Sofia?" Nelson asks, his heart in his throat.

"Take me with you," she says, not so much a question as an insistent demand. She has heard the exchange between Nelson and her father, is determined to accompany this man to the ends of the earth to find Diego if that is what is required.

"Sofia, this is sheer lunacy," Nelson responds. He is about to argue that this is no place for women, that what lies before them is a territory of a most dangerous kind, but he sees immediately that it will be impossible to dissuade her from the idea, and, knowing that time is of the essence, consents grudgingly to her request with pursed lips and a warning that she must do exactly as he says.

"I will, Mr. Nelson, I will," she promises, climbing into the coach quickly, excitement and concern coursing equally through her veins.

They travel to the hacienda, each immersed in their private thoughts—his suffused with foreboding as he considers what may be awaiting them there, hers full of questions she is too frightened to ask.

He thinks: *Can it be possible that my own obsessions have led Diego to this madness? Has he been infected with my tortures, my longing to set the impossible to rights?* He looks quickly at Sofia, thinks fleetingly of the pigeons, curses the moment he drew the map of Don Victor's hacienda with a stick on the ground.

And she thinks: *What mystery lies at the heart of this? What could Diego be doing at Don Victor's hacienda so early in the day? And why?* For weeks she has been trying to unravel the tangled threads left behind since Don Victor's ball, but no matter how hard she tries, things resist coming free.

And what could Mr. Nelson have to do with all of this? She looks over at him now, sees his ashen face, attempts to glean the thoughts that lie behind his clouded eyes. A thought strikes her then. This man, the man she has admired all of her life, the man she had once dreamed of following to the very ends of the earth in search of a specimen, a theory, a skin, the man who has taught her more than anyone else in the world—this man is a complete enigma to her, as impenetrable as a stone wall. *And how have I not seen this before?* she asks herself. *What levels, what depths lie in this man's soul?*

He looks at her now, meets her curious eyes with his. "Sofia," he says and then he pauses as if measuring what he is about to say next.

"Sofia," he repeats sighing.

And then: *It is about two birds . . .*

*

Inside the aviary at Don Victor's estate, Diego has been trying to find a way to carry the pigeons out. The birds are housed in a cage that is much too large to be picked up. He opens the doors and holds his hands out to the two of them, which are chattering and kecking loudly as they circle frantically about.

"*Venga, venga,*" he whispers, "come to me, my friends." He puts some seeds and berries in his hands. "*Venga, venga,*" he says, more frantically this time. *The time is running out,* he tells himself. The smoke is getting denser, the cries in the distance are growing fainter as if the estate has now been emptied of all but those who are trying to raze it to the ground. No matter what he does, however, the birds will not come to his side.

It is then that Diego has a thought. *What is more beautiful a song,* he thinks, *than the one that lures a lover close to one's breast?* A siren song, the one with the promise of the present and the future fused in a single note, in a single breath—the mating song that accompanies the fluffing of feathers, the squealing, the fanning of a tail, the bobbing of a head and the raising of a leg.

So it is that Diego begins to *coo* and *cluck* and *keck,* just as Mr. Nelson had once shown him, making a song from tinkling sounds that resemble the distant ringing of bells, trying to attract the pigeons to his side with their own mating call. And after some time, an eternity in Diego's mind, the birds do come to perch on his arm, first the female, and then the male follows closely behind.

Holding the birds tightly to his chest, Diego stumbles out of the aviary and heads back to meet Very Useful, who has now been joined near the entrance of the hacienda by his frantic *patrón* and la Señorita Sofia no less, both demanding explanations, both trying to make sense of the conflagration before them, the sight of a wounded Don Victor being attended to by a servant nearby and their fear for Diego, making the situation seem all the worse.

Now, from outside the aviary, one of the insurrectionists, a short stout man dressed entirely in black, watches as a figure emerges from the building with something underneath each arm. *The son,* the man thinks, *there before me must be none other than Don Victor Blanco's only son.* Carrying out something of value, no doubt, hoping to escape unperceived, his body shrouded by the smoke, a fleeing figure that seems already ghost. The man picks up his gun, aims it at Diego, shoots once, twice, three times.

Diego feels something burn into his side. He tries to focus all of his attention on walking, on holding onto the birds. *Concentrate, Diego,* he tells himself as he makes his way to the gates, his eyes failing him, his hands growing weaker with every passing step. *I must keep walking,* he tells himself, *get the birds out.* He is moments away, he knows, from escaping what seems now to be the very pit of hell. He starts to turn around then, suddenly confused, no longer sure of which direction he is walking, which way is down, which way up.

From beyond the grounds, Nelson spots Diego as he attempts to make his way across the path. *Why is he tottering around like that?* he asks himself. The smoke, it must be the smoke. He begins to run towards him and it is just then that Diego stumbles, wading in a sea of delirium, forgetting suddenly what he is doing, where he is.

Is it ever really possible to leave the past behind? Because in the confusion of that moment his mind has catapulted him back to another place in time. Seville. He thinks then he can hear the music, see the women with the roses in their hair, that he can smell the oranges and the jasmine, the faint scent of olive from the distant groves, that he can feel the cobblestones as he tries to take one step and another and another one yet, each more difficult than the one before it, a mountain to be scaled. He thinks of Emilio then, his beloved father hiding beneath the counter of the Librería Alfonso, lost in one of his books of poetry, reciting those hallowed English words to himself. And he thinks of Mónica, poor Mónica, condemned to live in the half-light of failed promises, failed dreams; a woman made old by all that she desired and that lay forever beyond her reach.

Is this how it all ends? he hears his Uncle Alfonso say, outrage in his voice. Are we merely the playthings of the gods?

The birds, Diego says to himself now, *the birds.* He thinks then of the way Mr. Nelson had once described the beauty of the pigeons in flight, how swift they were, how graceful they appeared as they ascended into the open sky. He raises his arms up and releases the pigeons into the air, watches mesmerized as the birds rise up, flapping their wings, now slowly, now powerfully, until they have flown over the main arch and into the forest that surrounds the hacienda, vigorous, elegant, a most wondrous sight to feast the eyes upon in such a maelstrom of confusion and despair. He sighs in contentment, watching as the birds disappear into the forest canopy for good. *Free,* he whispers, *the birds are free.* It is then that Nelson appears before him, in time to catch Diego just as he topples onto the ground.

"Did you see them?" Diego asks, wonder in his eyes. "Did you see the birds fly out?" And in that moment, with everything shrouded in smoke, his mind delirious from his wounds, he thinks it is Emilio who has picked him up and is now holding him in his arms.

"*Ay,* I did, Diego, they were indeed a spectacular sight," Nelson replies, cradling the young man's head in his hands, trying frantically to stem the blood that is escaping from his side, watching horrified as Diego's smile fades and his eyes slowly close.

Madness, Mr. Nelson will say later, agony in his voice, trying with all his might to console a young girl who will not be consoled. It is madness all, he will repeat, over and over again, to himself, to her, to the world. The smoke, the rage, the futility of one man's quest and no bird spectacular enough on earth to make the matter less unbearable, to bring his wounded soul comfort or relief.

Ah, but at least the music remains—the scratchy *krrrk* of a Keele-Billed Toucan, the thin whistle of a Rose-Throated Becard, the *coo coo* of a Mourning Dove that sings its sadness to the world at large.

THE CURTAIN CALL

Another five years would pass before the Revolution fully arrived in the Yucatán. In 1915 General Alvarado entered Mérida leading his troops in their Stetson hats, rifles in hand, ammunition belts criss-crossing their chests, a *norteño* mariachi band at their beck and call, a band that would park itself in the courtyard of the governor's palace and play "La Cucaracha" over and over again every day from dawn until dusk. Alvarado would end slavery in the Yucatán, he would outlaw pimps, eliminate bordellos, deprive the Yucatecans of their wicked pleasures—cantinas, bullfighting, their raffles and their lotteries—would even bring in the American big guns under the guise of the Boy Scouts. He would transform churches into schools, empower the rural *maestro*, would start a "great books" program. He would punish the abuses he found perpetuated freely by the *hacendados*, would even go so far as to publicly humiliate the daughters of a prominent planter found guilty of coercing their former slaves to kiss their hands, which had been strictly prohibited by then.

He would not, in the immediate future, however, be able to keep the *henequeros* from continuing to amass their enormous wealth. Politics was one thing, revolution another thing yet, but economics ruled the world and in this realm the luck was still running high for those who cultivated henequen. The First World War was on and the Americans wanted their bread, needed rope to bind the sheaves for their wheat. The Yucatán was their only possible source now that the Philippines and other markets had been closed to them. So it was that the *henequeros* made their final stand, reaping the last of their outrageous fortunes, for the War would soon end, synthetic fibres were waiting in the wings and the slave labour that had once made their product cheap to produce was no longer an option available to them.

Using primitive glass plate and early cut-film cameras, hundreds of photographers descended upon Mexico, risking life and limb to record the images that were transforming the nation for all time. Their negatives were printed on postcard stock and distributed far and wide, visual testaments to the revolution that had been unleashed and that would continue raging for years—its aims in many ways still unmet today, almost a century after the guns were fired for the very first time.

*

Stuffed in one of our grandmother's many boxes were dozens of these postcards, grainy and weathered by time. Among them, there were a few that we especially prized. One depicted perfectly the divide across the Rio Grande with some Americans standing on the northern shore—the women in pristine dresses, the men in dark suits—while across the river, facing them wearily, stood a group of Mexican insurgents, rifles in hand, sombreros on their heads. Another featured none other than Pancho Villa himself, riding a horse furiously into the camera lens. Our favourite though, was the picture of a young boy, no more than eight, sword in one hand, gun strapped to his waist, an ammunition belt wrapped around his arms and chest, all the fervor of a true revolutionary in his gaze.

Our grandmother gave the last performance of her grand opera when the oldest of us was only ten. A stroke felled her soon after and she was confined to a bed for a year until her death. By that time her hearing had grown weak, her English and Spanish had become all mixed up so that a woman who had once prided herself on her verbal acuity could no longer remember when it was appropriate to speak one language and when the other was called for. In that last year it was the music that consoled her, the arias, the *bulerías,* the *rancheras* that told of another place and time.

Our Abuela died peacefully in her sleep but not before asking to hear one more song. We prepared ourselves for her beloved "Liebestod" from *Tristand und Isolde* but instead she requested the song she had once played for our grandfather when he too had stood upon the threshold of death:

> *Y todo aquello pasó,*
> *Todo quedo en olvido*

> (And all of that is behind us
> Everything is but a memory now)

The years passed and the opera faded into the recesses of our minds like Mozart's *Idomeneo,* waiting in the wings to be rediscovered by the opera cognoscenti and performed once again to cheers and applause.

In the end, it was not the music that brought us back to the opera but a discovery made by our cousin Lily while researching

Mexican birds. Edward William Nelson, we were astounded to find out, had been no creation of our grandmother's fertile mind—he had indeed travelled the length of Mexico in the late-nineteenth century and, together with his assistant, Edward Goldman, had classified countless mammals and birds. Later, he would take a leading role in spearheading the many measures that would aid in the conservation and the general administration of wildlife in his own country. He would be instrumental in the negotiation of the *Migratory Bird Treaty* with Great Britain and Canada, the *Migratory Bird Conservation Act*, the *Migratory Bird Hunting Stamp Act* and the *Alaska Game Law of 1925.*

Nelson died in 1934 at the age of seventy-nine, never married and with no known descendants, resigned like Absalom to leave the earth with no son to keep his name in remembrance. Nevertheless, he did leave his mark in many other ways. A man who had never been trained in proper laboratory techniques, who had never finished an official course of study at a university, a naturalist in the old style, self-motivated, self-taught, has today over one hundred mammals, birds and plants named after him as well as a number of geographic features in the states of Alaska and California.

Of Diego Clemente nothing remains except the recipes for Bautista's stews, the map and a yellowed photograph, which are still in our hands today. Did he really exist, we ask ourselves, or had he been our grandmother's invention, her alter ego, her unlived masculine self?

As for the fate of the Passenger Pigeon—that, alas, is all too well known. In 1896 the last significant chapter for these birds was written in the state of Ohio. By then, only a quarter of a million remained of the billions that had once filled the sky. In April of that year they came together in one last great nesting flock in the forest on Green River near Mammoth Cave. Recently installed telegraph lines were used to notify the hunters of the appearance of this flock and they arrived by railway from far and wide. The result was catastrophic—two hundred thousand carcasses were taken, another forty thousand were mutilated and wasted, one hundred thousand newborn chicks were destroyed or abandoned to predators in their nests. Only five thousand were thought to have escaped.

The hunters' efforts were wasted in the end. The birds—packaged for shipment to markets in the East—rotted under a scorching sun when a derailment prevented them from being shipped as planned. The putrefied carcasses of the two hundred thousand birds were disposed of in a nearby ravine.

The last bird of its kind, Martha, died alone at the age of twenty-nine inside the Cincinnati Zoo at about one o'clock on September 1, 1914. There were few then who understood the significance of what had just come to pass. A bird that had once thundered across open skies had been vanquished for good—driven to extinction by man's ignorance and greed.

But there are the other two still left unaccounted for, the two pigeons freed by Diego Clemente in the early hours of a late December day in 1910. In our minds we can see them flying majestically over the imposing arch of Don Victor Blanco's hacienda, their wings flapping now slowly, now powerfully, up, up until they have disappeared into the forest and into a new life in the wild. They are our very own Adam and Eve, the founders of a new line that remains hidden in the forests somewhere in North America, biding their time until the terrain has been made safe for their return.

Years after our grandmother's death we still perform the opera, are thankful for what life leaves behind—a *corrido,* an aria, a *soléa,* the early-morning song of a cardinal that announces itself to the world.

On the chair where our Abuela once sat, weaving her story note by note, silencing our titters with the wave of her hand, on that chair we sit and take turns now, relating the tales of our ancestors, the good and the bad, to our own children, who scoff and cheer and laugh.

After all, as you once said, Abuela, what else of ourselves do we leave behind? Just a story, scattered scenes from an often-complicated life, a tidbit from an arduous journey, a song that surges, thrills and fades into memory after the last word is sung.

Acknowledgments

I am eternally indebted to the many wonderful writers of Mexico who first introduced me to their enchanting country and made me love it from afar. They include Juan Rulfo, Carlos Fuentes, Octavio Paz and Carlos Monsiváis. I am especially indebted to Ermilo Abreu Gómez, a Yucatecan author too little known outside of his own country, who wrote the masterful *Canek* and without whose "Cosas de Yucatán" my own book would not exist.

I am also indebted to Christopher Cokinos's *Hope Is the Thing with Feathers: A Personal Chronicle of Vanished Birds* and to the works of historian Gilbert M. Joseph on nineteenth-century Yucatán.

We in Toronto are very fortunate to have one of the best opera educators in the world, Iain Scott, living among us. Iain has infected many with his love of opera, and I feel extremely blessed for having been able to study with him over the years.

A special thank you to Iris Tupholme, my editor at Harper-Collins Canada, for the energy, brilliance and sense of joy she brings to her work. Thanks also to Noelle Zitzer for overseeing the manuscript's transformation into book form. Jackie Kaiser, my agent at Westwood Creative Artists, provided much needed advice and encouragement along the way. Nicole Winstanley, also at Westwood, worked very hard pitching the novel to publishers abroad once it was all done. A heartfelt thank you to both.

In Los Angeles, Jerry Kalajian has shown that if there is a mountain to be moved, he will do all that he can to move it. Thanks so much for your enthusiastic support over the years, Jerry—it has meant much to me.

Finally, this book would have been completely impossible without the inspiration, wisdom and unconditional support of my husband, Andrew Graham, who gave me my first pair of binoculars, took me to the Yucatán and forever changed my life. *Gracias, mi amor.*